Judy,

Both End in Speculation
A Vena Goodwin Murder Mystery

For all our mysteries —

Nancy Avery Dafoe

Published by Rogue Phoenix Press, LLP
Copyright © 2018

Names, characters and incidents depicted in this book are products of the author's imagination or are used fictitiously. Any resemblance to actual events, locales, organizations, or persons, living or dead, is entirely coincidental and beyond the intent of the author or the publisher. No part of this book may be reproduced or transmitted in any form or by any means, electronic or mechanical, including photocopying, recording, or by any information storage and retrieval system, without permission in writing from the publisher.

ISBN: 978-1-62420-401-2

Credits
Cover Artist: Designs by Ms G
Editor: Deborah C. Day

Dedication

This novel is dedicated to my Pen Women friends Judy McGinn and Karen Hempson, who read early versions of the book, and Mary Gardner and Bobbie Dumas Panek. To my husband Daniel who traveled with me to Rome, Italy and to my son Blaise for his inspiration and conversation about how to solve the crime.

"The unknown is the largest need of the intellect."
Emily Dickinson

"What shocks the virtuous philosopher, delights the camelion [Chameleon] Poet. It does no harm from its relish of the dark side of things any more than from its taste for the bright; because they both end in speculation."
John Keats in Letter to Richard Woodhouse, October 27, 1818

Chapter One
Woman on the Arch of Constantine

    Seeping from a post-mortem wound at the lowest position of the body, aided by gravity, a drop of uncongealed blood fell from the Arch of Constantine. No one saw or heard a drop fall twenty-one meters and hit the ground. Even the most observant, sleepy tourists did not notice in dim morning light, a slight discoloration in hard-packed earth below the Arch as they walked the fence's perimeter. An evening storm kept most excited tourists in their hotels, but hard rains had finally stopped, with scattered showers descending.

    Less than five hours after her murder, the once beautiful woman was cruelly carried, then hoisted up with a rope and pulley by a burly man who painstakingly ascended an inner staircase to the Arch's attic. He had meticulously planned, read schematics, knew particulars of the monument before his grisly acts and treachery. Far more knowledgeable about his city than a tourist, he was aware the Arch's roundels were sculpted for Emperor Hadrian over two hundred years before Constantine declared Rome to be a Christian kingdom. He knew the statues at the top of the Arch were stolen from the Forum of Trajan, one hero supplanting another. This information was acquired incidentally after he decided he must know everything about the structure. Aware of difficulties inherent in his plan, he was also certain the elaborate scenes he created would throw off authorities, a red herring in the making.

    Setting out signs reading, *Riparazioni* and Bulgari, in front of lighted areas facing the Arch, he then sectioned off the monument with orange plastic fencing. He knew enough about construction and restoration to explain his presence if a guard or *Polizia* questioned him. After years of practicing deception, he was skilled at projecting confidence in any situation. The murderer's scheme was also aided by the Ministry of

Culture's decision to outsource restoration projects to corporations in exchange for advertising, linking historical sites with various companies. Romans had grown used to construction around their crumbling, ancient monuments.

A few hundred feet from the site, a guard saw obvious construction equipment, Bulgari's corporate name, and continued his rounds. Shaking his head, the guard moved off, thinking about the expenses of preserving these decaying treasures of *Roma,* but feeling his city and country should have taken care of her monuments rather than outsource their maintenance. He was aware private contractors were taking public jobs, anticipating his own would be next.

Webcams set up around the Coliseum would show images blurred by rain and streaks of unnatural light, but the murderer had disguised his face. In the event an image of him could be clearly viewed, he could not be positively identified. Bulgari's logo on his truck would be evident, but by then the stolen truck would have been dismantled.

Depositing the young woman's body at the top of the Arch filled him with a kind of power his life of crimes and anonymity had deprived him. The risky nature of his plan appealed to him. Discovery of her body would confound any and all authorities tasked with solving her murder. He imagined their perplexity, a scene which kept a smirk on his face as he cut through the fence gate and placed a stepladder between the columns of the great triumphal Arch in the *Colosseo* district.

A Herculean and brazen feat. With her body in a black bag draped over his shoulder, he first ascended to the doorway enclosing a staircase on the west side of the Arch, facing Palatine Hill. The stairway was confining. A light attached around his forehead gave off enough of a glow to lead as he stopped several times to catch his breath. The entire enterprise was more difficult than he had anticipated, so he set up a pulley mechanism to haul rather than carry the body to the top. Finally, ascending after the body, he pushed it to its position near Constantine's Frieze. He went about his appalling business in rain and relative darkness, without paying homage to Constantine's great exploits which were gouged into grey and white Proconnesian marble under panels. Placement of the woman's body was not the work of heroes, epic battles, or great vision.

Wearing a black, hooded coat with the Bulgari logo stitched on the back, he panted heavily but moved with an athletic grace belying his large frame. Neither statues of Trajan nor Augustus at the top spoke a word about what they witnessed in the middle of the night. Even evening stars hid in shame as the man descended, gathered his plastic fencing and drove to his next destination.

A few hours after the young woman was shoved through an opening to its locus slightly above spandrel reliefs; an eagle-eyed, German tourist, out for a dawn excursion, studied the monument. His camera was still in his pocket because of the rain. Something drew him to stop at the Arch, and he had been studying the sculpted panels for several minutes before noticing stains on marble, an anomaly he considered a natural process of age, weather, and pollutants. In the moment, another drop oozed from the body and fell. A sudden gust transported a red pearl beyond fencing below where it struck the man on his hat before the blood bubble slowly sank down his face. He brought his left hand to his cheek, thinking a nasty bird had defecated, or perhaps rain water heavy with dirt or pollutants was loosened from a crevice.

Then the tourist examined the color of the substance, a thick, half-congealed liquid on his fingers, rubbing them together to test consistency. Blood. He did not panic or startle but looked up curiously, more carefully examining the area above the left lateral arch. Tilting his head to the side to alter perspective, he thought he could make out a hand or body part, not decorative or made of stone, but human.

~ * ~

Once a method of recovery was decided upon, it would take much less effort to lower the young woman's body than the labors taken to hoist her body atop the Arch. By the time *Polizia* responded to the horrific scene, there was a small crowd gathered in spite of renewed rains. Their heads moved, their hands rose then fell before coming to rest over their mouths because a young woman's slender arm could now clearly be seen dangling from the edge. Dueling sirens from ambulances and *Polizia Municipale*, *Polizia di Stato*, and *Carabinieri* vehicles rang out in early morning. All responded until authority over the case was sorted and assigned.

Casting a reddish hue, a rising sun suggested something more ominous than daybreak as dark clouds continued to roll in over Roma.

Young officers concerned themselves with keeping people back and craning their necks to stare in astonishment before finely dressed, military *Carabinieri* assumed operations. There was a brief discussion as to whether the *Direzione Investigativa Antimafia,* or DIA should be called, but after initial confusion, Dante Canestrini determined making an assumption about *Camorra* or *'Ndarangheta* mob connections to the murder was far too early.

A coordinated, if slightly overlapping, strategy was devised and would be carried out for removal of the body from the Arch before examination of the remains. Investigation began the moment her body was discovered, and *Polizia* proceeded slowly, not disturbing evidence, finding a bit of cloth from a body bag still caught on the fence. They hoped to find something or someone identifiable from webcams, in addition to fingerprints; but they would be disappointed with muddied results from cameras filming through rain, and the careful, hooded murderer had been wearing gloves.

When rains ceased temporarily the area began to fill in with tourists. "How did she get up there?" asked an American woman to officials who repeatedly demanded in crisp Italian to step further back.

Dressed in bright green stretch pants, the overweight woman pretended not to understand, repeating questions in English, "Who is she? Shouldn't someone have noticed her being dragged to the top of this thing?" she asked loudly. "Are terrorists involved? Should there be a curfew?"

"This thing, as you call *Arco di Costantino*, is a national treasure," stated an Italian man in perfect English mixed with Italian. He swept his hand upward, and the woman noticed his cufflinks and the fact he was wearing a fitted blue suit, accentuating his musculature and tapered waist. She could not have known the suit was Dolce & Gabbana and worth more than her plane fare.

"You speak English? Oh, good. Finally. Could you tell me how to get to the Spanish Steps?"

"Ah, of course. American." The handsome, immaculately dressed Italian shook his curls, as he turned from the tourist and walked briskly away.

"Yes, I'm American. How rude. I guess he either didn't understand me, or he's extremely nasty," she said, turning to a policeman. "Which way to the Spanish Steps? I'm trying to get to the Spanish Steps, but what's going on here? She's dead, right? Who is it?" An officer near her motioned with his hand for her to move back.

"How awful. Dead people everywhere. No one will help me get to the Spanish Steps. I was told Rome was safe to travel to, and yet here I am with murdered women. Is this how every day starts here? Doesn't seem very safe to me. Anyway, I want to get to the Spanish Steps. I need a taxi." Another officer refused to engage with her and simply pulled the line of tape back further, stretching the tape in front of her protruding belly. Following several more attempts to get an answer, she left in disgust with her newly purchased plastic bag, serving as a raincoat, pulled closely around her body. Stumbling on uneven ground, she waved her arm frantically, hailing an unfortunate cab driver.

After initial confusion regarding enclosing the Arch with crime strips, the monument was finally surrounded not by tourists, but by yellow tape with black letters; a message clear even if you could not read Italian. Repeatedly, *Carabinieri* were forced to expand the area blocked off from prying tourists and even a few Italians who were drawn to the noisy, confusing scene.

"Thank God it's raining again," said Dante Canestrini, the *Carabiniere* who appeared to be in charge until the local chief of police, *Questore* Enzo Rossi, arrived on scene. They would decide together who had authority. In the meantime, Canestrini was speaking to several officers who looked to him for guidance and orders. Unfortunately, Dante Canestrini had planned to attend an official ceremony later in the day and was dressed in his long cloak and Napoleonic hat. Unsettled by the strangeness of the murder and initial confusion of various security reporting to the scene, he removed his hat, ran his hand over the top of his balding head several times, and experienced momentary regret at the loss of his once beautiful, thick black hair. He thought of his youngest brother and the idea of Elio, not him, who inherited their father's genes for charm, good luck, and a full head of hair. Their uncle on their mother's side of the family was as bald as a cue ball. Dante reddened with chagrin for ruminating on the absence of his hair at such a macabre scene.

"How do we get the body down?" recent recruit Flavio Grillo asked him directly.

Canestrini returned to the crisis at hand and brought his full attention to engineering problems, directing a crew of *Agente di Pubblica Sicurezza*, police, and crime scene investigators. After a confusing discussion with too many voices, they devised a fairly simple method of bringing the body to the ground; testing the mechanism before lowering her. Their efforts, however, caused them to comment on the ingenious murderer who had created such a horrific scene. A few careless *Polizia* openly admired the methodology of the murderer who had brought his victim to such heights.

"Bastard must have had a reason for putting her all the way up there," said Grillo. "What do you think the positioning means?"

"Let's not make determinations or speculations yet," said Canestrini, aware any type of conjecture could lead in the wrong direction. Experience had taught him even very violent crimes against women were often the result of an angry boyfriend or cuckolded husband. A good starting point would be to find this young woman's husband, fiancé, or boyfriends. Often, initial questions led the guilty man to stammer then break down and confess before he was formerly asked.

Despite the early hour, rain, and tragedy, Canestrini was pleased to be temporarily stationed in Roma; a rarity, and the murder might lengthen his stay. Flavio had no idea how fortunate he was, thought Canestrini. *Carabinieri* were moved all over and seldom were stationed in Roma for long.

"Follow the evidence," said an officer behind him, as if he had heard this speech from Canestrini before.

"Something in her hand and a paper pinned to her chest," said another.

Initial examination, based upon physical findings before an autopsy, was the young woman had been bludgeoned to death. Paying attention to seemingly insignificant details when dramatic damage to the woman's body sucked air from his lungs, Canestrini knew sometimes the least became a point of discovery in a murder investigation. But stapled to her torn clothing was a slip reading, "finanziamento dei migrant."

"Funding migrants? A political statement? Internal terrorism?" asked the young officer, leaning toward Canestrini.

"Maybe. Let's not jump to conclusions yet, and let's keep this particular factor quiet for now."

There was another detail bringing forth information. In the dead woman's clenched fist was a bit of torn paper with the slightest mark in elegant hand, inked across the scrap. Of course, the paper, which appeared to be aged, naturally or unnaturally, might mean nothing, but Canestrini saw this snippet clutched in her fingers and immediately thought of his brother's girlfriend Vena Goodwin. Such amateur help, as Vena could provide in an official investigation of so grave a crime, would have to be off the record, but he decided to give his little brother's woman a call.

Dante was not even sure his hot-headed brother had made up with Vena after their break, which all of them knew was temporary. The older brother had been made aware the young couple continued arguing since Vena's unexpected trip to America. Shaking off a chill caused more from the horror of the young woman's death in front of him than the rains, Dante believed he would have been more solicitous of Vena than Elio had shown himself to be. What was wrong with his spoiled brother sometimes?

Yes, Vena might be interested in this case. She had previously shown an eye for minutia others missed or dismissed and had an ability to navigate even the most intricate crimes all the way to solution. He had seen her in action. Perhaps what impressed him most about his brother's woman was her bravery. Dante was aware of the absurdity of asking for an amateur's help in the midst of all of these experts who tended to get in one another's way. Vena had the good fortune to work outside of any kind of bureaucracy. She didn't have multiple personnel to report to or consult with before arriving at a theory.

Reluctant to admit it to himself, Dante was attracted to Vena. Of course, his desires would be nothing he would act upon; he was after all, a married man with two small daughters, and a good Catholic, unlike his philandering father and most of all, he was a Carabinieri. Dante loved his wife. They were married when they were eighteen and Francesca was a good woman. She had grown heavy after the girls were born, but her eyes were as pretty as the day he first spotted her. Francesca deserved his fidelity, yet his mind wandered, led by his eyes. When he looked at Vena, however, what he saw was her sharp intellect, what he heard was her quick laugh, and what he felt was a connection somehow painful.

One thing the eldest Canestrini brother knew for certain: this murder was no ordinary act of violence. Depravity, coupled with oddity, covered in a blanket political statement, immediately separated the case from those more easily categorized into domestic violence, robberies gone wrong, or obvious Mafia-type crimes. After he studied the young woman's badly damaged face; her nose, cheekbone, and eye-socket crushed, he thought about the kind of ferocity behind such an intimate and barbarous act. A man who struck a woman in her face in such a way? It was personal. Most likely the murderer was a man, Canestrini thought, based upon the force of the imagined blows and the task of lifting the body up the ladder and interior stairs. Why had the murderer gone to such lengths to stuff the young woman's body atop the famed Arch? As Dante was considering the bizarre case, Mosconi approached him.

"What do you think? There must be a connection to the placement of the body? Home-grown terrorism? Could be domestic. Outside group or individual?"

"Better not to theorize yet. Let's collect all the evidence, get this scene photographed and secured," Canestrini responded, but realized all of them were thinking the same thing.

"The act is symbolic, but a symbol of what exactly?" asked Mosconi.

"Funding migrants certainly hints at the political, but the phrase could have been used to throw off our investigation." Canestrini had to consider a fringe group, perhaps sympathizing with Fratelli d'Italia or another right-wing political alliance, as having supporters capable of such acts. Still, the placard on the body insinuated something else. What connection did the young woman have to migrants?

When the rains let up the place would be crawling with tourists, and

Rome's young Mayor would want this solved as quickly as possible in order not to greatly impact tourism trade. At the moment, Canestrini saw no reason to call in DIGOS, the anti-terrorism police division, as there was no definitive indication or claims. Still, the strangeness was disturbing. Someone or a group certainly wanted to be heard.

Here, again, he wished to talk with Vena before conjecturing as to possible emblematic statements and motive. Vena would likely have some theories. A bit embarrassed, he thought of Vena's ability to ferret out the truth before he had even given himself time to consider the crime. There had to be historical connections or significance behind this act of placement. Why not dump her body in the River Tevere? There were so many ways to get rid of evidence, or a murder victim's body. Why would this killer leave, so obviously, a dramatic trail? Canestrini surveyed the scene and remembered cameras. Of course, video tapes would be examined. Perhaps this case would be more easily solved than he anticipated, but the more he thought about particulars, the more he wanted to talk to Vena. He was glad she was finally back from America, but this was not what he would tell her. No need to let her think she was essential.

As Dante was about to call, Vena was waking next to Elio, responding to his early morning caresses, still tired after a long night waiting for a student, her new friend, who never arrived.

Chapter Two
Movements of the Moon

The second to the last time they met, Sabine Esposito flipped her blue linen neck scarf over her shoulder with casual elegance. Although she had worn scarves as a graduate student at the University of Rochester, Vena never felt as comfortable with one wrapped about her neck as her European friends. The natives instinctively knew how to wear a scarf artlessly. Vena studied the young woman's movements as Sabine approached the alleyway table covered with green vinyl checked cloth. The street was noisy and crowded but less so than inside the café.

When she arrived at 8 *Via degli Uffici del Vicario*, in a tailored white shirt and a pair of European jeans, Sabine looked as if she had come from a fashion shoot after changing into her chic street clothes. Even from a distance, Sabine was stunning. Seeing her student offered an example of one of the few times Vena experienced a twinge of jealousy over another woman's beauty.

"Oh, good," she said, greeting Vena with a quick embrace. "I love gelato. You can get the most delicious ice cream here, too." Sabine disappeared into the shop, while Vena sipped sparkling water, waiting again for her student. Vena's eyes returned to the narrow, stone-paved street where their table was positioned, then the tutor glanced at her notes. Sabine had asked her about the John Keats' poem "Endymion," a most difficult work whether in Italian translation or original English. Most challenging; Vena admired her student who wanted to discuss poetry in the most sophisticated language. Sabine's bravery caused Vena to like her student even more. Most of Vena's students were Italian businessmen hoping to advance their career interests abroad; mastering English, they hoped to grasp the nuances of financial terms in order to complete their deals. Such tutoring was boring to Vena, but she could not let them know.

With Sabine, Vena had an opportunity to touch upon material she loved. Sabine was educated and already attending a university, but required someone to help her with English and English literature. She was not studying the subject at Sapienza but wanted to be versed in English literature before leaving school.

"I want to understand this poem," Sabine said, crossing her long, thin legs and licking her ice cream like a kitten, "but it's so complicated and…"

"Difficult?"

Sabine laughed like a child. "How did you know what I wanted to say but was too embarrassed?"

"Don't be. Keats' 'Endymion' is roughly 4,000 words in length—written in four parts or 'books.' I imagine he wanted to make sure his name went down in the annals of poetry, rivaling other greats. Shelley knew Keats' work would be immortalized before nearly anyone except Keats himself."

"Shelley?"

"Percy Shelley, another great English poet, who was a contemporary of Keats. Strange, they both died so young, one here in Roma and the other off her coast, and within a year of one another."

"Off the coast? What happened?"

"Shelley died when his sailing boat sank off the Gulf of Spezia. He had gone out in bad weather and was apparently very stubborn, insisting on the adventure. A tragic drowning. Keats and Shelley had an uncanny ability to gauge their works from a historical perspective. I don't think Keats would be surprised to know he surpassed even Shelley and other English poets, with the exception of Shakespeare, of course."

"Too much dying young. I don't like it. So sad. Let's change the topic, please. Does anyone read Keats' whole poem, 'Endymion'?"

Vena laughed. "Yes, but few undergraduate students, typically mistaking Book I for the complete poem." Studying Sabine relishing her ice cream, Vena wished she had ordered either ice cream or gelato instead of her water. The afternoon was particularly warm for early November, even in Roma where weather was often unexpectedly hot. There had been no rain in a few days, which was unusual for the month and Vena anticipated a downpour in the coming days.

"Must admit, I stopped reading after Book I. I tried, but too many unfamiliar words. All those names. You must think I'm lazy or a terrible student."

"Definitely not. I've read 'Endymion' multiple times and still struggle with the poem. I keep discovering new entrances, and English is my native language. You're doing remarkable, really." Although there were a couple of years difference between Sabine and Vena, the tutor had adopted the mentor/mothering posture. Both young women accepted the dynamic without question.

"Here, in Book II," Sabine held out the text and pointed to the lines. "This moon."

"Ah, yes, the poet's persona is speaking to the moon. Selene is the Goddess of the Moon, and she is in love with Endymion who is sleeping. All of the characters in this narrative poem are references to Greek or Roman mythology. Jupiter, Amalthea, Ariadne, Pomona, Vertumnus, and Endymion, of course." Vena had forgotten her momentary jealousy, wrapped up in the sumptuous language of Keats' poem.

"Too many names for me to remember. I'm not unfamiliar with the gods, however." Vena recalled Sabine was studying the classics at Sapienza. "It's not Keats? This persona?"

"The voice could be, but typically poets adopt a persona to move the reader through a poem. The poem's speaker may or may not suggest the poet. In other words, poets too invent characters, like novelists, fantastic inventiveness. Keats once wrote about his imagination in a letter to Shelley, stating, "My imagination is a Monastery and I am its Monk.""

"Ah, what a perfect metaphor. I would rather my imagination be a party *selvaggio,*" Sabine laughed. "He was severe, this Keats."

"Certainly, he could be obsessed, but perhaps not severe."

"How do you know all this? About him thinking he is like a Monk in his imagination? You're a genius."

"Oh, no. I wrote some notes and was reading them over as you walked up."

"You're smart. Do you have notes about Keats' poem 'Endymion'? The persona is not Keats' voice? Selena is the moon?"

"The words, 'cooler light' above his head. Follow those silvery traces...Keats' own words, his lines become evidence in the mystery. Reading a poem is a little like detective work. The evidence is all right there if you know what to look for, I suppose."

"I like mysteries, but this is impossible. Moon imagery and mythology. It's too much for me today." Sabine could be a spoiled child but then changed her tone again. "I really do want to learn, but I feel *stupida* when I try to read this Keats."

"Oh, no, no. Don't. This poem is so layered. You have this complex mythology on top of the English language to take in, then there are words no longer used, archaic words, such as 'burthen of mystery' for 'burden of mystery.' We could find a much shorter poem of his."

"How did you know I stumbled over phrasing? Couldn't find 'burthen'. I know mystery, of course," Sabine said proudly. "It's all a mystery, isn't it? This sleeping boy, the moon in love, moonlit landscape. Everything beyond reach, even his life. Our lives."

"You are a philosopher. One of the things I love about poetry is the inherent mystery in implicit language," said Vena. "Supposedly, in mythology, Endymion is the first to notice the movements of the moon, almost as if he was an early astronomer. If you trace the moon imagery…"

"I see the words now: 'silvery,' 'cool,' 'starlight gems.' There is 'midnight.'"

"When you follow these images, the meaning begins to unfold."

"He is unhappy, 'despairing,' this Endymion. He is in love."

"Ah, yes."

"I know the feeling." Sabine said dramatically.

"You are in love, too? Love can lead to despair, but I certainly hope not in your case."

"Oh, I have known the grief Keats writes about."

"One of the many reasons Keats' work still resonates today."

"'Hatred and tears,' yes, but now, joy. I have my sleeping boy, and I am feeling very appreciative, like the moon gazing down upon him,"

"Yes, then you are truly in love."

"I am. He is why I was almost late, and I never want to keep you waiting."

"This boy has a name?"

"Antonio." Sabine moved one shoulder lower, tilting her head to the side, widening her eyes, as if her young man was at the little round table in the alleyway with them.

"Saying his name and you break out smiling. Your whole body reacts to the suggestion of him. He must be very special."

"Oh, yes. Handsome and smart. He reads books in English, too, so you would like him. He knows English almost better than me. He is the first young man who has not been intimidated by me." Sabine had already discerned Vena's particular biases. "But I'm not going to introduce you yet because I don't want him to fall in love with you, too."

Raising her eyebrows, Vena intuited Sabine was a little jealous of her. A passing man called out to them: *"Buona mattina, bellezze."*

"See," said Sabine, turning her head from the man to Vena. "This is what happens when men see you."

"Of all the women in this beautiful city, you have no reason ever to be jealous of anyone." Both women were aware of their beauty. Yet neither demanded recognition of their gifts. "Does he treat you well? Antonio? Does he respect you and your scholarship? Most important."

"Yes, yes. Is it okay if we talk about Antonio instead of Keats' poetry?"

"Your love for Antonio or poetry? Maybe they are the same in the end. Of course, practicing your English on any subject will help you master the language. What do you want to tell me or discuss relating to Antonio?"

"Antonio Lagorio. His last name. What do you poets call it? Ass…" Sabine laughed at the language joke.

"Assonance, when the vowel sounds are repeated. He has a beautiful sounding name."

"Don't you think, even if his name means 'green lizard' in English." Sabine laughed, throwing her head back slightly, her throat long with perfect skin revealed from beneath the scarf. "His family was originally from the Genoa region, he told me. So many Italian names point to the region families once lived. Now, everyone finds their way to Roma."

"Names are fascinating. Yours, Esposito, means exposed, I've learned."

"Ah, I have exposed myself here with all this talk of love. What about your name? Do you know the origins?"

"You have hit a sensitive spot. My first name, Advena, in Latin, means 'alien' or 'foreigner.' I don't like my first name very much, hence, Vena."

"I like Advena. You should be Advena now. But I won't use the name if you don't want me to."

"I don't."

"Ah, but you are a foreigner here. What a good name you have. A description of you in Roma. Lovely to be foreigner everywhere…you are all the more mysterious to everyone."

"Definitely forget I told you. To identify me as an outsider always? Perhaps not so good. Here I am, trying to fit into Roman life and culture. I want Roma to be my home."

"Sorry. I see. Is the meaning the reason you shortened your name to Vena?"

"Yes, but enough about my name. Antonio? You wanted to tell me about him?"

"He kissed me last night." Sabine pursed her lips unconsciously.

"For the first time?"

"Oh, no, no. But this kiss was different. Kisses tell stories, you know."

"They tell stories? What did this one say to you?" Vena was amused to have a student who was becoming a casual friend.

"His first kiss, the story was, 'I'm a sexy, virulent Italian man, and I want to show off my finely mastered skills.' All tongue and showoff. I was still impressed, but not in love. I've heard this tale many times from so many boys."

Vena suddenly re-experienced those kind-of-kisses on her mouth. The story of every man she had ever dated at one point in the relationship. "But the story progresses or comes to a conclusion? I presume the narrative does not stay at showoff?"

"No. Not at all. No longer a showoff. There is no conclusion yet. The story is still developing in an interesting way." She had finished her ice cream and touched the tips of her fingers to her mouth to check for ice cream at the corners. "Do I have any on my mouth?"

"You're good. Perfect."

"Then there is his plaintive kiss, a kiss telling the story of desperate need, sexual urgency to fuck. May I say fuck in front of you?"

"Of course. It's natural…the act and the vernacular."

"You know I wouldn't share this if you weren't more than my teacher. You are my friend, no?"

"I am." Vena decided on the spot she would allow it, a line she typically did not want to cross with her students. Although, recently she noticed this tendency in herself. Perhaps, she had to admit she was lonely in some way.

"There is the story of his sad kisses, who say, 'I've been feeling all alone in this crowded, cruel world, so come and make me feel less sorrow, those soulful, long kisses like Keats' words.'"

"Like Keats' words," Vena repeated with envy. "It's your eyes," said Vena, surprising herself. "Your beautiful eyes say you would take away his loneliness. They are what first drew him to you."

Sabine tilted her head and wagged her index finger. "If I didn't know you had a boyfriend, I would say you are flirting with me."

"I'm sorry. Not at all, but you must know you have extraordinary eyes."

"I do, and thank you. I come back to Keats for a moment." Sabine raised her hand to make the point. "His poem about the moon as lover, and what you tell me about Endymion, reminds me: last night, Antonio drove me out into the country, away from Roma's lights, to see the moon. We drove on forever in order to look up at the moon because she was 'full, like a lover,' he said."

"He is indeed a romantic, your young man."

"Shall I tell you about Antonio's other kissing tales?"

"By all means, if you so desire."

"Desire. Yes, but 'by all means?'"

"Oh, by all means, definitely yes." Then a waiter interrupted them and asked if he could get anything else for them. "An espresso, please."

"Me, too," said Sabine.

The waiter stood longer than was necessary, smiling at them, pretending to write down notes, trying to decide which one he preferred. He was leaning toward Sabine and physically moved closer. "Anything else I can do for you, ladies?"

"No, and go get our espresso quickly," Sabine scolded. He turned away, embarrassment and disappointment worn on his face. "Sometimes you have to be cruel and not encourage them."

Vena thought about this comment and her American friend Warren. In truth, she never really let him off the hook completely. When she became braver then it would be time to let Warren go…fully, allow him to find new love in the world, and forget her entirely. "I suppose it's true."

"What about your man? Are you in love?" Sabine leaned in conspiratorially.

Hesitating, Vena said, "Yes." She leafed through pages in her notebook absentmindedly.

"Ah, but you had to think for a moment. Why?"

"Love is not always so clear as it appears to be."

"There is trouble in your relationship?"

"Confusion, uncertainty."

"Confusion? Doesn't sound good."

"It's not bad either. I had days when I smiled with a glow you are showing today."

"So, you are not in this warm place anymore? Did he hurt you, your man?"

"No. He is definitely not at fault here, if there is fault to be found."

"Then you are attracted to another man? I know your face."

"Let's not talk about me anymore." Vena touched her forehead, brushing away a strand of hair falling across her eyes.

"Oh, no. You don't get off easily. I'm laying my heart on this table for you, and Keats has exposed his jealousies and longings for everyone. You have a confession beneath those dark eyes of yours. I'm waiting."

"Sorry, but agitation and discomfort are what you get today. All I can rally right now because I don't know exactly what I want."

"This young man of yours, does he know he is going to lose you, yet?"

Vena pulled herself up straighter, opened her eyes wider. "I didn't say I was leaving him. Life together has become very complicated."

"Complicated always means another lover or would-be lover, so who is this other man?"

"Not always. You're so absolute." Vena's smile let Sabine know her comment was not an insult. "Tell me more about your love. What has led you to such unconditional happiness? This man who has captured your heart is, indeed, most fortunate."

"Antonio, ah, Antonio. I was telling you about his kisses. His kiss last night was not communicating any of those other stories. This one said, 'I am in love and devoted to you alone. I will wait for you forever, if necessary, but I do not want to wait at all.'"

"All that in a kiss?"

"Of course. I sensed this, heard love even in the long, slow movement of his warm lips."

"Did he say anything afterward?"

"He didn't need to use words. Sometimes we communicate better without them."

Vena wasn't sure she agreed with Sabine's last statement. After all, she had spent the better part of her young life surrounding herself with words; reading and writing. "You're so certain. From where does this certainty come?"

"Naturally. I come by it instinctively. Ah, why I am so happy today. Nothing could upset me. Today is perfection."

Chapter Three
Missing Person, Missing Poem

With rain descending, opacity ruled. *Polizia* appeared truly miserable in their wet uniforms, but not as uncomfortable as Carabinieri in their formal dress. Although rain was infrequent in Roma, November was always the wettest month of the year; but the rains seldom lasted all day. Vena never minded damp and cold in Roma, partly because she had been used to the snow and bitter winds of Upstate New York in late November. What harm was a little rain?

As usual, she had forgotten her umbrella but knew one of the dozens of umbrella salesmen would be waiting for her wherever she landed. Immigrants selling such items was a fact of life in Roma, and a circumstance she still had trouble getting used to since making the city her home.

"Five Euro. Five Euro."

"No, three."

"Five."

"No, two."

"Okay, three."

"Deal." The umbrella was hers for the day. How the negotiating was done she thought, the bargain not really a bargain, but the seller would leave her and move on to the next soaked tourist. Even after two years in Roma, Vena could still be spotted as an American, she thought with some disdain.

She had chosen Italy, but her choice meant she would continue to be a stranger in her adopted home. The name her perpetually absent mother Greta had chosen for her, Advena, had never seemed more apt.

When she fled Gould and New York a couple of years earlier, she sought movement, tried to become a blur of time passing. On the train to the Amalfi Coast from Roma, she imagined she would take in the countryside in its glorious ascending and descending sunlight, but the train was set within walls, blocking much of the view. What she saw was the story of non-paying passengers on the train, those trying to avoid the ticket taker. A man or woman would duck into a restroom, somehow knowing exactly when to disappear, then reappear again, sit on the step to the upper level or take the seat of a passenger who had stood up. After someone returned, a quick volley of insults in Italian would end the siege, and the ticketless passenger would roam again. Vena was not thinking of the murderer Gould two years earlier but the hustle of those without tickets as passengers in life.

On her fateful journey, she had written down Paul Theroux's words, "I sought trains; I found passengers," but at the time, she believed she was seeking people and finding the means of escape. Self-aware to a fault, she knew when she wrote about Italy she described it as a tourist, albeit an observant one. How to let go of the details long enough to breathe the air, walk compressed streets without too much attention to the ancient stones beneath her feet? As much as she loved Roma and her people, she would remain the foreigner, the watcher rather than one inside experience.

~ * ~

Pulling up on her blue scooter, Vena carried her helmet and a small, vinyl purse slung over her shoulder, then began trying to inch her way through the crowd. Quick and agile, she had reached the inner perimeter within several moments. At first, she had been unable to see Dante and tried to duck under the crime tape when an officer abruptly stopped her. She told the officer, Canestrini had called her to the scene.

"No. No one moves into this area," he said.

"Please. Officer Canestrini," she yelled. With her protestations, the officer became confused and searched for Canestrini himself, his eyes giving away the location of his superior officer. Spotting Dante in amongst *Polizia* and *Carabinieri* around the monument, she gestured frantically.

"Dante." Vena waved her arms, helmet still in hand.

Canestrini motioned for the officer to let her through, and Flavio

Grillo lifted the tape for Vena to proceed. Already aware of a murder investigation from Dante's early morning call, Vena scanned the area beyond the yellow tape. Instinctively, she knew whatever they were looking for was no longer at the scene.

Despite the nasty weather, the crowd of police, security and crime scene, Vena and Dante hugged and kissed one another on the cheeks before addressing the situation. They were both genuinely glad to see one another.

Joining Dante as he moved through the spectacle of blaring sirens, hustling personnel, curious sightseers, Vena whispered, "Good to see you, even under these circumstances. What do you know about the victim?"

"Everything about this murder is strange," he said, nodding toward Vena but directing another officer by his hand motion. "Right now, we're getting her name which may or may not be who she really is, but we found an identification card in her skirt pocket: Sabine Esposito."

Vena stumbled in distress.

"What is it?"

"Sabine? Sabine Esposito? My God, Dante, I know her. She was my student. I was her tutor, her friend."

"I...I can't believe this." The coincidence seemed too impossible for Dante to take in, even though he unreasonably half expected Vena would help lead him to the murderer. "Your student?" he repeated. "Do you think you could positively identify the body, for confirmation?"

"Yes, I'll try."

"I have to warn you. She is badly disfigured. This will be very upsetting, as some of our officers can tell you." Dante motioned toward a young officer bent over and heaving up his breakfast.

Vena steeled herself as they made their way closer to the tight crowd of officials around the body which could not be seen from the outer circles. Sabine's face had been smashed and was unrecognizable, but her ripped, bunched up skirt and open shirt, once white with blue flowers, were too familiar. Vena had seen her wear the chic outfit before.

"I can't be sure because of the damage to her face, but those seem to be her clothes and her hair, I'm almost certain. What happened to her?" A slip of paper between Sabine's fingers caught her eye.

"This is what we must find out."

"There's something else I must tell you", Vena said hesitantly. "She might have been trying to reach me last night, Dante."

Canestrini turned. "Not here. We'll meet at Elio's. Not another word now."

Vena made her way back to the scooter, then held her head down for a few moments. Willing herself not to burst into tears, she breathed deeply. After the nausea passed, she jumped on and raced through the city, darting in and out of traffic lanes as if she had lived there all of her life.

~ * ~

Even before arriving at the crime scene, before Dante's call, before she climbed into bed with Dante's brother Elio, Vena experienced the sensation of something missing and something amiss. Her understanding was visceral rather than abstract, coming to any kind of reasoned point from deduction. The thought, or really, the sensation, had woken her in the middle of the night. Was her unease related to what she had been reading or the fact her student had not shown up at the appointed hour?

Vena read all the time, but she had given away most of her books when she left for Roma. After moving to Italy, she made a practice of not acquiring material possessions, including books. Although she loved both the feel of a book and content of literature, Vena had moved from apartment to apartment, from one country to another, and tried to reduce her possessions in order to fit them into a box or two and a backpack.

Yet, absence, the physical deprivation of books, their hard and soft covers, their old vellum pages, smooth finishes of glossy paper stock were all experiences necessary to her happiness. She knew having no books around was a perfectly reasonable way to live in a small space, but she quickly came to regret the loss.

As a result of her new Spartan lifestyle, she borrowed books and reluctantly returned them, wishing instead to stash them away. After recently reading Patrick Modiano's *Missing Person,* she had an urge to quote a passage, but remembered the book was not hers and Modiano's words disappeared as elusively as Guy's past. The desire to quote at will, having memorized lines from various texts, was a skill she did not come by naturally, like her old professor, the monster Gould. Spontaneously, a thought of Gould would resurface with old fears and revulsion, but she also remembered her admiration of the professor's wit and intelligence in the early days before she knew too much about him.

Sabine. The young woman's face came to her when she woke or in the moment before waking. Could smart Sabine really have found an original Keats' poem? Then paid a horrific price for her discovery? Such a finding was almost too incredible to imagine. Vena was not upset her student had not shown up. Simply, she was unable to get ahold of Sabine to ask what had happened. After the second hour of unreturned calls, Vena decided Miss Esposito chose not to share the supposedly valuable manuscript with her tutor. Perhaps the lover Antonio had sidetracked Sabine.

Missing, lost ideas and possessions were on her mind when she woke to Elio's kisses followed by his brother's phone call.

"I have to leave," she said.

"What? You just woke up? Who's calling you?"

"It's your brother."

"God, him. Do you want me to come?"

"No, I'll be back quickly. He has a question about a case."

"A case?"

"A murder."

"Good Lord," Elio sighed and rolled over, pulling a pillow over his eyes.

~ * ~

"So, where are you in your investigation?" Elio asked as he poured a glass of Merlot for himself, then reached to fill Vena's glass again.

"Too early for conclusions, almost too soon for reasonable speculation," Dante said, leaning back in the overstuffed chair. "This is strictly confidential, as you both must know." Elio ran a zipper finger across his lips. "There are some disturbing signs, political, perhaps, in addition to the murder itself."

"'Ndrangheta?"

Dante said, "I don't know. I don't think so. Might be the work of a political group. There was a note affixed to her clothes, reading, 'funding migrants.'"

"Too far north for Ndrangheta or no? Politics over migrants? What did Vena's student have to do with migrants?" Elio asked, having heard his brother talk about Mafia moving into businesses in Roma.

"Calabrian mafia has made inroads here. Maybe I should be focusing in their direction, but their involvement doesn't make sense on some level. I guess the murder is brazen and brutal enough to be their markings, but not likely. This note about helping migrants, rather "funding" migrants, I don't know. Dangerous to assume too much yet but tempting."

"Sabine was not political. I never heard her talk about helping migrant groups. The symbolism and staging of the body feels forced, even deliberately misleading." Vena spoke for the first time about the crime in front of them. "She was so lovely and full of life. She was interested in poetry and learning English. I can't see her involved in some political group, but she did have a good heart."

"Forced staging? Symbolism? Meaning what exactly?" Elio looked at her with slight annoyance, regarding why his brother had asked for his girlfriend's advice before his own brother's. "And how do you know your student wouldn't be secretly helping migrants? What makes you think she would have told you?"

Overlapping their words, Dante interrupted while Elio was still speaking. "Meaning, the murder doesn't seem to be their signature, despite the brutality," Dante said. "The temptation is to associate the bizarre location with statement. Why the Arch of Constantine? So many possible implications. Could read as a warning to Italy to stop the great migrations."

"Perhaps a ruse? Something to throw off the investigation into her murder?" Vena interjected.

"On top of Constantine's Arch? A statement on military victory with the body of a young woman? Hardly. We have a clue in the form of a paper with the words 'funding migrants' we have to consider." Dante responded, shaking his head.

"But why Constantine's Arch?" Elio asked.

"A nod to the old gods, Apollo, Hercules, meaning what? Dante, the migrant statement doesn't seem right. The paper in her hand..."

"No. The paper between her fingers was nothing. The words 'funding migrants' was pinned to her blouse."

"Nothing about this is right. What military victory? Old gods no one believes in. How could a student have been paying the migrants?" Elio jumped in again.

"Suppose we set aside the symbolic associations of the monument? The act of placing the body at the top might mean nothing at all, if they, or he, wanted to throw in a red herring—a double red herring with the political statement about migrants," Vena said.

"You're kidding, right," interjected Elio. "If the placement meant nothing, why would anyone go to such trouble, and I'm assuming this staging was rather difficult to get a body all the way up there?"

"Must have been a strenuous feat." Vena tried to be analytical and not think of Sabine's death so personally.

"I would say a high degree of difficulty. I know this sounds callous, but our men were almost admiring the murderer's ingenuity." Dante weighed in with gravity. All three were silent for a moment.

"As strange as this sounds, a poem is possibly at the heart of this, as I told you Dante."

"C'mon, Vena, I don't want to be insulting, but you're being ridiculous. I know you love literature and all the intrigue, but this is overreach." Elio was feeling a little left out and showed his exasperation.

"I'm not so sure yet," said Dante as Vena tried not to allow a smile to register, aware of the seriousness of the crime on an intimate level. "There was something behind this murder—there always is. If the murder is not political, then the killing was likely out of jealousy. But why go to such lengths over jealousy? Perhaps a murder out of greed, but I, too, am having trouble believing a poem could be worth this kind of trouble and level of violence."

"Imagine, the *objet d'art* we are discussing had been something by an Italian artist, a Caravaggio, a Bernini, a Titian, a Michelangelo, rather than an Englishman? Would you be so skeptical?"

"You made your point. Maybe it's because I don't know the work of this Englishman, this Keats. I can't quite believe a piece of paper could have the kind of worth you steal and kill for. And I don't think we can ignore the obvious sign on her body, this 'funding migrants.'"

"You already talked about this, about a poem?" Elio stared at Vena.

"Broached the topic really. At the crime scene, right after identifying the body." Dante turned to Vena, leaning toward her. "We couldn't say too much in front of the others which is why I came over here. You'll have to explain a bit more to me if I'm going to take this theory at all seriously."

"First, consider this political angle. Sabine barely had enough money to attend school. She was always thinking of ways to save in order to pay for her tuition and my small fee, which I altered for her, on a sliding scale."

"Vena," Elio protested. "You promised to stop undercharging your students."

"I know, but, really Elio, this is not the time. I don't think Sabine could possibly have been involved in funding any group. This sign feels like something to throw us off. Imagine for a moment: if Sabine was actually the last person to hold a John Keats' poem, as she told me, a work written right here in Roma. The original document would be worth an astronomical amount."

"Astronomical…again, for a poem?" Dante was trying not to sound incredulous.

"Yes, a poem," added Elio. "An original Keats' poem, one up until now undiscovered."

"I know, this may seem strange to you and most people, but think about an undiscovered Caravaggio painting, a work no one knew existed, suddenly turning up in an attic. What do you suppose would happen at or before an auction? Would thieves be intrigued?"

Shaking his head slowly as if still trying to decide the possibility, Dante said, "I need to know more about this supposed poem as motive. How would selling a poem work? Even if this Englishman's poem was as valuable as you imply, couldn't someone fake a poem? How would you or any of us know?" He picked up a scrap of paper on the desk and held it up for dramatic effect. Elio's smile told him he already knew how Vena would respond.

"I'm not sure I would know immediately, but there are experts who could accurately identify the work of the poet," Vena spoke more rapidly as her words spilled out. "Of course, we're talking about an amazingly gifted poet and forger who would be capable of approaching the task. Then the Keats' scholars would examine the poem's rhythm, the diction, rhyming, line lengths, iambic meter, repetitions and deliberate omissions, his preferred word choices, stanza construction and patterns, line breaks with enjambment, number of articles, alliteration." Taking a breath, Vena continued as Elio leaned forward and Dante raised his brows. "There would be an examination of the metaphors...the choice of vehicles and tenors...the subject matter, naturally. His similes. Even if a contemporary forger was clever, seems unlikely he or she would be able to avoid using contemporary terms and expressions, accidentally allowing the current vernacular to slip into the poem."

"Hah," yelled Elio, delighted with this smart woman with whom he had fallen in love.

"I hate to break your rhythm, but then, Elio already did," Dante said with a wry smile. "I'm afraid you lost me on a couple of those terms, but I get the point. An expert could figure out if this poem is really an original or not."

"But I'm just getting started. There is Keats' handwriting which would be analyzed against known representations from his letters and poems. The paper...there are tricks to aging papers, but we are fairly well able to precisely date such things now."

"All right. All right. We'll know if it's really the English guy's poem."

Elio clapped, half in mockery and half in genuine approval of Vena's victory. He loved the fact she never averted her eyes—a murder, an ugly situation, a grotesquery and still, Vena would train her eyes on the task.

"Thank you," she said, turning from one brother to the other and nodding at Elio.

"There's something else. Vena, you're going to have to come in and explain why you were meeting with the murder victim and what your alibi is during the time period she was killed."

"Sabine Esposito, not the murder victim."

"Miss Esposito. Okay, you're not a suspect, but you're going to need to verify your whereabouts."

"Easy," Elio jumped in. "I'm her alibi."

"What?" Vena and Dante said at once, starring at him. Dante was relieved, but Vena was surprised.

"I didn't tell you. I was tailing you all night. I know confessing doesn't sound good, but I wanted to make sure you were safe. You wander about this city as if Roma is your own."

"Safe? From my student?"

"She was murdered, wasn't she?" Elio protested.

"You have to stop following me, Elio. I don't want…"

"Hey, you two can work out the dynamics of your relationship later," Dante interrupted the lovers, "but for now, I'm glad you were there, bro. Make things easier when Vena comes down to answer questions about what she knows."

Vena rolled her eyes. "When do I talk to…"

"I'll call you. Don't do anything before I call, and Elio, you come with her."

Elio sat on the arm of the overstuffed chair Vena was sitting in. "Should we get an *avvocato difensore*?"

"No. Nothing like a defense counsel; I don't think it's necessary. They make people appear guilty. Vena has nothing to hide." Turning from his brother to Vena, Dante asked, "What can you tell me about Miss Esposito? Any detail you left out?"

"As I said earlier, she was trying to reach me. Sabine was supposed to meet me to show me this original Keats' poem. She was very excited about the prospect of finding an original and certainly believed the poem to be authentic. Wait, when I think of it, she was going to share the document with her classics *professore* first. Pavoni is his name. Yes, I encouraged her to share the poem with him before showing me."

"What? You didn't tell me. You were in all this intrigue and you say nothing about it until now?" Left out, Elio worried he was unaware of some possible danger to which Vena had exposed herself.

"I didn't tell you because I was unsure of what she had. The document could easily have been a forgery or a copy of something she was unfamiliar with but merely guessed incorrectly what she had. Once I confirmed what the paper was, I would have told you. I asked her to verify the poem with someone from her university, someone at Sapienza."

"You suggested Pavoni?" Dante asked.

"No, I suggested she contact a literature professore, and she said something about her classics *professore*, Pavoni. I'm certain Pavoni is his name."

"I trust your instincts on this, Vena, even if the poem idea doesn't seem to make much sense to me yet. If there is some documentation you could show me on what such a poem could be worth, then I'd be able to explain the situation, your theory, to the other officers without them laughing." Dante turned from Vena and put his hand on his brother's shoulder. Vena would be a handful as a girlfriend.

Within moments, she and Dante were deeply engaged in the possibilities of a surfaced and invaluable poem. Elio sulked, feeling entirely left out. At moments like those, Vena questioned whether she had fallen for the wrong Canestrini brother.

Dante and Vena would have conferred longer, but his phone rang.

"Scusami, ma devo andare via scappare. Mi dispiace, ma adesso devo proprio andare."

Dante stared at them in amazement. They had found another body in the *Fontana dei Trevi*, another victim of a bizarre murder.

"You're coming with me to the professor's office tomorrow morning," Dante commanded, back in control. "Let's go for a walk and talk about what you know about this Pavoni and anything else you can think of about Miss Esposito."

"Yes, I will," Vena said, already knowing she would go.

"Me, too." Elio grabbed his jacket.

Putting out a hand, Dante stopped him. "Not now. Not this time. And not tomorrow morning either. I can't have this inspection appearing like a family holiday. Let's keep the investigation to Vena this time."

Sensing Elio's need for reassurance, Vena reached over and put a hand around the back of his neck, drew him to her, before kissing him in front of his brother. Elio smirked and began humming, a curious habit he had. Humming was at first endearing but then became cloying to Vena.

"Settled." Dante turned and went out with Vena right behind him. Elio stood in the open doorway looking after them, unsure of himself, uneasy and uncertain as to whether or not he should be doing something more. He stuck his head out the window and yelled out to them.

"What time are you going to be back? Should I wait for you to prepare dinner?"

Vena turned first to Dante then yelled back, "No more than a couple of hours. Yes, please do wait. We'll make dinner together."

"All right. Bring wine."

"Red or white?"

"Are you going to go over the entire menu from here, too?" Dante asked, moving off more quickly.

"Red," Vena yelled back toward Elio then caught up to Dante.

In *la Strada* below, Dante said, "Let's go over exactly what you are going to say when they question you. I never expected you would be a potential witness."

"I'll tell the truth. I have nothing to hide."

"Not the point. You have to be consistent in your answers and never waver." Vena's proximity to the murder victim made him uneasy and concerned for her. Then more quietly, Dante said, "I really can't believe this is about a missing poem. A poor Englishman's poem." He started walking more rapidly then said, "And, are you really in love with my brother?"

Chapter Four
Vena Returns to Keats-Shelley Memorial

"*Prego. Prego.*" Vena Goodwin moved past a woman and her child, smiling, and they smiled in return. Prego turned out to be the most useful term Vena had ever learned. The Italian word seemed to work for any number of situations: I beg your pardon; please; you're welcome; of course; the check—please; and some ill-defined contexts when no other word would quite do. For whatever reason, as soon as Vena said *Prego*, everything had the aspect of appearing to be fine.

At Roma airport, Fiumicino, Vena searched for Elio Canestrini for a few seconds after deplaning. She had not yet told her lover when she was arriving, but, still, she couldn't help scanning the waiting throng of expectant faces. In unreasonable anticipation, she thought he would somehow intuit her return. Although she did not want to admit it, she missed him and wished she had not been so stubborn and Elio so jealous.

Stopping to sip a thimble of expresso at a coffee bar, Vena readied herself for the trip into Roma. Already very warm, she thought about how body chemistry changes with the environment. A number of men of various ages turned their heads in her direction, flashing their white or yellowed teeth and winking with their beautiful eyes. Sighing, then turning away from strangers, Vena was aware of her shoulders dropping. Then she adjusted her backpack and pulled her long brown hair into a ponytail to avoid catching strands beneath the shoulder straps. Cooler already.

A couple of years earlier, Vena Goodwin was the girl with short-cropped, purple hair and a struggling graduate student in New York State. She was as natural in unnatural color hair, and as unnatural in Rochester, New York as she was in Rome. She rather liked changing her physical appearance and discovered she loved changing her physical venues. Her tan had faded during her return trip to New York, and she knew she again appeared to be an American tourist. The way to avoid being an obvious target for anti-American sentiment and pickpockets was to set out for the train with confidence and a quick pace. An hour-ride into the city practically begged her to shut her eyelids, but the stares of strangers kept her alert; not afraid, but hyper-aware.

Termini Station was an entirely different experience in Rome than the U.S. city train stations Vena had traveled through, with homeless men sleeping on the floor, graffiti lining walls, African immigrant hustlers desperately trying to sell trinkets, key chains with miniature Coliseums. She was, however, wiser than the first time she entered the city. Termini was not merely a place of departures and arrivals but a destination for some who made their way into the thick movement of humanity in order to eke out a living. The hustlers were both anonymous and ubiquitous. Not making eye-contact, walking quickly, attempting not to notice the camps of young, hopeless men along the walls, some moving toward her, she made her way. Merging into a large family or tourist group gave her easier passage. Never hesitate was her method. She remembered the second time she had entered the city, and Elio had followed her to her good fortune.

There would be a journey to arrive in Rome proper. She toyed with calling her lover in a moment of weakness and fatigue, but she wanted to shower and rest before seeing him again. Along the ride she was saddened to see an increase in the number of shanty constructions of recent immigrants, both for their despair and the city's inability to handle such an overwhelming influx. Perhaps there were not more tents, but the sight of them required getting used to again. Riding on a plane for all of those hours made her feel as if she had been working out all night, aware of beads of sweat at her hairline, at the back of her neck, beneath her breasts. Ah, for a cool shower.

During the interval of traveling between the airport and Rome, she thought again of her last trip, nearly two years earlier, and the young man who respectfully followed her at a distance; finally introducing himself before offering to guide her on a tour of his city. He was so proud and confident. How could she not have been attracted to him? Part of her decision not to call Elio this time had to do with stubborn resolve in proving she could take care of herself. She was allowed one indulgence on arrival in the city. As tempting as it was to move back into Elio's one bedroom flat in Monti, she would rent a lovely, spacious room for a few nights before calling him.

Navigating the narrow streets, scooters, rush of traffic and pedestrians, Vena pulled her bag along and considered walking an opportunity to collect herself. She noted the spill from trash containers leaking contents. There were never enough of them for tourists who were used to tossing their refuse every few feet. Then she recalled reading something about a rubbish collection strike in Rome. Ubiquitous litter blew down streets in such abundance the remnants suggested a party had passed through, but the litter remained a marker of the city's growing indifference to degradation.

Roman roads did not fare much better; potholes always seeming to grow larger, and teen prostitutes from West Africa and Eastern European countries stepped gingerly in their spiked heels and mini-skirts along broken pavement. How much better to get a pair of flats she thought, as she moved past a particularly young girl standing on the corner.

Wordlessly negotiating a path through the city, Vena was not surprised but a little dismayed to see so many spray-painted walls, more swastikas than she remembered, as if hatred and anger were increasingly encroaching onto every façade in Rome. With a flood of recent immigrants came a counter surge of neo-Nazi sympathizers and organization members. Even awash in corruption and decay, Rome was a work of art, still one of the most beautiful cities in the world she thought. She adjusted her shirt sticking to her back. If she was to be a part of this city, Vena had to start adopting Roma as her own.

Why Vena loved Roma was not an easy answer, but the rush swept her up as soon as she first stepped on the streets again. Mediterranean blue of the sky juxtaposed against ochre walls, jutting ancient stone, green burnished statues of bronze Caesars and gods. An unexpected trellis covering a south-facing wall with deep green, crawling ivy, dust on her bare toes exposed by sandals, speaking of another age, columns and majesty crumbling from within and without but still standing proud, defiant. Animated ruin was part of Rome's endless appeal. Street musicians were playing violins, guitars; a man balanced on a chair, and woman in white paint and a pink tutu pantomimed at a corner. Finger puppet man was in the middle of a show. Good to be back.

By the time she reached her hotel Vena was tired and wanted nothing more than to fling herself down on a bed and sleep for half the day, but the hotel clerk explained the room was not yet ready for check-in. Sunny and warm, Roma was welcoming despite Vena's exhaustion and observance of the city's physical flaws, so she set out to find a little place to drink a glass of Merlot and get something to eat. It had been a surprise when she first moved to Roma and found a good bottle of wine and a bit of delicious, fresh cooked pasta were the norm, not the exception.

Walking in the city she found temptations impossible…not to be drawn into restaurants with odors of fresh fish and olive oils, basil leaves and garlic, a newly peeled onion simmering, arancini dipped into the deep fryer. Vena's tongue was already moving in anticipation as she quickened her pace in her best traveling blouse and skirt. Everything was close but still foreign: the people, buildings, cars, conversations of lives overlapping her own. Even laughter expressed itself in a resistant tongue, and she began the process of immersing herself in Italian again. In the span of a few months, the Romance language had slipped into another part of her brain, but began reemerging like a cat slowly stretching upon waking.

When she lived in upstate New York, Vena seldom thought about wide-open spaces around her. Distances were pronounced outside of the cities, marked by wide, deep landscapes of hills and valleys of forests, undeveloped, untilled lands, characteristics almost unheard of in the density of Italy. Vast stretches of pines, maples, and other trees were one of the few things she really missed about New York, other than her father Bill and long-time friend and former lover Warren.

There would be days and nights to come she would long for the openness of her American home, but then laughter bounced up to her from a group of young Italians, rapidly conversing and flirting, intimacy unknowingly shared. History of a past always reemerging followed her everywhere in Roma.

"*Signorina, Signorina,*" a young man called after her until Vena ducked into a *trattoria*. Colorful glass grapes hung on ochre colored walls, that held a tall leaded glass window and whole cloves of garlic strung along sides of an open doorway. While the trattoria was welcoming, a building on the opposite side of the street boasted a recently painted swastika which unnerved her for its boldness here in the beautiful heart of the city. Checking behind her, she was relieved no one was still following, and she leaned her head back against the rough, plastered surface of the interior room...the first time she was cognizant of feeling relaxed in days. The doors were flung open, however, and street noise poured in like water as a group of German tourists entered. For some reason, the waiter escorted them to another section of the restaurant. She was left alone.

After her second glass of Merlot and feasting on a plate of grilled octopus on potato crème, she said out loud, "It's good to be back." The waiter suggested puzzlement until she repeated herself in perfect Italian. He smiled.

"Ah, you know Italian. Good. From where?"

"From here now, but I'm an American. I will never speak the language as beautifully as Italians do," she said in Italian.

"You speak Italian well."

A few minutes later, the waiter brought her a plate of stuffed zucchini and cherry peppers. "For you, from the chef."

"But, I," she protested weakly.

"On the house." Curious as to whether this was gratitude for her efforts to learn their language or because the young waiter was flirting, Vena accepted the gift with relish.

"Then, an extra tip for you," she responded in Italian. Pleased because she was still hungry, Vena bit into the stuffed pepper and tasted its sweetness. Aroma of garlic and olive oil drifted around her, and she smiled with pleasure.

After her time in the U.S., she knew her Italian was feeling a little unnatural in her mouth, words rolling around then jumping out from behind English. Warren's fault, she thought. He had refused to try to learn Italian and spoke in English during her visit. Of course, her visit with Warren drove Elio crazy with jealousy, no matter how many times she told her Italian boyfriend, "Warren is my friend, not my lover."

"But he wants to make love to you, so there is no difference," Elio yelled into his cell. Bill, however, had been a good sport, trying to learn the

Romance language, and practicing Italian with her every day of their visit. Vena reflected upon the fact after her leaving that some of the longest conversations of her life with her father had been in Italian, and those attempts to express ideas in another language. She considered the oddity of growing closer to her father as she was moving further from home. Bill actually teared up when she left, telling her to stay in touch. He even promised to write, in Italian. He had given her two gifts; the first, a silly thing from her childhood wish list, a recording pen, and the second, a gold necklace, surprisingly pretty.

"*Scrittura ancora?*" Bill asked sheepishly, conscious of the fact his Italian was flawed.

"I am, and I expect you will write to me. I will hold you to your promise," Vena responded in English, kissing him on his bearded cheek.

Vena's first night back in Roma she booked a room in The Inn at the Spanish Steps at *Via Dei Condotti* 85. She didn't regret the impetuous decision to return to the first site chosen during her undergraduate study of this ancient city, even though her room was far too expensive, making a long stay problematic.

Tourists were everywhere, but the location provided proximity to where she wished to begin her next journey. The drawback was this section of the city in *Piazza di Spagna* automatically gave her away as a foreigner, particularly one from England or America. After living in Italy for almost two years, however, she was intrigued by the feeling of newness again, seeing *Roma* with a kind of excitement and awe experienced in the past. Everything was fraught with mystery.

The Inn also gave her temporary distance from Elio whom she missed more than she wanted to admit. She was, nevertheless, fairly certain of where their relationship stood. Before coming home to the Italian capital, she had called him and neither was ready to assume they should move back in together right away. Vena obsessively thought about how to cure jealousy as she flew over the Atlantic and came to the conclusion distance was not the ingredient in the recipe after all.

Elio advised her against renting an upscale bed and breakfast room or staying in a tourist hotspot, but she immediately began arguing with him and stopped herself before she could say anything hurtful. He had been moody and pouting because she had gone to America without him, not showing him off to her friends and few relatives back in the States. He could envision this slight as a signal she was not proud of their relationship or, much worse, she did not wish to continue their liaison.

Of course, Elio had many young and beautiful women who were interested in him, he reminded himself and her. In hurt and anger, he thought it might be best to explore his options when Vena showed up at his door, knocking loudly and toting a book as a gift. He instantly forgot his intentions to fall in love with another woman.

~ * ~

While she was still a student at the University of Rochester, Vena made her way to Keats-Shelley Memorial House, even before she saw the Coliseum, the Roman Forum, one of the city's famed arches, or museums of which she was so enamored. Keats was an important part of the reason she made her way to Rome the first time. She had been tasked with researching for a professor at the university, one who became a villain of great proportions.

Vena was not the first to speculate on the possibilities of such a calamity as a lost Keats' poem. When she was researching for Professor Gould at the University of Rochester, she made notes in margins about a possible missing poem. Could the wildly prolific Keats really have spent the final few months of his life in this ancient, storied city without even once taking a pen to paper? Keats had been aware of creating a legacy, wanting to live on through his poetry. Suppose Keats had managed to grip a writing implement and scrawl lines from his head onto paper. Vena could conceive of the poet waiting for Severn to read his work, unsure of the value of this poem; he probably thought the construction hurried. Keats knew his mind was roiling with fever, but he placed the poem between pages of a book of Shakespeare's plays and pushed the tome back onto the table by his bedside.

~ * ~

Entering the *camera da letto* where Keats died, Vena was struck by

Both End in Speculation

the narrowness of the reproduction bed—his original burned along with his other possessions after his death and the dimensions of the small room. Other than a few prints, and a glass case, the bedroom remained spare, and the ghost of the English poet still there, a presence after the boarding house had been turned into his Memorial.

Copying down lines of *New York Times* correspondent A.C. Sedgwick, Vena added the note in her pocket journal: Keats' death room holds, "the smell, more of England than of Italy, or so one thinks, of leather bindings...There was quiet, peace, pause..." Vena reread Sedgwick's words again and determined she would return to Keats' Memorial as soon as she was situated.

On the long plane ride across the Atlantic, she read and reread several of Keats' poems until she knew at least the odes by heart, the way Professor Gould had shown his students. Whether thinking about the villainous Gould again or the fact she had been alone for some time, she was struck by a feeling of absence, a lingering of something, even more than someone missing.

~ * ~

"This is ridiculous," Dante Canestrini said, clapping his youngest brother on the back with more force than he intended. "Isn't it time you called Vena instead of sulking about her absence? She's back, right?"

"She should call me." Elio stood up and walked a few paces from his brother, turning away.

"Elio, have you ever stopped to consider why you've never acted like a damn fool over a woman before Vena?"

"So, you think I'm a damn fool." Elio studied his older brother and was slightly amused despite his demeanor.

"At the moment, yes. Listen, plenty of us have been struck stupid over a woman, but you surprised everyone because you never really seemed to care before. Maybe your cool detachment had more to do with your feelings about the girl or woman than your control? Maybe Vena challenges you in ways which are good for you but hard on the ego? She might be the first woman not to fall on a bed with you and stay after you left."

"Might surprise you to know I don't have any need or use for your advice or lectures."

"Fair enough. I should have been there for you more when you were growing up, but the old man made up for all of it, didn't he?"

"Leave Vincenzo out of it. I was seven. He had no choice but to do something."

"Can't do. I have a little history with the man, and I'm not nearly so forgiving. I seem to recall he left our mother when she had cancer with three boys to care for. It's why I went in the military, remember?"

"I didn't say you should forgive him. I know you hate him."

"No, I don't hate him. I hate what he did. There's a difference."

"I don't want to talk about our father anymore," Elio said, gesticulating fluidly.

"He was good to you. I get it."

"Not exactly; he shouldn't be what comes between us."

"He doesn't. I don't like to see you so unhappy."

"I'm not unhappy…curious, maybe annoyed."

"Curious?"

"About why you are suddenly so concerned, and what is your interest in Vena? When is Francesca coming to Roma, anyway?"

"Leave her out of it. My interest in Vena is related to my concerns for you, nothing more. Don't insult me or imply something else. Your insinuation conveys the impression you are worse than you are."

"I'm not going to apologize, but I didn't mean to insult you either."

"Whatever you say, little brother."

"I don't know. Maybe I'm too sensitive on this subject. Vena and I…I'm not exactly sure of myself with her."

"Now, I understand. Let's go get something to eat. It's not often I'm stationed here."

"Then it's my treat," said Elio.

"You're a teacher. Why don't we split the check?" Dante was aware Vincenzo still offered support to his youngest son, the one who had not turned away from him.

Elio let the mild insult slide, reached up and wrapped his arm around his brother's shoulder as they went out into the night.

~ * ~

Considering her return to Roma, Vena recalled the first time she ventured into the city with a laminated guide/map and John Varriano's *Rome, Ten Literary Walking Tours*. Varriano's book served her well. Over the last two years she had walked the outlined steps, returning to some again and again. "I don't care if I appear to be a tourist," she told Elio when he teased her.

"Can't you pretend you are going to get some pasta? At least try to pretend to be a French tourist, not so intent on seeing everything, and put the book away."

"I could, but then I would not be myself. You don't have to come with me."

"But I do," he said half-joking but wearily.

Opening the book to its middle, she began with the Sixth Walk; following Keats and Shelley to the Keats-Shelley Memorial House where prints and documents relating to Keats adorned the walls and were secured in cases. Two prints striking her most powerfully were the death bed drawing of Keats by Severn and Keats' own drawing of a Grecian Urn. In a glass case a lock of Keats' hair was preserved, and she thought wanting to hold his hair between her fingers was at once morbid and exciting. After finding Shelley's, Milton's, and Barrett-Browning's locks of hair in cases in the Memorial House, Vena considered the practice bizarre, but was fascinated as if the strands of hair held their stories.

Leaving the Keats House again and again over time, both in her imagination and repeated trips, she always made the next stop the crowded Spanish Steps. Called by Hugh MacMillan, "a glorious flight of stone," those steps continued to offer a paradox of movement and permanence. For many, Rome called to mind glorious battles, emperors, gladiators, the history of violence and civilizations. Rome also called to hundreds of the world's greatest artists; Keats, Shelley, Joyce, Melville, Henry James, Stendhal, Elliott, Elizabeth Bowen, Woolf and scores of others were drawn to Rome as if by some magical force. The city's paths conveyed the impression of awareness of those who walked upon her stones, retaining memory of their presence.

Vena once told Elio, "Roma is an ancient woman."

"No, no," he protested. "Consider our sculpted emperors and warriors found in the architecture, statues, and designs. You must know of Romulus and Remus, in laying the foundation of the city?"

"I know the mythology, but Roma's resilience in the face of repeated degradations, the way the light filters through her dust creating changing views of her face; this is the city's experience as a woman."

~ * ~

Overlooking one-hundred and thirty Spanish Steps outside his third-floor window, Keats must have gazed at people below with an understanding of how his position in the world would be elevated after death. English poet John Keats knew how to make an exit, which was paradoxically, theatrically dramatic and peacefully poetic, but he couldn't avoid the pain. Yet, he could not have staged his leaving better: the *pensione* where he died, a boarding house since then designated a landmark in a city ridiculously rich with them.

~ * ~

There were one-hundred and fifty Keats' poems and fifty-four published in his short life, but none were produced in Rome, at least, in the known version of events.

Vena tried to imagine those last months of Keats' life. He would have been in pain, but his mind was still working. Severn would surely have left a note or directed someone to Keats' last poem if such a marvel existed.

No poems could have been written in the city in which he chose to live briefly before dying. How was anything else possible? Then Vena answered her own question. Anything is possible.

~ * ~

"Your morning coffee."
"Get out of my face. I can't even swallow without spitting up my lungs." Keats picked up the coffee cup and flung the cup with its contents toward Severn, hitting him and splashing hot coffee across his chest.
"My God, John!"
"Get out. Get out." Keats began violently coughing, spitting blood into a bowl at his bedside.
Severn left the room to change his stained shirt and allow his dear friend to recover his senses and temperament somewhat. The night before had been particularly trying for both of them, he thought. He almost expected the fear and frustration would spill over into the next morning. Joseph decided to go for a long walk through the city, giving his friend time to compose himself somewhat. "Poor bastard," Joseph said under his breath, but Joseph was also upset with his friend who did not seem to appreciate his sacrifices.
"Not up to Dick, dear friend," said Keats to himself, knowing his actions had hurt his most loyal companion. In his cramped, hot room with the smell of blood and sweat, John Keats pulled himself up slightly. He picked up a quill pen and a paper resting on Severn's chair. In those brief moments of lucidity John scratched out a few lines, dipped the pen in the ink bottle again and wrote with the kind of ferocity he was capable of at any point in his brief history.
During an interval, Keats' hand had miraculously stopped shaking. His lungs stopped demanding. When he set the pen down, his coughing began in violent spasms again. He knew this work would be his last, and he scarcely hesitated before tucking the draft inside the thick volume of Shakespeare plays on the little table at his bedside. Joseph would see the poem he reasoned, before falling back on the pillow. Although he would never apologize for abusing his companion, at least Keats would leave him this gift, he thought with momentary satisfaction. Joseph loved the Bard's *Hamlet*, so his decision would be natural. He would turn to the right page

and discover this last gift from the great poet.

~ * ~

In his returned feverish state, Keats imagined Severn and others extolling technical and thematic virtues of his last poem. Yes, Joseph would make certain the man and his literature were not forgotten. Keats counted on Severn even as he abused him verbally in the agony of dying so young.

Severn, however, did not follow the script of Keats' hoped-for scenes. The young English painter and portraitist was distraught, alone in a foreign city after John's death. His return to England would not be easy either, having previously defied his father, and having been knocked to the ground by his old man before leaving for Rome with John. At the time of their journey Joseph never imagined witnessing the agonizing, slow death of his dear friend. He had hoped, no, expected, Roman air would do wonders for the gifted young poet, and Keats would be restored to health. Severn imagined at the time they would go back to England after travels, triumphant.

Joseph could not take in the beautiful face of John Keats in death mask and most certainly paid no attention to Shakespeare's text from which he had read to his friend until a fateful day on February 23, 1921, when Keats breathed his last.

Before leaving the room and hotel forever, Severn impetuously grabbed the heavy Shakespeare volume and handed the book to a student in the street. It was Severn's one indulgence. He had everything else in the room burned to make sure the infection was not spread.

"*Prendete questo. Apporteneva adun grande uomo.*"

"Take this book? From a great man?" asked the surprised, young Italian in his native language. He could neither read nor write in English. He scrutinized the volume as the stranger disappeared in a crowd. After opening the cover he abandoned it. He had been given something of worth, even if he could not decipher it and the young man offered the strange and unexpected gift to his younger sister, Isabela, who was attempting to learn English.

"Perhaps you will learn enough to enlighten us both," he said in

Italian. Isabela was always the brighter one, the one with a quick mind and tongue.

"*Ci, proverò*," she said.

Sadly, it was not Isabela's fate to become a student of English or a student at all; at 15 she was married off to a much older man with sufficient means and money to offer Isabela's father a dowry for the arranged marriage. Isabela, nevertheless, kept the thick volume of Shakespeare until her death many years later.

During the rest of her long life, she never opened its pages, embarrassed by her inability to understand the words but too ashamed to tell anyone. She would keep the book, however, because the foreign words were a gift from her beloved older brother who was to die a few years after he fought with their father over her arranged marriage. She also held onto the tome because she persisted in believing she would master English. She considered the Shakespeare volume a treasure, but had few of those in her life. From time to time she bought the book out when no one was around and simply examined its cover, not quite daring to peruse the pages.

In her dreams, Isabela would read Shakespeare's plays from cover to cover. Yet Isabela passed away after a long life with many sorrows and scant joy...the death of two stillborn children and one in infancy...before the birth of her healthy daughter, without reading any of the English plays in Shakespeare's book. The weight of the book alone, not even figuring the obscure and foreign language, often made her turn away from the text in shame, yet she allowed no one to touch the book. Her brother would have been so disappointed in her. The book, left to Isabela's sole daughter to survive to adulthood, held the undisturbed secret of John Keats' last poem.

Chapter Five
Man Thrown into Colosseum's Hypogeum

"Oh, look at you. My beautiful boy, now a professor at Sapienza. So smart. Such a fine man."

Giancarlo heard the echo of his dead mother's words in cruel mockery every time he found himself further in debt. She would not understand the world in which he operated. Nothing was as simple as the woman imagined with her limited skills, he thought; his mother gone a year earlier. If she could have saved a bit more, had something substantial to leave him at her death, but there was barely enough to cover her funeral. In the end, he inherited a few of her trinkets and bubbles. With everything in her house sold, there was no way out of the financial hole he had dug himself in, unless Sabine's surprise turned out to be true. Giancarlo thought for once he had finally stumbled upon luck. The Fates cruelly mocked him for much of his life, then arbitrarily, decided to grace him with the precious gift of a valuable poem.

~ * ~

A day earlier, Pavoni had made a note in his iPhone about *Idi di marzo*, the Ides of March, marking the assassination of Julius Caesar. He had meant to discuss the significance of the day with his students, but he set out to meet a seedy gold broker about a very valuable poem. This appointment had kept him in a state of near perpetual agitation since making contact with the man Pavoni suspected of having ties to organized crime. Pavoni believed the thuggish man who called himself a gold broker was the key to his freedom from debt, from the threat he faced because he had somehow managed to turn considerable losses into an impossible mountain.

Pavoni also believed the life of a young woman, a student in his class, had worth, of course, but not as much as his own life. Sabine was not even aware of the actual value of the paper she had in her possession simply by serendipity. Her Shakespeare book could easily have been in his own mother's attic, a cluttered little space in which not an ounce of gold or treasure from antiquity was buried. Other old women kept things tucked away, like Sabine's grandmother. How many years had he waited for such an opportunity to present itself? Giancarlo had an innate sense of hierarchies and social order, even as he sought to achieve a higher level in his own life.

~ * ~

Giancarlo Pavoni had never walked the labyrinth below the Coliseum floor although he had stood staring at the ancient realm. This realm, a space uncovered centuries after burial, offered an opportunity for imagining. During those speculative moments of his life, Pavoni considered the degree of panic men and animals must have experienced as they nervously paced in tight confines before being lifted by a complex system of cables, ropes, hoists, pulleys, and metal mechanisms into a sunlight too bright. The sun would illuminate their deaths. The spectacle would have been amazing, even if their gory ends were not also brutalizing for the crowds in attendance. "Imagine attempting to fight a lion or other animals, surrounded by tiers of cheering or jeering fans of either lions or men," Pavoni had once said to his students.

Being a man given to fanciful visions his entire life, Pavoni had drawn an imagined scene of himself at the Coliseum, besting a magnificent lion before he turned to the crowd in victory. But the fatally wounded lion lunged and swung his enormous paw, his claws raking across Pavoni's shoulder and through his stomach. His shield wrenched loose, Pavoni shuddered in death. With his associative orientation, he could create a fantasy with a great deal of realism before redirecting his thoughts to analysis. Backing up, he recognized he would have likely died of fright at the first sight of the charging lion. This was not a scene he would ever paint for his university students.

Of course he would never have bested the beast, even for a moment. His head hung low before his resilient mother buoyed his spirits with her flattery. He was her only child, two others dying in utero, a fact of which she never ceased to remind him. Giancarlo's father was also long dead; the result of an early heart attack, leaving the family with very modest means. Still, his mother had such glorious hopes for her son.

"Oh, my boy, all the girls must love you, but don't you listen to the first pretty one who comes along. Wait for the right one."

Pavoni never had the heart to tell his old-fashioned mother of his interest in young men which was far more salient than his interest in young women. Although he meant to someday reveal his sexual identity to her, the old woman died before he could have such an awkward conversation. In some ways, he thought her death a relief. Even during the brief and sparsely attended funeral, Giancarlo never shed a tear for the mother who had loved him so deeply. For most of his youth he was frequently embarrassed by her dress and old-fashioned manners. Then he learned she had spent all of her money getting him through school and there was nothing left after her demise. These facts caused him anxiety, even disgust.

~ * ~

How a man of his prestige and knowledge could get so deeply into a fund-raising scheme which ended badly was something troubling to anyone who knew him. Pavoni had, however, managed to keep his financial and legal trouble from the ears of his associates and professional acquaintances. Still an impeccable dresser with style, he was able to keep up pretense and few, if any, would suspect he had fallen on hard times.

If he was honest with himself, and at the moment, Giancarlo was being honest, he had no real friends. Life in academia dictated a competitive course. He had made feeble attempts to become more than friendly with another man who taught the classics, but his awkward gestures determined the outcome. The other *professore* told Giancarlo he was engaged to be married even though Giancarlo knew the excuse wasn't true. What could he think after such lies? Giancarlo had compiled a lifetime of misinterpreted gestures. One man he might have been in love with,

Giuseppe, hanged himself in his bedroom three years earlier. Another colleague with whom he had been friendly for some time turned against him when he broached the subject of a loan, not even a considerable sum.

More than lamentable, what followed the moment *Signorina* Esposito walked into his office was that Giancarlo had been considering a number of illegal activities as a means of extricating himself from his recent misfortunes. Poor girl, he thought, how was she to discern the sort of trouble into which her *professore* had landed?

~ * ~

"I have found an original poem written by the English poet John Keats," *Signorina* Esposito blurted out breathlessly. "This sounds kind of crazy, but the poem reads like much of his literature. It's an Ode, and I happen to know the paper in question has been in this book for nearly two hundred years."

Then, she had his full attention. *Professore* Pavoni knew Keats' work and had recently read about an auction at which a portion of a Keats' poem sold for 262,000 Euro. Strangely, Pavoni had even mused upon the idea he would find a rare treasure and end his difficulties. After all, he lived in Roma, and the city still held historical gems buried beneath its stratified floor. Every day of construction they would turn up something.

Perhaps if Giancarlo had not been so severely worried about money and his reputation, if he had not been a professor of the classics, if he had not already thought about various illegal means of removing his burdensome debt, everything that happened next might never have happened at all.

Unfortunately, *Signorina* Esposito had piqued more than his literary interest with her nearly unbelievable story.

~ * ~

"What are you saying? I apologize if I sound incredulous, but how can you? Where did you find this poem? Where is this paper?" His questions flew out as if all part of one thought.

"Seems unbelievable really, but I opened a volume of Shakespeare's plays and there, inside the pages of *Hamlet,* was a paper with beautiful handwriting. I thought at first, the page in English was merely a note written by a student of Shakespeare, but then I looked again and saw the unmistakable signature at the bottom: John Keats."

"How do you know Keats or his signature? How you could think…"

"I'm studying with an English tutor; she's American, but she is teaching me English literature, and she's a Keats' scholar."

This was most unwelcome information. "What is this woman's name? Perhaps I am familiar with her work?" Without knowing exactly where he was going yet, the *professore* intuited this tutor, this woman, would be a competitor in his barely hatched plans.

"You wouldn't know her, I'm afraid."

"Don't be sure."

"She doesn't teach here at Sapienza University but at a private language school and tutors on the side. But this is not important how we met. The American woman is helpful to me, and we had been reading and discussing Keats together."

"Why would you be taking a course at a private language school?" The way in which Pavoni said the words showed his disdain.

"I'm not enrolled in a private language school. I take lessons from her. She is a better teacher than…" Sabine stopped herself from insulting Pavoni.

"I am certain you would do better to get a professional here at the university if you require help keeping up with your studies. I hardly think you should waste your money on a private tutor while you are a student at Sapienza."

"I'm sorry, I…"

"Never mind." His impatience showed in his tone and curtness. "Why don't you let me decide what is important or unimportant here? I don't want to sound dismissive, but if this…this woman is merely teaching at a private language school, she probably does not have her doctorate or the training necessary to assist you in such a delicate authentication. I doubt very much she is a Keats' scholar, as you claim. Further, I find this difficult to believe she would have the expertise to determine whether or not you hold an original Keats' work."

"Oh, but she is—a scholar. She can recite his poetry by heart. I am amazed by her talent. She has been studying and writing about his work for years."

Pavoni was clearly perturbed and trying not to demonstrate it. "My dear *Signorina* Esposito, recitation is not really a difficult skill to master. Almost anyone could learn to recite with a little time and practice. You are a student at the best university in Roma. Why then wouldn't you go to the best and most professional source for help identifying documents?"

"I am. I mean, I'm here. I do plan to show the poem to her, too, but I thought you would better understand what to do with such a find here in Italy because she is not Italian. I believe you will be able to authenticate the origin. I mean, if the poem is Keats' original, the work could be worth a great deal."

"Ah, yes, but let's not get ahead of ourselves talking about specific amounts." Sabine appeared confused, since she had not mentioned a number. Pavoni was indifferent to her reluctance. Finally, the girl was coming to her senses, he thought. "Of course, you are correct. I know what to do with the document, but don't foolishly speculate on monetary values, *Signorina* Esposito."

Sabine hesitated. "I think…"

"The idea of finding an original Keats' poem no one knew about…its existence secret for, let me see, slightly less than 200 years…such a find would involve astronomical odds. I'm afraid this is highly unlikely. One should be realistic."

"But I…"

"To have such a manuscript floating around Roma for nearly 200 years, and no one aware of anything about it?" Although doubting the authenticity, Pavoni was already speculating about the possibility of passing off a forgery at considerable profit. "Do you see the likelihood of a forgery or simple misidentification of a copy?"

Sabine thought of all the treasures Roma still had buried beneath her surfaces. "I realize…. Our city…we have so many buried…"

"What is conceivable is this paper you found is nothing at all…some student's attempt to write one of Keats' poems in his or her hand, perhaps practicing calligraphy."

"No," said Sabine, resolutely. "It's not."

"No?" Pavoni was as shocked as Sabine was by her daring to correct him so sharply.

"No, I mean, it's not a forgery. I'm almost certain, and it appears to be in Keats' own writing, I believe. I almost feel the certainty."

"Almost certain? You believe? You feel? You have qualified a number of dramatic statements framed as if fact. How, may I ask, do you consider yourself an expert in Keats' handwriting or the investigation involved in detecting forgeries?"

"Please, sir, I am trying to find out if this poem is original, and I may have mistaken something in my excitement. The book was in the possession of one family…my family, all these years. If you would rather I take the volume with Keats' poem to someone…" Sabine turned as if to leave.

"No, of course not." Pavoni stood but did not yet move toward her. "Such an action would be foolish. You were quite right to bring the matter to me first and tell no one about this document yet. You've said nothing to anyone, right? Not even your tutor?"

"I may have hinted at the discovery with my tutor, but as a hypothetical." Sabine's face reddened with her lie, yet she considered the lie a form of protection for her tutor. She had no idea why she needed to protect Vena Goodwin from her classics *professore*.

"I would like her name. The name of your tutor?"

"Why is her name important? I thought, foremost, we should find out if the poem is authentic and discuss what we should do with such a treasure."

"Quite right, *Signorina* Esposito, I meant there are many thieves in this world who would try to take advantage of you, of such information for their own gains. I would hate to see this tutor lie to you or try to trick you to extort money. I would imagine she is in need of money, considering her circumstances. When you are ready, I assume you will share with me the name of this tutor. She's a foreigner, an American, you said?"

"I am not a fool, *Professore* Pavoni. I'm aware I must be careful, and I have been. I'm afraid I have misrepresented my tutor in some way because she is absolutely honorable. In fact, I would trust her with my life."

"Oh, please do not be quite so dramatic. I will take your word for it. This American is not intentionally trying to rob or deceive you. I'm sure she has some interest in the poem for the sake of scholarship." Sabine focused on Pavoni as his sarcastic tone warranted some kind of response from her.

"I don't..." Her right foot pivoted toward the door, and Pavoni jumped in quickly to prevent her departure.

"Of course, you do not know yet. This is a painstaking process, and we will see great care is taken to get at the truth."

"That's all I want here."

"Good, good. You may bring this poem to me for examination. I will determine whether or not you have a forgery. Once established, we can proceed. When we have authenticated the document, you may wish to discuss our finding with your tutor."

"And how should we proceed?" Sabine's emphasis on the word "we" betrayed suspicion.

"Sabine, please allow me to finish." Pavoni cleared his throat in preparation. He instinctively knew this was a test. "I will contact top repositories of Keats' writings. I suppose we should begin by notifying our administration and perhaps the Harvard Library in America, the British Library, the Keats House in London, and weigh public good against what such a find might mean for Italy, for Roma, and what these repositories might be willing to pay the University or our city for housing this treasure, even if temporarily. We might launch a bidding war. Such an enterprise could be very helpful to our university and our students." Pavoni stopped momentarily. "Are you expecting some kind of finder's fee?" Then he realized he had gone too far with the "fee" comment, and he had been doing fine up until then.

"No. I'm not expecting a bidding war? A finder's fee? I was not even considering this kind of payment. I want to find the right situation for this gift from literary history."

"Hypothetically, you must know I'm simply positing here. Good to run possible scenarios before we consider the next moves."

"But I thought the idea was to bring Keats' poem to light? Share his work with the world. At least, my intention…"

"Quite right. Mine too. Perhaps the best home for such a document would be our own Keats-Shelley House here in Roma. Who better to appreciate this last act of the English poet than the citizens of the city in which he chose to spend his final days? Most fitting. Yet, such an exploration will take time and much research before a gifting can be made."

Sabine smiled, and Pavoni was suddenly surprised this attractive young woman had not in the least piqued his interest earlier in the semester. He stared uncomfortably at her large, dark eyes made more pronounced by her smoky eye make-up. There was, however, a young man in the class for whom he had grown overly fond without making any explicit gesture. "I knew you would be able to help me," she said with evident relief.

"How does the poem open, may I ask?"

Sabine's face reddened. "I'm sorry. I have not memorized it. Perhaps I…"

"Never mind. I am curious. What makes you think the document is an original?"

"When I read it, the poem's rhythm and word choice appear to be like Keats' other poems. There were multiple allusions to mythological gods."

"Yes, those kinds of references would have found their way into nearly any poem during that time period. I'm afraid we will need to do more than merely feel the originality. Now, let's set up a time and place to meet when you will bring me the document. Come alone. Let's put the date in our calendars but tell no one. Take very good care of the document and don't touch the actual instrument with your fingers before the work can be authenticated and archived, or dismissed as a forgery."

"Of course, yes, I treat…I am very careful not to get my fingerprints or damage the paper in any way. I wore gloves when I picked it up."

"Very smart."

"I placed the document back inside the pages of the Shakespeare text where I found it."

"For the time being, your action seems wise. Now, to meet…"

"Couldn't we meet in your office here?"

"No." Pavoni knew his negative response was too final and quick in coming. "Until we know exactly what we are dealing with, we should not involve the university. These things could end up embarrassing our standing, particularly if the poem is a gross forgery. Until later, until we have absolute proof of authenticity, let's keep this between the two of us."

Sabine looked at him with a hint of suspicion once again. "Not involve Sapienza?" If she had followed her instincts and fled, run down the hall, out of the building, and never returned, she might have lived long enough to graduate and pursue her dreams.

"You see, we would not want to bring any kind of negative publicity or notoriety to Sapienza in the event of an imitation or some other kind of scheme, you understand. Such errors could be damaging to the University's reputation. We must keep this very quiet…between the two of us."

"I guess." Sabine remained uneasy, but unwisely dismissed her distrust. "I'm not involved in anything unseemly, *Professore*. I would never…"

"I am not suggesting you are. Simply better to take precautions when we don't yet know the origins of the document or with what exactly we are dealing. There will be a time and place for involving the University, for sharing this discovery joyously should the work prove to be an original."

She nodded in agreement. "But I don't see how anyone could be trying to create a forgery and profit from this by sticking a poem in some old book in my Nonna's house? The book has been in the family for nearly two-hundred years."

This new information caught Pavoni off guard. "Does your grandmother…is she aware of the poem? What have you told her?"

"Oh, no, no. My Nonna died years ago. As far back as I remember, she never mentioned either the Shakespeare text or the poem inside of the book to anyone. She did leave the Shakespeare volume to me, however."

"So, neither your mother nor father are aware? Have you had a conversation about…?"

"My father Gianluca passed away last year, before the semester. I thought I told you." Sabine considered him with growing distrust. How could he have forgotten their sole conversation before this? A conversation in which she laid her soul bare and told him of her difficulty keeping her mind on her studies after the trauma of her father's death.

"Yes, yes. Of course. I'm terribly sorry. I remember our conversation." Pavoni recalled nothing from the earlier exchange in which his student tearfully explained why she had been late to class. He had so many students. How was he to keep track of every student's parental situations, their endless tales of woe and stream of problems flowing down the hallways? This was not a primary school. "Your mother knows nothing about the poem? We must be sure of this."

"Why? My family would not care even if I told them." She nearly laughed at the thought of her widowed mother Lia questioning the authenticity of a Keats' poem, as if her mother had ever heard of Keats or knew of any English poetry at all. "My mother doesn't read very much really and certainly does not read English poetry. She does not even speak English. The book was in my Nonna's bedroom."

"For two hundred years, you say?"

"Sounds strange, I know, but our family home…we've been in the same building in Trastevere forever. Her room was filled with little personal possessions Nonna could not part with. My Nonna never liked to throw away anything, and my mother and father moved in with her years ago. We recently sorted through her things, after her death, after my father's death."

"Hoarding. Yes, I appreciate the problem, but in this case her habits may have been a bit of genius on your Nonna's part if the book ends up holding such a rarity."

Sabine was suddenly missing her Nonna and thought, if she were alive, she would grasp the situation and advise her. "You really think I should not discuss this with my mother? Perhaps she could tell me why the book was kept all those years? I don't see any reason not to share this with my mother, particularly if the poem has real value."

"Precisely for the reason you have articulated, you do not want to share this information with anyone. I understand your desire to share with your mother, but better not to say anything to anyone, even her, until we can authenticate this document. And, as you stated, your mother does not read English. There is reason not to worry or excite her at this time. Why make her anxious over a piece of paper when the paper may, in fact, be worthless?"

"Of course."

"You are to be commended for your honesty and perception, even if the document turns out not to be credible," he added.

"I believe you will find the work credible."

"And again, to avoid any embarrassments or worse, please do not share this information with anyone, even your English tutor. This is imperative." The mention of the tutor worried Pavoni. A third party could wreck his scheme before he had even finished devising it. He could persuade Sabine's mother of the paper's worthlessness, but an English professor might be far more difficult to trick.

"I understand."

"Good."

Sabine left Pavoni's office unsettled but excited. Air outside his cramped office space was easier to breath. The amount of old and new paper in his little den nearly overwhelmed her. She sized up the room and puzzled as to how he found anything in such clutter. Her mind racing, she could not wait to have the document authenticated, but why was Pavoni so suspicious acting? The more she thought about it, the more she wanted to share the paper with Vena Goodwin despite Pavoni's warnings. What she had not shared with Pavoni was the fact she had already mentioned the poem to Vena and promised to bring Keats' original to her at an appointed time.

~ * ~

Although Vena already knew about the supposed Keats' poem from an earlier conversation with Sabine, the tutor was not nearly so suspicious when her student told her. In fact, her English tutor suggested Sabine contact someone at the University first. Sabine smiled, thinking about Vena's generous reactions and the fact Pavoni did not realize she had already shared the information with Vena. Still, he would likely be the best person to figure out whether or not she held an actual treasure or some worthless piece of paper. What might such a discovery mean for Roma? For poetry? For scholarship?

Sabine's feet barely touched the stones on which she danced home. Even as she stepped lightly, she thought of the history still buried beneath the city, artifacts lying in wait for rediscovery. Her optimism filled her being to such an extent she thought she might actually leave the ground. Then a plan occurred to her: she had not told Antonio about the poem or Vena about Antonio's proposal, the student with whom she had fallen in love. Yes, the discovery of the poem was akin to falling in love, she thought.

~ * ~

Giancarlo Pavoni could feel his heart beating too rapidly after the young woman left. Had he been too insistent? Better to be casual, but then, if she offered the valuable document to someone else? Who was this American woman, this, this tutor? Suppose she was able to place her hands on the paper before him? Could he trust Sabine to honor her word? How ridiculous I am, he thought. He worried the girl would run home and tell her mother, share the paper with the American woman, and alert authorities. Breaking out in a cold sweat, he leaned his head on his hand, balancing his elbow on his desk, feeling faint.

In a twinge of regret, Giancarlo realized he had barely noticed the attractive young woman until she asked to speak to him after class. Even then, his attention was divided over concerns about a debt he owed. He recalled when Sabine first made herself noticeable to him. He could hear himself whisper her full name.

What he planned to do with the poem was beginning to form. Yet, instinctively, he knew this document was genuine. The Keats' work could be worth more than he had ever dreamed, and there was now a way for him to pay off debts he owed for his gambling. No one would be breaking his fingers or face. He was also fully aware he never should have become involved with a pawn broker whose deals always made him feel dirty and nervous. But the gold/pawn broker was where he would attempt to change his life. The man was unscrupulous and would not care about turning a valuable document over to libraries, or repositories of literature. They would not argue about whether or not the University should be involved.

Both End in Speculation

Dealing the Keats' poem would merely be another transaction for the burly man Pavoni had already visited too many times.

Perhaps, the poem would bring enough to enrich him, not merely pay off a debt. What he would tell Sabine was a kernel in his skull, but the lie had been planted. Convincing her the poem was a clever fake would not be difficult.

The solution. He knew now he would claim the document was a forgery, but he would tell Sabine he intended to use the poem to show students how a document could be counterfeited. Sabine would go home saddened, but no worse for the information he gave her. Then, he could sell the work through Guerra on the black market. Ah, he thought, remembering the wide gap in the gold broker's smile. Guerra was the source demanded by the situation. Unfortunately, he had used him before to pawn some of his mother's jewelry. There were a few pieces of his mother's meager treasures left, and so little over which to bargain. Now, he had something, or almost had something. He could taste the wealth like the finest wine swirling in his mouth before swallowing.

At one time in his life, Giancarlo was distinguished for careful forethought, for planning, and moderating his behaviors to get ahead. Those were the early days before his obsession with gambling began. As he watched his student walk down the hallway, he turned and shut his door again, considering how like a hallway his life had been…long and cold, nearly deserted, but possibilities awaited.

Once he knew she was out of the building, Giancarlo clicked on his computer and began searching Keats' poems. Fortunately, as a classics scholar, he was at least familiar with Keats and all of his allusions to the Greek and Roman gods, filtering out Keats' passionate poems. Would he really be able to tell a forgery from an original? He doubted it, but all he had to do was trick the pawn broker, convince the fat, ignorant man the poem was worth a fortune. Cite a few lines, point to some classical references, confuse the bastard and all would be fine. How much should he ask for?

Searching for figures on the Internet, Giancarlo began a chase. He planned to find a way to use Sabine's document to enrich as well as extricate himself from his terrible debt.

~ * ~

Professore Giancarlo Pavoni had been to the Coliseum more times than he could count, but on the evening of March 14, Giancarlo was lying in pooled blood inside a body bag at the lowest levels of the Coliseum. From a historical perspective, the Coliseum had always impressed the young university professor of Greek and Latin studies.

A hulking figure dressed in black, pulled up the construction vehicle in pouring rain, and dragged Pavoni's wrapped body out and, with considerable exertion, lifted the bag over his shoulder. Indifferent to the Coliseum's night lights and cameras, pictures blurred by the downpour, the mysterious man was thinking about body weight. The city's carelessness about farming out construction on their monuments made everything possible. This man's specialty was dismantling and dismembering anything and everything. Of course, he could pay a couple of mechanics to do his bidding on a stolen truck. He knew they could be trusted because they owed him money, and owing Guerra money could be a death sentence.

Guerra was surprised the middle-aged man was nearly as light as the young woman had been when he climbed steep stairs inside the Arch of Constantine. Comparing body weights was the straightforward but determined thought process of the man who was immune to risks; a man who knew Webcams would capture his photo, scenes of his crimes, his construction truck. None of the physical evidence mattered because they would not find him or link him to the scene. He had, however, left a conspicuous clue, one designed to confuse authorities. Stapled to Pavoni's shirt was a note reading, "*cazzo di migrant*," fucking migrants.

On a stormy night, *Professore* Pavoni was quickly and unceremoniously dumped into the Colosseum's Hypogeum. Giancarlo's handsome head, with its sharp long nose, and high smooth forehead, and large dark eyes, struck ancient masonry walls of the labyrinth several times in descent, breaking bones. His damaged body fell into an abandoned capstan where a mangy lion once climbed from its cage straight into the arena above. If he had not already been dead, *Professore* Pavoni would surely have died from his brutal fall. He would also have been outraged at the lack of ceremony, but perhaps, pleased he would land in the midst of ancient Roman rituals.

~ * ~

After the discovery of the body, the rains finally stopped, the sun came out in force, casting artistic shadows along the broken walls of antiquity, but no one commented on the majestic beauty of the scene; horrifically murdered victims becoming the focus of the day. Even gradations of coloring in the ancient stone took on a sinister note.

Chapter Six
Luciferous

"When's the last time you wrote?" Elio yelled over his shoulder as he tossed a red checkered cloth on their little wooden table, his manner of helping with dinner.

Vena laughed. "Hold onto the thought for a moment." She was finally writing creatively again after the turmoil of uprooting her life; learning Italian, finding a steady job, making her way in a city in which she would always be a foreigner no matter how long she lived there. She had also learned to cook, not merely adequately but like a gourmet. "Thanks for caring, darling," she said playfully pecking him on the cheek.

"I do care. You should spend half your day writing, not constantly teaching and trying to solve murders."

"Unfortunately, not a ratio possible for most of us with our feet on the ground and five Euros in our pockets," she said setting down the plate of Trattoria al Moro, a dish of snails in ragù sauce she had nearly perfected. "And I don't seem to be solving any murders or mysteries lately. I've really been of no help."

"Ah, *squisito*." He lifted his fork, then stopped himself and waited for her to sit down and pour the wine. "Five Euros? Do you need more money?"

"No. Of course not. Thanks for waiting. I did notice."

"I will always wait for you." He hesitated, and the statement hung in the air too long. "I really don't think you should be worrying about trying to discover a murderer. In fact, I don't want you involved because your amateur investigation could be dangerous. What would happen if you come across this person? Suppose he is armed, and Dante and his officers aren't around?" He picked at the food. Unnatural for Elio to wait for much in his life, he had been thoroughly spoiled by his mother before her illness, and

Both End in Speculation

later by his father, who indulged his youngest son's every whim. Elio was the son who did not hold blame against Vincenzo for leaving their mother during her illness.

"I'll be fine. I'm not venturing off on my own, anyway. Let's not think about the murders tonight. You asked me what I have written lately, and I have something to show you after dinner."

"What? A poem?"

"Yes, I wrote about the four fountains. May not be any good, but the writing came to me as if the stone was speaking."

"I remember you telling me how much you loved our dirty old fountains at the corners, but they are personable, right? Did you write in English or Italian?"

"English. I tried to write in Italian first, but I kept getting stuck. I'm ashamed because I went back to English. Too many imprecise words."

"It's natural. Maybe in a year or two you won't even think about writing in English. I will read all of your Italian poems and ask when your English disappeared."

"Maybe." Vena recognized Elio was projecting them being together in a year or two and knew she was still unsure.

"So, why the fountains?"

"They surround each other. I feel as if they must be talking to one another when no one is around."

"My beautiful Vena, such imagination. And a good cook, too. After dinner, you will show me your poem." Occurring to Elio in the moment, he realized he wanted to propose to Vena, but somehow asking to marry her over a dinner she had cooked did not feel right. There would be a grander setting for his overture.

When she finished the dishes, Vena thought about how many young men her age in America would have cleaned the dishes, maybe made dinner too, but Elio had been used to being waited on. There would be time for him to change habits, or he might never change them. If he had proposed to her then, she would have turned him down.

Returning with her poem, she said, "You don't have to say anything, but it's my interaction with the fountains. I'm glad I wrote about the fountains anyway."

Elio began reading the poem out loud, but Vena stopped him. "No, silently first."

Via delle Quattro Fontane

"[S]ome fountains can be quite stupid, like, for instance, those which give its pretty name to the Street of the Four Fountains and which consist of two extremely plain Virtues and two very dull old Rivers." [William Dean Howells]

Unexpectedly coming upon the Four
Fountains on Quirinal Hill in Rome, I
was struck by these Baroque sculptures,
unearthed from ruins of the Baths
of Constantine, then resurrected
at the intersection of Via del Quirinale
and Via XX Settembre by Pope Sixtus V,
the Fountains operating in concordance
at intersection of busy streets. Unlike
the rivalry of architects Borromini
and Bernini of the churches which they
adorn, the Quattro Fontane suggest an
intimate yet apathetic knowledge of one
another: like husbands and wives long
ago used to sleeping in separate quarters.

Diana sleeping still, one hand resting
against her stone head with its austere
curls. Her female cohort Juno gazes at
none of them, nor at us, as she freezes
her look downward at a lion the size of
a dog, its mouth the opening for a thin
stream, the suggestion of a once mighty
river. Juno's right breast is bare; her
hand holds the lion's crown about to be

Both End in Speculation

bestowed. Behind the Goddess is a bird
with its wings spread wide, representing
Fortitude, and above the bird a tree with ornate
leaves intricately encased in the grime
of ages. Neither Goddess seems
concerned with her male counterparts
Arno and Neptune, also in repose.
They know them both too well.
Neptune leans against a male lion,
peers out from behind his left shoulder.
The index finger on his left hand is
missing a last digit, a casualty
of existing much too long.
His body and face are deeply pocked
and darkly discolored with exhaust from engines
of centuries. Neptune lies in front
of the suggestion of corn or wheat stalks
written into the wall. Bas-relief
so much simpler in design than
Arno's tableaux. Arno, accepted
personification of the Tiber, with his
exaggerated phallus sprouting fruits,
perpetually looks out at pedestrians
and motorcyclists, while a she wolf scans
streets for prey. Arno, too, is missing
fingers, but his brow, unlike the others,
is knit with concerns.

Howell's critique may have been
right for a young country developing
its own voice and ironic style, but not here
in Roma, where these sculpted Gods
and Goddesses, defiled by contemporary
exhaust, long ago swam out of rivers
of imaginings, their dark memories etesian.

"I thought you said poetry should always be heard?"

"Yes, but not mine, at least the first time through."

"You don't sound very confident."

"Read the poem please; say whatever you wish." Vena waited for him to finish for a couple of seconds, then left the room to make tea. When she came back, he was staring at her. "You're done. I'm waiting."

"It's prosy, not really like a poem," said Elio. "I'm not saying, I don't like this work, but Four Fountains reads like description. Is the effect what you intended?"

"I can't speak to intent at the moment. I wrote the poem because they spoke to me."

"They…the fountain sculptures spoke to you? Okay, but these mythological creatures are so distant from one another, isolated even in proximity in your poem," Elio said, his brow raised in slight anxiousness. "'Apathetic knowledge.' Should I read anything into this phrase? About the two of us?"

"What? No. Of course not. You're not a stone god."

"But the female statues are not even concerned with the males in the poem. They've grown entirely disinterested."

"Are we talking about the bas relief or us?"

"Maybe both."

"If I was concerned about us, would I have asked you to read it and stand around until you responded, fidgeting? You don't like the poem. Fine. I'm not offended."

"Did I say I didn't like your poem? No…it's the statues' attitudes that are bothering me. They're indifferent to judgment. You should not care what I think."

"I do. The Four Fountains are not a blanket statement on all of our intimate relationships or anything," Vena said.

"Fair enough. Give me time. I might get to like this poem."

*

Vena gulped a Coke too quickly and nearly spit the carbonated soda back up while waiting for her Eritrean student. Not entirely sure he would show, she thought about all he had to go through in order to survive in Roma. Fitsum said he could not afford her usual fee, so she adjusted the price dramatically. Elio reminded her to stop under charging her clients.

"Charge the African the same fee as you would a Roman. Why are you drinking Coke for breakfast? It's bad for you."

"I'll get a coffee, an Espresso on the way."

"You're not independently wealthy. These private language schools are notorious for not paying on time, shorting their teachers. Even tutoring, you don't bring in much."

"Thank you for telling me what I know. Are you complaining about my rather pitiful help with the rent? I'll do better."

"Stop it. Of course, not. You know what I'm saying. Besides, you don't really know this guy. Eritrean? He could be from anywhere. He could be a criminal on the run, a mugger or some kind of schemer. What makes you think he really wants to learn English?"

"Because he already paid me for a lesson even before I had given him anything. He is eager to learn and remarkably adept at languages."

"All the more reason not to trust him. I don't trust any of them."

"Them?"

"These Africans. Too many of them coming in. I don't want you meeting with him alone." Elio was pacing their tiny kitchen, pleading.

Vena stopped her movements, tilted her head slightly. "I don't want to upset you, but let me ask, if he was an Italian, a Roman, would you be asking these questions?"

"No, maybe, I don't know. You make me sound racist."

"Elio, you are racist. These are difficult times for Italy and for the migrants fleeing horrific situations. Nearly everyone is racist to some degree. The humane response is to at least be more aware of it."

"I'm not a racist, but you've been here a short time. You don't fully understand how... Africa immigrants flooding into our country have changed Italy, altered all of Europe. They've washed up on our shores without means, without anything but desperation. They are hungry and poor, and we haven't the resources to take care of them all. We don't even have the resources to help all of our own people, to fix our own economy, our monuments." Elio knew Vena would connect with his last comment since the bodies of the murder victims were placed at monuments under construction by private business.

"I'm not oblivious to the complexities of the issue, but your statements are racist even if you don't intend them to be. 'Washed up on shore?' Think about the metaphor you used to describe human beings."

"Maybe I do intend it. Why? Are you condemning me? I'm tired of the problems resulting from this influx of migrants. What are we supposed to do? The rest of Europe doesn't want them. We don't have the kind of space, the land you have in the U.S. We don't have the jobs either."

"Of course, I'm not condemning you. I recognize this is a disaster, but a human disaster with people who are going to die if they remain in their own countries. Prejudice exists in some degree in probably all of us, but I want you to think about another way of looking at this multi-faceted issue."

"Trust me, I've thought a lot about it. We can't take in any more. They are changing my country. I almost don't recognize Roma anymore."

Vena bit her lip slightly, then drew in a sharp breath. "You know, Romans went into Africa not because the native people asked them to come. They came as aggressors to colonize free peoples. One of the long-term effects of colonization is destabilization. I'm sure Africans did not recognize their homes after Europeans came, enslaved them, and stole their resources."

"Damn it, Vena, I don't want a lecture."

"I didn't know I was giving one."

"You were. You're not Italian. You don't understand what they've done to my country. Let's not talk about this anymore before we end up in a fight."

"Because we disagree?"

"Because I don't want to have a fucking fight with you, and I don't want you in danger. Don't you get it?"

"Give me some credit. Even if you don't trust Fitsum, trust me. My student and I are meeting in a very public place, and this young man has to pay for his lessons upfront. He is an individual, not all of Africa, not a representation of all migrants."

"Then I'll go with you," he said, suddenly leaning over and stroking her hair.

She pulled back. "No, don't you see, it's foolish. You can't follow me all over the city."

"I already did, remember?"

She did remember. His obsessive following her was how they met nearly two years earlier when she was running away from a crazy professor. Her professor had come after her in order to try and silence or punish her for the discovery of his murders.

"Elio, I have shown I can navigate this city on my own. Show me a little faith and confidence in my judgment."

Throwing up a hand in a gesture indicating he was done, Vena left their apartment.

~ * ~

Meeting Fitsum at the Almost Corner Bookstore on Via del Moro 45 in Trastevere, Vena was still carrying the argument with Elio in her head. As soon as she exchanged greetings with her Eritrean student, she spotted Elio already in the bookstore. He was standing against the wall of books, peeking around a display. If Fitsum had not been there, she would have confronted Elio and had a real fight with him right then and there. Instead, she shot him a glance of annoyance but refused to acknowledge him further. Perhaps they could talk during lunch together after she met with her student.

"*Buona Sera*, hello," Vena called to Fitsum. "What do you think of this book store?"

"So many books," Fitsum offered after his greeting, bending back at the tall wall of books facing him. "Every book in English," said Fitsum surprised, as he glanced around.

"Yes. I thought I would introduce you to a place where you can find lots of books written entirely in English. I discovered this amazing store a year ago. You don't have to purchase anything. Pick them up and read a few. Feel free to browse."

Immediately, as if given permission to touch the books, Fitsum chose a text with a colorful, green and yellow decorated cover from the crowded, waist-high bookcase in front of the stacks. "*Africa39*," he said out loud. "I like to read a book."

"This book," Vena corrected, peeking over his shoulder at the cover. "New Writing from South of the Sahara," she read. "By Ellah Wakatama Allfrey. Oh, wait, Allfrey is the editor not the author. This is an anthology of many different writers."

"Anthology?"

"A collection of numerous works by different authors," Vena brought her hands together foolishly, as if to demonstrate the concept of anthology. "I'm sure the work is remarkable."

"Too much," said Fitsum, dejected, as he noticed the price, then put the book back in its place, neatly arranging the volume upright.

"Write down the title and editor. Perhaps you will come back for this book at another time."

Fitsum looked at Vena with incredulity, aware she could purchase books when and where she wanted. Vena was, in the moment, tempted to buy the volume for him, but she remembered being chastised by Elio for her overly generous tendencies. As long as she was economically struggling in Roma, she had to be conscious of not giving away what little she had.

"Maybe another time, we will buy this one," she said to the indulgent owner or manager who was standing nearby. Elio gave her a wink which she noticed but refused to respond. She found a Henry James volume on the shelf and let the book cover fall open. Fitsum positioned himself behind her so he could glance over her shoulder this time. "Here." She handed him the book, and he looked tentative. "Open to any page. What do you find?"

"Words I don't understand."

"Don't give up."

"I'm tired. My head spinning."

"All right. Let's go get some air. We'll talk…in English. You'll practice."

When they walked out along the alleyway, they ran directly into a festive little parade of people dressed in colorful shirts.

"African," Vena said. "They must have come to save you from

homesickness." They moved to the side, and Vena waved as the short parade danced past.

Fitsum shrugged. "Not my people," he said. "Not sick for home."

"Of course, presumptuous of me."

"Presumptuous?"

"Oh, meaning, I didn't respect the boundaries. My statement showed my ignorance and prejudices, I'm afraid. I'm sorry."

"Do not be sorry. I do not feel at home with them. Maybe never feel home anywhere, not here, not in Eritrea."

Vena understood but nearly stuttered before telling him, "My real name is Advena, and the name means foreigner, migrant, interloper, so the name has always made me stop and think about what home calls up and what being a foreigner feels like."

"You do not like your name?"

"I'm afraid I've never been fond of Advena."

"Ah, why you say your name is Vena?"

"Yes, my mother Greta chose Advena before leaving me."

"I will change my name, too, when I get to England."

Vena imagined his name would be changed for a very different reason than hers, but she said nothing. They walked to a bench where they talked about Fitsum's urgency to learn languages.

"If I know more languages, I fit better."

"Yes, knowing the language helps anywhere. It's why I've studied so hard to learn Italian, too."

"I am like the cats here."

Vena knew he meant feral cats populating the ruins in Roma, but she was not sure how Fitsum intended the analogy. She was also aware of the municipal effort to get rid of cats from the historical sites, officials citing health concerns. Unlikely Fitsum intended a meaning in which Romans wanted to get rid of him, but she recalled Elio's words. "How you like the cats?"

"All your Roma cats, hiding in alleys, in corners, behind columns in ruins…they find a way to eat, catch what they can; a mouse, rat, scraps people throw, fish heads tossed from alleys behind restaurants, but they are still wild. Cats here belong to no one. I am like these cats."

"All of us should feel free, but you are not like the cats. You are a man."

Fitsum appeared to give up the argument. He handed her a paper. "This is what I work on for you."

Vena scanned the paragraph. "I don't think you intend the word 'peregrination' here," said Vena, leaning toward her student.

"Journey of families to come to Roma long and slow," Fitsum responded, "like peregrination," defending his choice of words.

"Ah, yes, but peregrination also means 'meandering' or moving about without an urgent destination or goal. You had a goal." Fitsum was perplexed. She tried again, "Meandering, moving carelessly or without aim." Fitsum then expressed understanding. "And you want your family members to arrive in Roma as directly as possible, right? A straight line."

Fitsum stood up in agitation and moved around the bench. "This is why I not so good in English. Too many meanings for one word." A passerby stood suspiciously staring at him before moving away.

"No, no. You are doing incredible. Your English is excellent, really. These are mistakes native speakers make, too. When did you leave Eritrea, may I ask?"

Fitsum sat down again, hitting his fist on the bench for emphasis. "Long story, and I say poorly in English or Italian. If you spoke Tigrinya, Arabic, or Bilen, you know better what I say."

Smiling, Vena asked, "How many languages do you speak or know?"

"Five, six, but some better. Eritrea, Italy's colony before, so I know Italian better than English, see."

"Perhaps you should be my teacher in Italian, then," said Vena, "I know four languages, and I struggle with expressions in all but my native English."

Fitsum rubbed the scruffy short beard on his chin then finally smiled. "I would be good teacher if you learn Tigrinya or Bilen. What do you know about my country?"

"Know of your country? I've never been there. I'm afraid I'd be lost trying to learn Bilen. The Italians gave their former colony Eritrea her name. You probably know Eritrea is a translation of the Greek word meaning 'red land.' I also know your homeland is in the horn of Africa, but beyond this paltry information, I remain ignorant of your country, other than reading about the diasporas. But you have made me curious, so I am learning."

"I did not understand all your words, but I like your teaching."

Vena had found one of the most effective means of tutoring her students was through conversation rather than writing and testing.

"Red land," Fitsum repeated in English.

"Yes, red land could be symbolically associated with…"

"With drought, death…maybe they see future when Italy named my country."

"I read there are over 5,000 of your countrymen a month who leave for other countries or Europe."

"Everyone disappearing in Eritrea."

"From, the word you want here is 'from' Eritrea. Prepositions are tricky."

"From. No job, no food, forced…is right word? Labor. Men are slaves to government. Made to be in Eritrean Army. Tortured. Disappeared."

"Yes, I'm sorry everything is so hard for the people in your country."

"Hard everywhere. I know many refugees from other countries, escaping, make life better somewhere, other home."

Vena thought many times before, but pointedly in the moment with Fitsum, about her ability to choose between cultures and countries. She could return to the United States or make Italy her permanent home. Choice, while intimidating, is a welcomed option she considered, but Fitsum and his countrymen did not share the luxury of choosing. From the marked bend of his back, his multiple broken fingers and bent nose, his thin frame, she could tell Fitsum was carrying burdens with stories hard to hear. Should she ask about his difficulties in reaching Roma? No, better not to delve into those waters.

"How did you do on your homework, your translation?"

Fitsum pointed a finger for emphasis, "I choose magazine news report, like you say. But I not find all words. This one," he said indicating the paper he was holding. "This word, 'luciferous,' what does this word mean? I look up Lucifer and read 'rebellious archangel,' maybe 'Satan?' Make no sense."

Vena smiled. "Great word, and one I think many people speaking English fluently would not know. Luciferous means emitting or bringing light. Lucifer is an entirely different word, although they share an etymology or word origin. Lucifer has its origins in the same history of words relating to morning star or bringing light; *lux* meaning light and *ferre,* to carry."

"Like sun?"

She showed approval. "I suppose you could interpret in that way, but more often the word is used in its metaphoric sense of bringing enlightenment, bringing knowledge. Understanding as light."

Fitsum said, "Too many words for me. You are luciferous." He laughed, and she joined him.

"Next week, we will meet at the Piazza Santa Marie," Vena said, trying to come up with something which would not tax the young Eritrean's wallet.

"Maybe not next week. Business. Two weeks at English book store. Okay?"

"Okay."

"You held a novel by Henry James today, an American author. The title, *The Portrait of a Lady*."

"Yes, but too many big words."

"James is difficult for native English speakers. I don't recall if this quotation is from *Portrait* or one of his essays, but he once wrote, 'One's destination is never a place, but rather a new way of considering things.'" Searching for the scrap of paper with James' quotation on it, Vena felt in her pocket and two slips of paper fell out. Fitsum picked up one.

"Is this what you are looking for?" On the paper was the address she had found in Pavoni's office."

"No," she said too loudly, then changed her tone. She reached over and grasped the paper before offering another. "Here is the quotation I wanted you to have." She had been so careless with the address, but she didn't dare leave the critical piece of paper at home or Elio would have questioned her about it.

Fitsum read the quotation to himself, his lips moving, then said, "I think Mr. James was in mistake. My destination…the destination of migrants is a place, but place keeps changing."

"You, sir, have taught me another way of regarding things. Do you know the poet Fessehaye Yohannes?"

"No."

"I thought you might have heard of him because he was an Eritrean. He died in a prison in Eritrea. They said, in complete isolation."

Fitsum winced. This part of the story was familiar to him. "Many prisons, torture, disappearances. I'm sorry I don't know this poet. You are sad today."

"Oh, I'm sorry. I was thinking about another student of mine. Something terrible happened to her."

"What happened?"

"She was murdered."

"This woman had a name?"

"Sabine."

Suddenly, Elio made his presence known. He was ready to go home. This Eritrean man was suspicious, he thought, knowing he did not like the way the young African smiled at Vena.

"There is man behind me looking at you," Fitsum said with his head perfectly still. "I should stay to make sure you not in danger."

Vena turned her head and made eye-contact with Elio. "No, it's okay. I know him. Everything is perfectly fine. I will see you soon."

Fitsum slightly bowed to Vena, then left without turning again. As he found himself in another narrow alleyway, Fitsum thought about Vena and was certain this would not be the last time he would see her. He knew the address in her pocket, and it deeply troubled him she held onto such a dangerous location.

~ * ~

Elio sheepishly made his way over to Vena and sat down. She was shaking her head.

"You have to stop following me, Elio. Even if I didn't mind, which I do, your shadow behind me appears to everyone as if you didn't trust me. How do you think your lack of trust makes me feel?"

"I know, I know, but"

"I'm not in danger. Fitsum is simply trying to learn English and improve his Italian."

"Maybe."

"No, not maybe. Stop being so suspicious, and most of all, please stop being suspicious of me."

Elio lowered his head and assumed the mantle of a guilty child. "What is it?" Vena finally asked to break the awkward silence descending.

"I've never felt this way before," he said. "I'm afraid to lose you."

Although she tried not to smile, Vena's lips broke into a curve. "If you don't want to lose me, then let me go. I don't want to be monitored any more than you do. Respect me enough to believe I will do the right thing for myself and for us."

"I respect you," Elio protested. "It's the rest of the world I don't trust. The African…there is something not right. He is suspicious, I'm telling you. He could be dangerous. What is he learning English for, anyway? Why did he come here? How do we know he's not some kind of terrorist?"

"Ah, Elio. Really? He is trying to scrape by, survive in a brutal world far from his home to which he cannot return, and so he learns another language to attempt to fit in and find employment. He's not a terrorist."

"You're so certain? What makes you think you know him? Because he talks to you in English? There's not enough work for Italians. I don't think you should help him. We don't want any more Africans living here in our city, in our country. We make it too easy for them. Give them food and shelter."

"I know you don't think Italy should help, but on this, we think very differently."

"On this, we do."

"Fitsum has a right to try to find a place in the world, and I want to help him. Imagine, this is not about a generic people, migrants, but about one person. I want you to think about what it would be like if you had to leave Italy through no fault of your own."

"I wouldn't expect everything handed to me."

"Neither does he. Suppose, you had no money and no connections, no Vincenzo."

"Vincenzo, again?" Elio said bitterly, feeling the irony of his own words falling off his tongue. "All right. My father helped me, helps me out, but his assistance is a matter between families, not between countries."

"I'm glad your father is generous. He has helped me, but this is about compassion for those who have nothing and no place to turn."

"They should turn to their own fathers, their own countrymen. Italy cannot be a father to the world."

"Nor Roma its mother," Vena said, thinking about her feelings of Roma as a woman.

"Roma as mother? What?"

"Consider for a moment, you were worried the government would arrest you and kill you for your ideas. Your father is dead. He was murdered in a raid by men who might have been government forces or anti-government. You don't know because they all murder. They had already taken everything from you, even your food and means to get it. Wouldn't you want someone in the world willing to try to help you get along?"

"If I left my country, I would make my way on my own as Romans have done for centuries."

"I expect they feel the same, but even then, you would not be on equal footing."

"Maybe not, but I don't think they feel the same. These African migrants aren't even grateful for what we give them. You are American, so you don't understand."

"Meaning what exactly?"

"America is so big. You have room and the economy to absorb these waves of people from other lands. Then you shut down your borders when you want. You talk about building walls, but you have a wide ocean between you and Africa."

"And you have the Mediterranean Sea. We also have planes, and people still arrive in America from all over the world. However, I know, this is not a fair equation. We are a much larger country."

"Italy is not so big. Our borders are porous. They cross the sea in leaking boats and expect us to save them. We cannot take them in any longer. Someone has to stop this exodus."

"By stop it, what do you mean?"

"Border security. I don't know exactly. I'm no expert, but something has to give. Italy is going broke, and we can't take any more Africans or Arabs."

"If Italy had never had a hand in colonialism, perhaps Italians, too, would have an argument for trying to remain uninvolved, but observe Eritrea."

"What about it? Long ago. You're not…you talk like a lawyer."

"Lawyer? On the contrary, I am being fair. I want you to consider…"

"I've considered enough. Why don't they try to fix the mess in their own countries instead of coming here? We should close our ports to them. I'm tired of this stupid argument."

"And let them all drown?"

"They chose to get in those damaged boats. It's not up to us to stop them. The rest of Europe, they'd as soon leave us with all of them."

"I don't think…"

"What? Are we supposed to take in 100,000 million Africans because their continent is drying up, their governments are corrupt, and the people are starving? I don't know of 100 million spaces in my country for them, do you? Maybe they could all sleep on our doorsteps, on the stairs, on the roof."

"Don't be sarcastic and cruel. I don't feel it's you."

"Not me? Maybe I am exactly the man who is aware of the migrant problem. Maybe I have prejudices based upon experience. Maybe you don't know me at all." Elio had worked himself up to the point he was pacing, clenching his fists, ready for the fight. Even his jaw was tightened.

"Such a terrible problem with no easy answer. Maybe a solution lies in helping to stabilize these countries, shore up their economies, and help them end internal corruption, but we seldom manage to do this difficult task well in our own countries."

"If you've an answer for broken economies, you should probably share such valuable information with the government because there are millions of us who want out of this fucking mess."

"In Italy, I think they are working on it."

"They'd better work a little damn faster."

"We all have hard work to do," Vena said.

Elio didn't know if her last remark was political or referred to Vena and her student, or the effort he needed to exert to stay with her. "We do," he finally responded.

Vena, however, was already preoccupied with returning to a murder. Who was the last person to see Sabine alive?

Chapter Seven
Passing in the Night

Daniel Solomon and Suad Kahsay left from Tripoli, Libya at 2:00 in the disorienting morning. They had marched along the coast from their original point of destination, and the migrants were exhausted. Zuwara had been effectively targeted by an EU military operation to stem the tide of human smuggling, so the traffickers in people temporarily moved operations to Tripoli until they could move back again. Daniel and Suad boarded a blue wooden boat with a chipped white stripe around it, the paint faded, but migrants saw a black shape in the water. "Blue," said Daniel, looking down at the sea and boat as they moved with the waves. He was nauseous but his stomach settled more quickly than those around him.

Captained by a wiry man who told them he had great knowledge of the sea, the boat appeared sea-worthy enough in the dark. "I was a fisherman for years. Now I'm a captain, taking you to Italy, to Europe, to a good life. I know these waters like my own city."

Daniel knew from the man's age alone, he was a liar. But the fisherman had taken on the character of a man who could still navigate a boat, and the rest lay with a higher power. So many promises. The smugglers talked of Europe as paradise. Even though Daniel knew they were all story tellers, hustlers trying to move people like merchandise, he liked to imagine such a place waiting for him and Suad.

All they had gone through to get to the launch came flooding back to them in the dark with wind drowning hushed voices and moans, anxious men and a handful of scared children. So few children, so few women. Mostly a boat filled with strong young men who were able to make the arduous journey to the sea. Foolhardy young men pushed and shoved, some even balancing on the gunwale, dangling their feet, tempting fate. The captain had cautioned them, but darkness was approaching, and they were anxious, anticipating.

Seventeen-year-old Suad lost her husband Kidane and father in Eritrea. Kidane's brother Medhane was also conscripted by the government and killed in Eritrea's endless, unofficial wars. Suad's infant and older sister died on the long passage across the desert. So much death in Eritrea and on the journey. Another young man, a friend of her husband's, Abdullah, was also gone. Abdullah had promised to protect Suad and her sister on their long quest, but he had been killed in a fight with a smuggler over an increase in the price of passage. Such stupidity, thought Suad, angry with her husband's friend. To be murdered haggling over so little when they still had some means. Why did he bring a knife if he did not know how to use it? By the time Suad found the missing Abdullah, he had already bled to death. She held his head in her lap but refused to cry again. Much later did she feel pity for him rise up in her, overwhelming her yet again.

~ * ~

After waking, Suad would still reach for her son who was no longer there. She turned her head to tell her sister something before the death came back to her. Ghosts were everywhere around her, calling to her. If she had not been with Daniel...

Daniel lost his wife Terhas early in the journey when they were on the run. She was so young. They had been married a year when he decided they must leave. If she had not married him, he thought, then perhaps she would still be alive, in her mother's home. He hadn't known she was so sick or they would have waited before setting out. Although he had chosen Terhas, she had not chosen him, and Daniel weighed the sadness of her discontent with his guilt over the loss of her life. He was selfish, he thought, wanting such a young wife, but then Terhas could not conceive, she told him.

~ * ~

"Forgive me, husband, I am so ashamed," she said quietly, her head bent nearly to her chest.

"There is nothing to forgive. I am a modern man and understand biology. This is not anyone's fault."

"Do you wish to take me back?" For the second time, Daniel saw fear in his wife's eyes.

Her fear confused him because he always thought she would want to go back to her mother's house.

"No. If you wish to go to your childhood home..."

"I do not."

"I want you to remain with me. We will manage without children. We live in a hard world. Perhaps better we don't have children."

Then, without movement on his part, Terhas threw her arms around the thin neck of her husband and kissed him. Such a passionate, unasked for kiss surprised him, but he never forgot her touch.

Months after their marriage, her father asked Daniel if he wished to return his bride, but Daniel told him, no. They would learn to love one another in time, and if they did not, then they could at least be good companions. "She is a hard worker and will be loyal," said her father, apologetically.

Daniel thought of the moment when Terhas decided she loved him. Her kiss came to him again before she died, her eyes wide with fear.

"Don't be afraid," he said gently. He swallowed. She was gone.

~ * ~

Partially out of kindness but more from loneliness and attraction, Daniel brought Suad under his wing after Abdullah's murder. The dead husband's friend had been careless. You have to know when to fight and when to swallow your spit. Abdullah could not keep his mouth shut even with two women and a baby to protect. Daniel thought him a fool, but would not say so to Suad because he understood loyalties of families and long-established relationships, even when unearned.

"You stay with me," Daniel told her, "I will protect you, and we will get across."

"I can't swim," she told him softly, so no one else could hear.

"You will not need to swim. We are riding in a vessel and will land on another shore. You will see. We go through Italy then maybe to France or even England."

"England?" She had never thought of a land so distant before this. Italy was as far as her imagination could take her. Even then, she suspected Italy was some far-off impossibility.

England had been Daniel's goal, but now he simply wanted to reach the other shore with Suad. His dreams, however, were tempered by the harshness of the journey. His throat dry, his body aching. Sometimes, his head felt as if it would explode.

Sleep came fitfully, and when he woke, always with a start as if someone was about to smother him or slip a knife quietly into his back. This woman made him want to continue, however. She was still beautiful even if she was worn and sad, and he thought he might marry her when they found their way to Europe. If they didn't reach England, they might live in Belgium or France. His cousin had made the passage to Brussels. Daniel still had enough to bribe an official or two. Like others before him, he had valuables sewn into his loose and baggy clothing. Although he was not proud of it, he had also stolen from the dead but never the living. What could a corpse do with treasures?

Suad didn't know if she would remain with Daniel, but he was kind to her when other men leered or pulled her down to try to rape her. These attempts had happened twice after the first time on their journey. Following Abdullah's death, she was raped the same night. In those few days before Daniel brought her with him, her life was a nightmare. She thought he, too, would rape her, but she went willingly, not knowing what else she could do.

Daniel was aware Suad was not a virgin but, unlike other men, didn't care. He had also made a vow not to touch her until she consented. This surprised Suad so much she realized she liked Daniel and would catch herself almost admiring him. But then such thoughts would vanish, and she gripped loneliness in a way, making her contemplate death with relief instead of fear.

Even in the middle of the night, she refused to allow herself to think of the first night of her marriage, her brief moment of happiness when she had been beautiful and her young husband was strong and good to her. After his senseless death in a war neither knew anything about, she thought she, too, would die yet found strength again when Eyob was born. Holding the boy child in her arms, Suad found the courage and power of giants for the first time in her short life.

~ * ~

At the end of the passage nearly across the desert, Suad's sister Sarama whispered something, but as Suad bent her own ear to her sister's mouth, those cracked lips offered no more words, releasing a horrible, dry rattle.

But when her boy died, too, so soon after Sarama, Suad wanted to give up, to do nothing more than to lay in the desert next to her sister and son and let the animals pick at their bones. Daniel had helped her bury her baby as deep as they could in order to keep scavengers away, but there wasn't time to bury her sister more than a few inches. The act of digging the shallow grave pained Suad terribly. She could not take her son or sister home for mourning rituals. To leave them in this place of desolation did not seem possible, but leaving them is what she did. At some point on the journey, Suad had lost her hope and her guilt as one casualty.

~ * ~

Pulling her up, Daniel put his arm around her. "We're leaving," he said, giving her no other choice. She thought if she made it, she would have to remain with this man even if she never married again. He would carry her if she did not comply, so she forced herself to get up again.

There was some trouble with guards near the shore. Several people were culled from the lines. Daniel placed something in the hands of a guard, and the larger man motioned for them to continue. "A narrow escape," said Daniel after they had passed out of earshot of renegade guards. "They are not really officials...robbers, but I had enough this time."

~ * ~

They reached the shores in Tripoli. Border patrols had largely disappeared, the result of civil wars and an exodus which could not be stemmed. Lucky ones were permitted to awkwardly climb into the open boats after sections of émigrés were again culled. These sessions consisted of muddled interviews resembling interrogations; many held against their will in an abandoned warehouse where they would be separated according to which ones could be ransomed for more money, which ones could be forced to labor for passage, which ones would be raped or sold.

Again, Daniel and Suad were fortunately sparred this torture. Daniel told the men who masqueraded as border patrol officers, he and Suad were married and offered yet another bribe. A quick pat down revealed nothing. Each time, he feigned the trinket was his last because even the suspicion he held out more would command a thorough body search of them both. Then they would take everything left. Suad learned to avert her eyes, cover much of her face and head. Perhaps for this reason, they left her alone. For this, Daniel and Suad were grateful.

~ * ~

All had set out over brutal desert sands. Death from thirst is an ugly, hard way to die, but at the end, at least quiet Suad thought. They had sand up their nostrils and in their ears, down their parched throats, between their teeth. Her tongue transformed into a thick, arid land. Her hair was caked with sand.

Not all made the harsh journey across the barren landscape. Children succumbed more often than women. Few old men or women attempted the journey. Some of the young women made it, but more of the young men. At the end, mostly strong young men boarded the boats for other shores. Those who could swim feigned confidence. They clung to one another out of desperation but had grown weary of human touch.

~ * ~

Suad said nothing as they boarded but held tightly to Daniel. When a large, brusque man motioned for them to move forward, Daniel told her not to look back at those crying because they did not have enough money to pay for their passage. A man with a limp screamed and tried to flee, but he was tackled and held down. There would come a time to help others, but this was not the time, Daniel told her quietly.

"What will happen to them?" Suad asked Daniel as he edged her along between rows of waiting émigrés. How they would all fit into such a vessel was a mystery to him.

"Put one foot in front of the other," he whispered. "They will get on another boat later. It will be all right for them, too," he said, although he knew many would remain and end up as slaves or worse until they worked off their ransom or died, or escaped again to some other misery. What more danger could the sea hold? Death was always ahead and behind them. He tried not to think too far out over the water. No use planning beyond the next moment.

Daniel and Suad were edged close to a group of West Africans who had come together in a gang, arriving from a different route. The West Africans took care of each other, and Daniel worried about coming up against them. He told Suad to keep her headscarf tightly about her with eyes lowered.

"I cannot swim, Daniel," she said as a statement of fact rather than out of fear. Shifting weights of men rocked the vessel with violence.

~ * ~

The sea would have terrified her once but no longer. Eritreans, Syrians, Ethiopians, Nigerians boarded every kind of boat at the port. Those weather-worn and proven by fishermen and those bound to sink part way over the two and a half to four-day journey at sea, depending on the route and the skill and good fortune of the captain. A group of strong young fighting men from Gambia and Senegal had made their way to the Libyan shores. Perhaps they had been in the military as they still appeared to be in training shape. Already, they were fending for one another, ready to fight to survive. Even false border guards were intimidated by this group of banded men.

The captain pulled a few of these men from Gambia aside and ordered them to work as crew. Daniel saw and understood the interaction even though he did not know the language. If these fellow migrants were the crew, he thought, what would become of them all? A few babies crying were hugged to their mothers' breasts for fear of giving everyone away. So few babies. Suad envied those women with children, but she should have known babies would probably not be able to survive for long even if they did find land again. Without reading news reports from European papers, she could visualize images of their little corpses floating. She saw her own son again in the black water's movement. After a day and a half at sea, she was already having delusions. She had not drunk any water since the morning they left shore.

Seasick passengers were moaning, men leaning over gunwales, hanging on tightly because a jolt from someone behind in the overcrowded boat could send a man, woman, or child over the side into blackness. If anyone fell, the boat would not turn back. The luckless or hapless going overboard would disappear almost without question. Ahmed, their young captain, had bluntly told them this fact. "We won't go back for you. No turning around." There was no protest; resolve in its place.

In the boat, bodies pushed against bodies until there was no space to move, barely enough to breathe. Suad peered in the one direction which did not hold more bodies. She watched the moon partially emerge from behind clouds and could see its light reflected in the eyes of those on board; a ship of luminescent, disembodied eyes in which fear and hunger and longing were stories untold. When she turned to Daniel behind her, she saw his eyes were fixed on hers. Comforting, if only momentarily.

Suad studied the man steering and decided Ahmed was a merely a boy, not a man at all. She did not tell Daniel but thought the boy would end up killing them with his greed and foolish bravado.

Death by his parts, his nostrils, his tongue, was on Suad's neck even when she slept standing. Some mornings recently, she resented Daniel for not letting her give up. Thoughts of the desert quiet came to her even as they set out over the moving sea, and she could smell sweat, salt and water.

~ * ~

Death was Suad's thought as Daniel held her hand with one of his own. She closed her eyes and nausea move around inside, her body becoming attuned to the waves. The warmth of Daniel's hand kept her tired eyes open for this last part of their migration.

Daniel hurt her fingers because his grip was too tight, but she never said a word of complaint. As the overcrowded dinghy lurched, she thought back to the long passage bringing them to this point of uncertainty. All the suffering, the death of her baby, her sister, her husband's dear friend, weighed like stones around her neck pulling her down. She understood they would sink her when the boat capsized. Waves splashed up and hit them in the face, soaked their clothes, and they shivered even on a warm night. She never thought of turning back. Like Daniel, she could see in one direction now even if the future held her death. She turned her face toward Italy.

When Suad and Daniel had boarded the dinghy, he was nervous, but most of all he was excited and hopeful. He knew Italy was out there even if he could not see land. He placed his hand gently on Suad's shoulder. In the current, he imagined their lives together, children running around them laughing, his own wide grin returned as he greeted his family with a fist full of fish on a stringer. In his vision, Suad was again standing straight and tall, proud to see her husband return with such bounty.

~ * ~

At last, the line of migrants was halted. They could carry no more; others tried to cling to the gunwales until a hand pushed them off into shallow water. If those who were pushed off could swim, they made their way back to the shore in hopes of another boat. If they were unable to swim they struggled briefly, flailing in the dark, swallowing sea water, fear and bitterness before death.

A human smuggler left shore after loading his wooden trawler with 180 men and a few women and children standing until told to sit, but there wasn't room for all of them to sit. He shouted orders at them in a language merely a few understood. Instructed the fleeing mass of humanity not to lean or move to one side or the other once they left the bank. The sinking of an overloaded dinghy the week before had made him more agitated than usual.

The smuggler had been a fisherman in the old days when he could still make a living tossing lines in the waters. The old days merely a phrase he used because he had been working as a boy too young; he didn't know his own age but had a rough idea. Providing passage was far more lucrative and a little more dangerous than fishing for a living. If they were lucky, the Italian Naval ships would spot them and rescue the lot. Once he escaped or was let go, he would begin this fool-hearty but lucrative passage again.

His friend Ahmed, a fellow trafficker, had drowned with all of the people in his dinghy a week earlier. Tareq had warned Ahmed about overloading the dinghy, but the fool hadn't known the sea as expertly as he had bragged, nor known how his boat would respond to the tests. Tareq was angry with his friend for dying, but he knew such a fate would not befall him. This knowledge was behind him, and human smugglers seldom questioned their decisions once made. Unlike the souls on his boat, Tareq was a strong swimmer. He was at ease in the sea.

~ * ~

If they are fortunate, Fitsum thought, as he waited for Martino Guerra to finish the forgeries, passports, identification papers, a ship would intercept their boats nearer shore. Everything is predicated on luck and the kindness of foreigners. Of course, the smugglers who know the routes best have a good sense of where the Navy boats might be and steer in their direction. A few believe they are clever and can find the way safely to the Italian coast. Those who reach shore have a shot at seeking refugee status or, in some cases, asylum. A few escape into Italy and move out across Europe without papers or means until they are detained.

The process was too slow, Fitsum knew. Maybe a year in CARA, and many would be turned down, sending them back or holding them in enclosures like animals for indefinite periods of time. "Why I do what I do is my business," he told the burly criminal Guerra in delayed response to a question.

"You are a fucking fool, negro, but as long as you are a paying fool, we can do business. I don't care at all. You get away or get caught; it's all the same to me, as long as I am paid." Guerra genuinely did not understand Fitsum's motives. Why the little negro helped these strangers he could not understand, but he did not let the man's actions trouble him. Fitsum was a steady supplier of gold items, many quite valuable, so their business was professional, profitable and quick.

Fitsum swallowed his spit. He detested Guerra, but was willing to do what had to be done, this business with a demon. Fitsum, too, was a mercenary, but there was more than one thing separating him from Guerra. The Eritrean provided passage and papers for compassionate reasons, in addition to money. Fitsum understood their hearts from watching their eyes before they spoke. There was the quiver at the edge of their mouths, the slight moisture around their nostrils, a shaking hand or hidden gesture. In all of those uncertain eyes, Fitsum saw his dead mother, his lost sister, his brother, his family. Yet, to Guerra, he said nothing more.

He could have made his way to England long ago. Practicing his English, he had even invested his precious money in a tutor, so he would speak adequately when he arrived on the island nation. His tutor was an American who was so innocent, he thought, but he liked her, though he generally had little use for Americans and their arrogant ignorance.

Traveling alone and with Euros, he was confident he could find an entrance, but there were so many others in peril. Crossing and terror seemed to change the shape of the migrants' pupils. Even hardened men had his sympathy and understanding. Whatever their circumstances and past actions, these people all shared something very precious with Fitsum: flight born in hope.

With Guerra, however, Fitsum found no common humanity, no sympathy nor empathy; in its place, a deep hole where greed and cruelty were stored, money accumulated. You were either worth something to Guerra or you were worth nothing. And if you were worth nothing— Fitsum saw in Guerra something his fellow Italians did not see: those who walked by the man or came to pawn wears Guerra would kill to survive, but also for profit, for spite, for amusement.

Fitsum was not a fool. He tried not to feel for any single individual in the group of émigrés he moved through the country. Better to sympathize with the whole lot. Some would get through and he would not sorrow over every individual death and those caught up by agents and returned; those young women who ended up in the sex trade. His efforts could not save them all, but if even a handful arrived in France or Germany or Belgium or England, they were worth his efforts and the daily risk of getting caught.

He knew what he undertook was dangerous work. Yet he made his mission to help those embarking upon this journey along the southern coastline and back up to Roma, picking up those who landed without authorities' knowledge, desperate to find a way further into Europe. He thought about these people, some from his own land, many more from other countries. All arrived on this foreign soil with temerity in their eyes, a stance narrating they would kill if they had to do so. They brought a parcel, something strapped inside their shirts or skirts holding value. This item, a last belonging, an inheritance or gift, would be traded for Euros, for papers, for passage. They seldom had enough.

Scanning Guerra's interior room, Fitsum noted irregular shapes in dark corners, perhaps an antique clock, a musical instrument, a case with gold rings; unlit parts of the shop suggested rather than told details. The bare bulb over Guerra's work kept even the men from disappearing into shadow. After a number of visits and feigned disinterest, Fitsum knew where Guerra kept cash, passports, gold rings and necklaces. He had watched Guerra open his safe. Then their eyes met. Both smiled but each other's smirks were difficult to interpret, a preference for working in darkness, a commonality. On everything else, Fitsum sought to distance himself from this criminal before him, the other man concentrating on forgeries, indifferent to desperate men but not their pockets.

"What will you do when I'm no longer in this business or refuse to trade with you?" Guerra looked up from papers to size up the much smaller man he thought he could crush with one blow. "You and your endless supply of fucking little Africans pouring into my country? What will you do then with your beggars and whores?" Guerra was smiling, but his words were not in jest.

"I will find another." Although Guerra was an intimidating presence in any culture, Fitsum had already decided how things would end between them. He fingered the handle of a knife in his pocket as a comforting friend. This brute would die at his hands, and Fitsum would feel nothing but contempt for this monstrous thief. Not so strangely, Fitsum never considered himself a thief although he took what was necessary.

"Hah. Or *Polizia* will find you first. You with your pitch-black, ugly skin. If you close your eyes in the dark, no one would see you. But in the daylight, ah, you stick out as the ugly toad you are. Even with all of you Africans running around Roma, you will be found and arrested. I would pick you up today and toss your rat's ass in a cell before deporting you back to Africa if I were *Polizia*. Then again, maybe I would sell you first, so be careful. What could I get for a rat your size?"

Fitsum did not allow Guerra's words to bate or distract him. "I think you are about as far from *Polizia* as any man," he stated calmly.

Guerra snorted a kind of choked laugh. "You might be right, but you are no saint. I'd kick your skinny ass outa here except you bring me some interesting gold pieces. Better than most. This strand." Guerra held up a necklace once sewn into the clothing of a Syrian man by his mother. The jewelry must have been part of some family's fortune. "How did this come into your grubby little hands again?" He turned to Fitsum with curiosity.

"The same way they all come to me."

"I'll give you a fair price for it," Guerra said before changing topics, "I know I've asked before, but I find your answers comical. Why do you care about them? You will never see any of these Africans again, and they will never thank you. They won't even remember you when they get to wherever they're going. You are a tool to them and nothing more. They might think less of you than I do. At least, I'm amused by you."

"They thank me," Fitsum said dully, unwilling to explain to this brute what helping refugees meant to him or why he did what he did. The Syrian who handed Fitsum the necklace told him the chain was stitched into his pants, but he was afraid his valuable gift would be found and stolen, and "all would be lost." With every encounter, the Syrian thanked Allah. The necklace was all he had, but its quiet presence sustained him. When Fitsum reached for the necklace, the big man withdrew it, his fingers closed tightly around the chain before finally extending his arm and releasing the treasure.

"You want one more look, fine. Won't change the price. I will give you what the market bears."

"We both know you take more than what the market bears." Fitsum carefully examined the gold chain one last time before relinquishing it. The man who once owned the necklace had tried to come with his whole family, but the family finally decided to give the money and jewelry to him and his wife and son alone. The woman, like so many others, died on route. Haalima made her husband promise to take their son to safety.

~ * ~

"I buried his mother with a little soil on top of her," the man told Fitsum, shame written across his face. "The thought of animals digging her up has tormented me since leaving her body behind."

"She will not know or care. You did what you had to," Fitsum responded.

Even if Fitsum wanted to forget their faces, he could not. The man placed his large, scarred hand on the child's head, and said, "We are here. For this, she would be proud of me." Fitsum knew their stories, those they had lost, girls and women who were snatched along the way. Although children died and women were raped or often sold, the horror was told best on the faces of the men thought Fitsum, because he was a man and because those surviving men bore witness to all done to each of them and all they did not do to prevent the atrocities.

~ * ~

Fitsum told Guerra nothing of their stories. "A decent price is all I ask."

"Ah, you are no more than an *idiota negro* but at least you speak Italian. Now, let me see what else you've brought, worm, and we'll talk deals…my price because, you see, you are not in any position to ask for market price." Suddenly, Guerra snatched the necklace belonging to a

Syrian family. "And to think they all trust a worm," he said, spitting on the floor of his shop.

In the moment, Fitsum knew it would be the last time he accepted such insults from Guerra.

Chapter Eight
Compro Oro

Compro Oro. A gold sign with black lettering, "I Buy Gold," was prominently set in a slender front window in the piazza Monte di Pietá. This reputable location in Roma was ideal for Martino Guerra. He paid to keep the veneer of respectability, not because he cared about such pretensions but because the address brought him more business.

His shop was still in one of the few areas where buildings were not covered with graffiti. Tourists occasionally wandered in carelessly or out of curiosity but were less likely to come to his store than head for the hot spots, the monuments. His primary customers were Italians who begged for some quick cash and were willing to make a bad deal to get it.

There were no migrants living on the street outside the doorway of his gold broker shop whom he would have to clear away every morning. This was a fact of location and police presence. Unlike the front of his sex shop, where the "negros," he said with contempt, frequently slept in rags until he kicked at them.

One morning, Guerra stopped at his sex shop on Via Adamello, later than usual, but still before his manager would show up. He couldn't wake the vagrant in front of the door with the usual nudge. After several swift kicks with his boot, one to the man's head, Guerra realized the negro was dead. He didn't think he had killed the skinny wreck at first but knew a couple of his first blows hit the man square on the temple. Maybe the negro had died from a heart attack or malnutrition? Who knew? But his boot had blood on it, and his kicks had been vicious. He wasn't concerned except for the fact he had to deal with a body which wasn't going anywhere until he moved the African.

Unlocking the shop, he quickly dragged the dead weight through the door and shoved the body in a storage bag, then stuffed the bag in a closet meant for supplies. Disposing of evidence always posed a challenge, regardless of how many times he had performed the task and the various ways in which he was skilled with making things disappear. There was also the aggravation of cameras on streets and shop fronts with which he would have to contend. Already the fiction was forming: the bum on his doorstep wouldn't leave when asked, so he kicked him a couple of times…the action discernible from cameras…then the beggar asked for food but wouldn't get up, so Guerra was forced to drag him inside in order to give him some of his own bread and cheese. After, he sent the beggar on his way through the back entrance, so he wouldn't attract negative attention and dissuade customers from entering. First, he had to make the negro appear alive. He decided to pull the corpse out of the closet; picked the man up to a slumped standing position and swung a dead arm over his shoulder. Then Guerra opened his door, waved with the arm of a dead man, and laughed, before turning back inside. His movements appeared staged, but the blurry videos would show only enough to provide cover for reasonable doubt should the films from street cameras be viewed.

    This death angered him because he hadn't set out to kill the negro. The act was pointless and without compensation. Guerra wasn't even entirely sure he had killed the beggar. Yes, he tried to talk himself into believing the fiction by repetition, perhaps the negro was already dead when Guerra delivered his blows? Except the blood made Martino think a dead man would not continue to bleed from a head wound. He knew less about biology than he supposed. As if his day would not be complicated enough.

    When Martino decided to kill, he typically relished the act, but killing this negro in the doorway was clumsy or misfortunate. He was immediately irritated with *Polizia* for not keeping out this homeless migrant. The government was to blame for allowing so many Africans to flood into his country. If Italia would not take reasonable actions, Guerro would. Too many of them in the streets, anyway, he rationalized. What did he pay his rent for if not to avoid this type of interaction? Now, he would have to devote part of his day and evening to planning disposal to be sure nothing led back to him. He noted the bright sun, and more businesses had cameras, but a beggar slumped in his doorway could not be his fault. A

Both End in Speculation

storm was predicted for the evening, however. The back alley was dim even in daylight and cluttered with clothes hung out to dry, extending from lines across the narrow street, providing more than adequate cover.

Already, he was altering his explanations for anyone witnessing the act. He went over his narrative again to check for flaws: the first story involved the migrant waking up, and he fed him out of the goodness of his big heart. Then he set the negro on his way, out the back door so as not to deter potential customers. The story didn't sound quite right, he realized, particularly the part about his big heart. No one who knew him would buy any theory about his kindness.

With an aching head, Guerra realized he had to come up with a better story. Martino actually contemplated turning the corpse over to the authorities and confessing he found the man already dead. Story two. Story number three, perfected story: the negro fell sometime during the night, died in his doorway. He simply moved the body out of the way with his foot. Story three sounded much better, less complicated, but the lack of details would garner the interest of *Polizia* or Carabinieri and questions. Officials would descend upon and snoop around his shop, and the next thing you knew, he was being cited for something. Choice four: tell no one. Dealing with officers—military or civilian—left a sour taste in his mouth, so he finally chose to conceal the body and incident rather than report it. If a store owner reported something seen on a camera, he would be ready with story one.

The door opening surprised him and a young woman came in early. Had he forgotten to lock the door again? Fortunately, he had already shut and locked the supply closet door, hiding the dead African.

"You're early," he yelled at Ilaria, annoyed he would not have time to dispose of the body until after all of the girls and clients had gone home.

"Sorry. Thought you'd be happy to see me early for a change."

He laughed even under the circumstances. This particular girl was typically late. "I'm always happy to see a beautiful girl." Guerra went up and slid his hand down her shirt to feel her breast, and Ilaria did not pull away. She pouted, defiant. He liked this girl. If there was time, he would do her later, but he had to get back to his gold store first. There was other business to attend to.

"Where's Tony?" His manager also made a habit of pressing the boundaries of work hours.

"Saw him coming up the street right behind me. I thought he was stalking me," she laughed with a throaty swell, speaking of strong drink and a young lifetime of cigarettes.

Even before she finished, Guerra's sex shop manager walked in, jingling his keys and whistling a tune. But he was limping.

"What's wrong with you?"

"Nothing really."

"You're fuckin limping like a gimp. What the hell happened to you?"

"Ah, a little scuffle after hours."

"What kind of scuffle?"

"Pissed off some sucker when I made a pass at his girl. I was in no condition for a fight, so I ran. Turns out, he did, too, right behind me. I had to climb over a fence, but the barrier was higher than I thought. The ground was not so soft and maybe someone had been digging a hole on the other side, but the dude chasing me gave up."

"Idiot." They both laughed. "Nothing broken?"

"Thanks for your concern, boss. Don't think so."

"Listen, I have some new toys I have to inventory personally, so don't get in the inventory room, or I'll take it out of your wages, or your skin, for the next month. You do, and you'll be limping on both legs." Guerra knew Tony

had keys to the door.

"Hey, I won't go near it. Got too much to do, anyways. The last thing I want is to inventory a bunch of new shit." Ilaria laughed now, knowing how much Tony hated real labor. She had her eye on Tony. Guerra had his eyes on her.

Guerra was uneasy leaving a body in a locked closet with people in and out of his shop, but he couldn't pull the skinny African corpse out and construct a tale on the spot about how he got there. He thought about trying out story one on his employees, testing their reactions, but the entire affair intensified his headache. This unexpected business was getting more complicated by the minute. He'd arrived at story three before going back to the first tale. Then he remembered dead bodies begin to smell very badly. There were heavy fragrances in the air already with Ilaria twirling her finger around a lock of Tony's hair. Ilaria liked to soak in perfumes, Guerra thought.

"Hey, I pay you to do the clients, not the help," he yelled at her, and Ilaria pouted, but then laughed. One of these days, Guerra thought, the girl would not be able to laugh her way out of a beating. "Get in the back where you belong and be ready."

"I'm always ready." Ilaria shot a naughty glance over her shoulder at Tony and stuck out her tongue as temptation more than insolence before exiting between the thick red curtains.

"Fucking little bitch."

"Yes, lovely, isn't she?" Tony smiled.

"I'll fuck her later," Guerra said. Tony was a little uncomfortable. He didn't like to think of Guerra on top of tiny Ilaria.

"Kick 'em all out early and lock up at least two hours before regular closing," Guerra said. "I've got some business to take care of. Come to think of it, hand over the supply closet keys."

Tony pulled the keys out and disentangled one, placing the key in Guerra's open hand. "C'mon, Boss, you can trust me."

"Like hell I can." But, for some reason, Guerra actually trusted Tony. Perhaps the trust arose because the young man was so eager to please. But Tony never really liked physical labor. They weren't very much alike, but Guerra decided the kid gave him a laugh or two every day. Still, better to be on the safe side and take the key.

"Your wish is my command." He was trying to keep his hair from standing up with spit on his palm, rubbing his hand over the tuft.

Guerra touched his temple self-consciously, then stopped abruptly, realizing he was stroking the spot where he had kicked the African. After Tony locked up, he would have to go back and get rid of the body. What a day and night ahead. Formulating plans both exhausted and excited him.

"Stop preening and get some customers in here. Put a girl on the street to tease. Set out a whole bunch of those scented candles, too. Place stinks."

"Sorry, boss. It's not me, I don't think." Tony pulled his shirt toward his nose.

"Don't forget to blow out the candles before you leave. I don't want the place burning to the ground." As soon as he said the words out loud, Guerra thought about allowing his sex shop to go up in flames, but they would still find the body, and his insurance didn't cover everything. He discarded the new idea immediately.

"Sure, boss. No problem." Tony loved his job. Girls and sex. Sex and young girls. Dumb and desperate clients. Money floating around, dropping on the floor. Steady pay, plus Tony typically pocketed extra cash every day and night by insinuating a client might get caught. A sweaty old businessman cheating on his wife would suddenly panic and stuff more Euros in his hand. And, he got along with his boss. An angry boss who was never as mad at him as he pretended to be. Tony thought he could tell when Guerra was putting on a show. Life couldn't be better.

Martino Guerra left abruptly, trying not to worry about the corpse. If Tony found it, he would have to deal with Tony later. He didn't like to think about offing his manager, but he would do what had to be done.

By the time Guerra got back to his gold broker shop, it was already afternoon, and he worried he had lost clients and money. Always something. He flipped his sign to Open. A man in an outdated, worn suit stood across the street, apparently waiting for his arrival. What was wrong with these people? Guerra motioned for the man to come forward. They were always uncertain. Maybe they really shouldn't sell their father's gold tooth right out of his living head, their aunt's broach, their remaining inheritance?

The boom in gold brokering had passed a few years earlier, and many brokers had closed their doors for good. Martino mused on the fact he was one of the survivors. With some heading out to suburbs of the city where rent was cheaper, gold brokers were finding their business was no longer an easy or profitable venture. Guerra, however, was pleased he had thought ahead and invested in something less reputable, allowing him to stay in the city proper. He had gotten his police license for brokering during better times, when a modest bribe was all that was necessary.

Construction on the recently torn-up street had discouraged traffic and business again. His practices, being what they were, favored him to be one of the few who prospered. Since the street construction project, more litter congregated in an otherwise tidy area of the city. He recognized his sex shop was more than a little insurance in an uncertain economy; he also enjoyed the business. Naturally, thinking about his sex shop led him to thinking about fucking Ilaria.

At ten minutes past two o'clock in the afternoon, Giancarlo Pavoni knocked, saw Guerra approach through a window, then open the door. Entering quickly, Pavoni was unsure if he was nervous about being seen or if he would rather be spotted in the event things went badly. He had never trusted Guerra but was running out of time on a debt. How he got mixed up with those thugs Giancarlo could not believe. If he had not gambled... Giancarlo was smart enough to recognize there were a great many things in his life he wished he could do over. He watched anxiously as Guerra shut and locked the door after he entered, then flipped the shop sign to Closed. The maneuver was one he had practiced in the event a client might have something unusual or more valuable to trade. There was a finality in the movement, further unsettling Giancarlo, but he was too desperate to be cautious or fully prescient.

"Let's see what you have."

"You're still open?"

"I am open for you alone. Wouldn't want our negotiations to be interrupted."

The *professore* followed the monster of a man to an interior room crammed with gold chains and necklaces, discarded or stolen wedding rings, gold earrings, gold tooth fillings, silver serving dishes, antique silverware, old coins, gold pocket watches and new, elaborate, designer wrist watches, musical instruments, artwork, gold-plated frames, antiques, clocks with gold inlay, old medals from some war, oddities and miscellaneous possessions of people who were as hopeless as Giancarlo in the moment. The last of his mother's jewelry was pitifully curled in his soft palm.

Guerra turned and walked over to Pavoni, a low-end client who continually brought items to barter for cash. Pavoni's recklessness was amusing to Guerra, and he found it bothersome to hide this fact from the snobbish *professore*.

Pavoni opened his hand with the ring. He knew the ring was not solid gold, but maybe Guerra would loan him something.

Guerra barely gave the ring a glance before offering, "You've got nothing left I want. What's in your hand? Junk. Why bring this cheap ring to me? I don't deal in pity. It's not even solid gold." He wanted to kick out the *professore* and get back to his sex shop where a dead body waited. The day had been particularly unproductive, and the lone piece the broker had to show was some old man's gold tooth and an antique but damaged pocket watch worth no more than $100 Euros.

"Wait. Hear me out. I think I have something worth more, more than anything I've ever brought to you. This could be in the hundreds of thousands of Euros, if not more." Pavoni was trained on the larger man, thinking Guerra reminded him of figures on an imitation frieze, head disproportionately large, legs short and thick; the gold broker, however, held none of the classical Roman beauty found in the ancient statues.

"My attention has returned, but briefly. What's this expensive treasure?" Guerra halted circling his prey, recognizing he would possibly kill Pavoni merely for the irritation caused.

"This is a little difficult to explain…let me ask if you have ever heard of John Keats, the English poet?"

Martino Guerra laughed, throwing his head back in genuine amusement. The second time he had laughed today, and both were belly laughs. Pavoni was nonplused. "A poet? A fucking poet? If we're not talking ransom, then we're done here. I don't deal in poets."

"Not the poet. I don't have the poet, for God's sake. Keats has been dead for nearly two-hundred years. Which makes this discovery all the more valuable: this poem of his was unknown. To have found an original Keats' poem—collectors, museums, treasure hunters will pay an exorbitant amount for such a rarity. I'm telling you this poem isn't simply any piece of paper, but the last work John Keats ever produced, and he created the work in Roma. Do you realize .."

"A poem? You're telling me about a fucking little poem on a piece of paper?"

"You don't understand. Not a poem, the poem. The last poem written by John Keats. It's…worth a fortune by any measure. Difficult to

Both End in Speculation

even calculate…"

"All right. I get it. Maybe, we can do business. Let's see this paper."

"Do you really think I would be so foolish as to carry this rarity around with me? An item worth perhaps a million. No, for now, the poem is safely in the hands of another with whom I am acquainted, but I will have the document very soon. You and I are in preliminary discussions right now, so I could get a sense of the market price and what you'd pay. I mean, I know its approximate worth, but I'd like to know what I can get for it."

"If you want to do business with me, you'll have the paper in your hands, delivered to me. I don't talk price on something unseen." Guerra didn't like the haughty *professore's* tone and menace entered.

Pavoni frowned, insulted. Even this big, dirty criminal looked down upon him. Straightening the collar of his shirt and checking his cufflinks, he followed up Guerra's threat with an inadvertent revelation: "Keats' poem is safe with a student of mine, a young woman, Sabine, and I will bring you a copy after we have made a bargain. When you see the copy, we can finalize numbers. After my finder's fee, then I will give you the original for your client."

"How am I supposed to know what someone would pay for this poem?"

"You're the broker. You get your buyer, and we will split the price, 50/50. I want half of my take when you make the deal, then I will get the actual artifact to you. We'll meet somewhere in a crowded place, the Piazza Navona, in the middle of the day. Not that I don't trust you, but this poem could be worth hundreds of thousands or more."

"A minute ago, your paper was worth a million." Guerra was already sizing up the man for a different reason. No weapons, no trailers in the street. Who might have known where he went? Sabine? He had a first name. What was the rest of it? Guerra was half-way to cutting out the middleman standing in front of him.

"The figure is most likely a million, but the buyer may offer something in the eight-hundred thousand range." Pavoni was throwing numbers out to sound like he had some certainty about the monetary worth. "Sab…my student knows nothing and has already offered me the poem."

"You're lack of trust is contagious. Maybe I don't fucking trust you."

"Let's not get into a series of insults."

"Half of what? I've agreed to nothing, and I never give half before I hold the item and have documentation about the price. In fact, I never, ever, give half period."

"Listen, merely a part of one of Keats' poems, a poem everyone already knew about, recently sold at auction for $250,000 Euros." Pavoni was relieved he had done some homework, researching the market value of the poet's art before approaching the menacing man. "We can do better with this, much better. It's difficult to even calculate what a collector would be willing to pay."

"Who has the paper, again? You say, your student…her full name? Sabine what?"

"I'm not going to tell you her last name." Pavoni suddenly remembered he had already blurted out the fact the girl was his student, and he withheld part of her name. Why had he been so careless? His nerves had gotten the better of his tongue where Sabine's name was waiting.

"I'm afraid this information is the only way we can go forward. Her last name? I'll take her name now. I don't play games, as you know."

"Why should you need her name? And why should I give the information to you for nothing in return?" Pavoni's face reddened and his shoulders grew hot. Guerra would take questions as a dare. Pavoni wanted to reenter the shop and negotiate from a better vantage point.

"I like to know who I'm dealing with…all the parties."

"You're dealing with me. The girl…she's an innocent bystander, a nothing. I asked her to hold the poem for me. There is no more to the matter."

"If this poem is as valuable as you say, why come to me?"

"We've done business before. Certainly, I could go to another…"

"Why have some nothing girl hold this immensely valuable item? Who did you tell you were bargaining with me? How can I be sure this is not some entrapment by *Polizia*?"

"What? Why involve Polizia? There's nothing illegal here…a transaction over a found object."

"I'll bet some officers might be interested in your found object?"

"Really? With your business, you want to bring Polizia in here? I happen to know something about you." As soon as the implied threat came out of his mouth, Pavoni regretted it. Never threaten a man like Guerra.

"I've got nothing to hide but seems you do."

"You can trust me."

"Who knows you're here? Who did you tell you were coming to bargain with Guerra?"

"No one knows I'm here. You think I'm proud of the fact I have to deal with…" A prolonged silence followed in which dynamics changed once again. They had been on their way to making a deal, Pavoni could feel it, and now he had pissed off the thug.

"Finish it. You're dealing with a gold broker. What you were going to say, right? Not 'some low life scum, some ignorant *teppista*?"

Pavoni's head snapped back. "Yes, a gold broker. All I would have said. You're dealing with me alone, not some child."

"A child? Aren't you a college professor, and she's your student? She's no fucking child." Guerra was circling him, getting between Pavoni and escape.

"Wait a minute, I need some assurances, some estimates on the price you can get before we go any further. And, I require an advance. After we agree on a price and the terms, an advance"

"You're way ahead of yourself, *professore*. You need, you need…you want an advance? How much?"

"A couple thousand Euro. Remember, this poem is worth hundreds of thousands, at least."

"The girl's name, the one with the poem, and where you were going to meet to get the paper, first. Then we'll see about an advance."

"There's no reason to complicate this. You'll make ten times over your time and trouble. I need a little loan for now, for today."

"You say you want two thousand?"

"A few thousand." Pavoni went out on a limb. He never expected Guerra to entertain the idea. Greed, once again, clouded his better judgment, making him forget Guerra had firmly maneuvered himself between him and an exit. "I'm afraid you're going to have to give me some money before I talk about meeting places or names of anyone I happen to know. Although Sabine has the poem, there are lots of Sabines."

"I don't know any," Guerra bore down on him.

"Did you stop to consider perhaps someone else is holding the paper for her now? Or do you always do business without thinking?" Instinctively, Pavoni discerned he had gone too far. He backed up, miss-stepping and stumbling.

Maybe what drew his rage was the fact he had never liked the *professore*, or the idea a poem made him feel stupid, the fact a dead little African was waiting for disposal. Pavoni's miss-step made him an even easier target, and Guerra's day had not gone according to plan. For all of those reasons, Martino Guerra suddenly spilled over like an erupting volcano.

Punching Pavoni in the face, Guerra knocked the *professore* to the floor, where the smaller man reeled before attempting to regain his footing.

"You've hit me," he cried out. "You fucking hit me." Already, too late, Guerra was down on top of him, pummeling with his large fists, then dragging the stunned, bleeding *professore* to a chair, where half lifting the little man up, Guerra pushed him down again. Pavoni was choking on blood filling his mouth from his broken nose but struggled to get out of the hold as Guerra wrapped a rope tightly around him. Too stunned to speak or cry out, Pavoni moaned piteously. Fear clouded all of his senses, and hot urine spilled down the legs of his expensive pants.

"You are going to tell me everything, little man; the full name of this girl, her schedule, number, address, names of her friends, where you planned to meet to get the paper. When I'm done, you will be begging me to take your every last possession, for which I will give you nothing in return. Now, let's start with the name of your friend holding this valuable paper. Take your time. I've got all night." At his comment, Guerra leaned over and turned on a sound system, trumpeting opera.

Pavoni at last gained his speech, raw terror rising up with vomit. At last, he found his voice. "I'm not going to tell you anything."

Pavoni's protestations were cut short with a blow to his abdomen. "This is the easy part," said Guerro. "When you don't cooperate, I make this harder for you," he said pulling out a pair of pliers.

Panicking further, Pavoni lost his last resolve to keep Sabine safe and, guiltily, quickly offered up her full name and address. He told the gold broker where she hung out, her class schedule, and where they intended to meet, the precise time they had arranged. She would be at a corner table. Even providing information about the poor student's widowed mother, except he couldn't remember the woman's name. Gasping for breath, coughing, and spitting blood, Pavoni even gave up her grade in his class, information in no way asked or relevant but he hoped would delay what he now understood was inevitable.

"Good progress," said Guerra. "Now, clean up a bit and sign a paper for me. Right here." He pulled out a blank paper and pen. "Write down the estimated worth of the poem as one million Euros, then certify the estimation with your name, your title, your university, *professore*." Guerra wetted a cloth and cleaned up Pavoni's face, then untied his hands.

This was the moment Pavoni should have reacted differently, fought for his life, dug his fingernails into Guerra's eyes, and fled, but he was uncertain, terrified, and almost paralyzed. He wrote carefully, buying time for what, he no longer knew. Somewhere in the back of his mind, he knew his betrayal of Sabine was enormous and the worst thing he had ever done. Yet he finished the estimate statement and signed his name with surprisingly elegant penmanship for the circumstances.

"Perfect." Guerra pushed him back and retied Pavoni's hands behind his back.

"You said you wouldn't, you fucking bastard," screamed Pavoni.

"A very big mistake," Guerra said. "Things could have ended quickly for you." Guerra tied a rag over Pavoni's open mouth. He had the girl's name and where Pavoni was to meet her. Now he even had his crude certification of the paper's worth. The rest of the time was his to explore the limits of the little man whom he immensely enjoyed torturing. For every smirk on the professor's face the first time he met Guerra, there were two more cruelties. For every advantage and privilege the professor had enjoyed in life, Guerra stole from the man double the payback. Pavoni's torture would have gone on longer except for the fact there was a dead African migrant to be taken care of at his other shop, and now a young woman with a valuable poem to meet and greet.

"You're a lucky fuck," Guerra said dully. "I have other business to deal with, so I will make your pain end too quickly." There was something about Pavoni's handsome face causing Guerra to want to smash Pavoni's it all the more. And the professor's arrogance would be stuffed so far back into him, there would be no retrieval.

Pavoni dimly heard Guerra's last words, all meaning already lost to him.

In the end, after Guerra beat Giancarlo senseless and finally killed the man with a blow to the back of his skull, the monster determined to drop the body in Trevi Fountain. He was already dreaming up elaborate staging to throw *Polizia* off his tracks. There were two bodies to get rid of, no, there would be a third: the girl Sabine would suffer the same fate after he had tortured her to get this poem. The dead migrant, however, gave Guerra an idea. Make the murders and their placement appear to be a political statement. Attach signs to the bodies and dump them in or on symbols of Roma. On the signs? Some word about migrants, these filthy Africans invading his country. Yes, the reference to migrants would throw officials off his track and bring heat on some political organization.

But first, he had to meet this girl at the assigned location, and there was a poem to steal, and such limited time. Going to be a busy night.

Although staging was not brilliant nor even terribly clever, the tableau pleased the criminal's sense of imbalance. For all the wrongs the world had heaped upon him, he would pay everyone back, make the beautiful in the city grotesque. Then blame the migrant invasion. Roma was so very proud of her fountains, her arches, and statues. Guerra would showcase the ugliness he lived with his entire life. The thought of tourists walking up to these grand monuments, then staggering back in disbelief and horror filled Guerra with a sense of power. He had thought of the scheme with no one's help. For some reason, an image of his old man crossed his mind. Never in all his father's life of petty crimes had the father concocted such a grand design.

~ * ~

After watching private companies take over repairs for expensive monuments in the city, Guerra knew all he needed was to do a good job acting. "Long day, officer. Wages aren't any better for the night work, either." He would play the part of a put-upon construction laborer, fixing what Roma could no longer afford to do on its own. He had stolen a truck, only requiring a fake insignia. If a police official asked him questions, he would plead dumb and go about his faux task before completing his real one. Roma could not take care of her own, yet she let all these negros into the country to wander about the streets. *"Maledizione."* They are a curse.

There was a girl to meet and take pleasure in killing. Suddenly, he hoped she was beautiful, but he could not be distracted. How long would he have to rape a girl? He had time. There was a stupid but valuable poem to steal and sell. A buyer to reconnect with. Already the name of a man came to him. An American buyer. Difficult to trace. All in a day's work, he thought, suddenly grinning.

~ * ~

Evening plans, however, were rushed after struggling with the woman. Disposing of her body on top of the Arch of Constantine had been more difficult than he imagined. The grand idea of deception had seemed so clever, to throw off investigating officials, but his plan was far more complicated and time-consuming to carry out than he had anticipated. Even a light girl like Sabine was heavy lifting in a dark, narrow staircase. Three bodies to stage in one night was far more taxing than he had imagined. All had to be done before the sun rose.

Proximity to the Arch made the decision practical. The Coliseum would be Pavoni's last tableau. Simple change of plans. No one would know where he had originally intended to dump Pavoni.

Last body, the vagrant, the negro, whose death would confound any investigation…had to be placed somewhere important in the city, Guerra thought. Then he hit upon the location. These Africans were flowing into his country, his city. He would place this one at the heart of a grand fountain. As he went about his grisly business with expertise and aplomb, he said out loud, *"Avrei dovuto essere un attore."* But Guerra was no actor. He had two sets of those skills: deception and channeling rage.

Chapter Nine
Sea-Horses, Tritons, and Monsters

Lovers braved the nasty night's weather and each tossed a coin into *Fontana dei Trevi*. Guerra pulled up in his truck, set out his construction signs, and hauled heavy blocks near the statue of Health. Stone snakes watched in relief. From his truck bed, Guerra brought construction tape and orange plastic fencing to rope off the area. His efficiency and speed surprised the few visitors who protested weakly to each other before turning away from the largest Baroque fountain in the city. Guerra considered the cold wind and drizzling rain an omen. The fates were smiling upon him. Typically, this fountain was crawling with tourists, even at night. One of the lights on the fountain was auspiciously broken and resulting shadows strengthened Guerra's resolve.

"Really? They have to work on this fountain tonight when we've one night left in Rome?" the English woman asked her fiance.

"Let them do their business. C'mon."

"Bulgari? Why doesn't the truck say Rome City Department of Works or something? Doesn't Bulgari make expensive watches or something?" Her mild protest was to drag her feet slightly as her fiancé led her away.

"Who knows? Who cares. Let's go." The couple finally wandered off, but the girl looked back twice at the menacing man unloading materials near the fountain.

"He's creepy," she whispered in the man's ear, stopping to untuck his twisted collar. "I want to take his picture." She pulled out her cell phone.

The tourist turned back once at the figure in black who strung tape all the way around Trevi Fountain. "He's doing his job. Put your phone away before you ruin it in the rain."

She complied reluctantly because she did not want to damage her

Both End in Speculation

iPhone.

"Shall we go back to our room?" He kissed her. They smiled and hurried off in the still dark hours before dawn. A few other tourists braving the blowing rain, pulled up their hoods and headed off as the menacing figure went about his construction business, ruining the ambiance.

"Seems fine to me," said one German to his Italian lover, his cold hands deep in his pockets.

"They are always under repair. Better we keep our treasures intact. Let's go get a Limoncello."

"Oh, yes, sounds delightful. I'm already warmer." The two drifted off in the night as Guerra pulled his hood further over the top of his head, partially covering his face.

At the center of the fountain elevated above the rest and standing sixteen feet tall, Ocean, with his long beard, was carried in a chariot held by two Tritons. From his spectacular vantage point, this personification of the river, Ocean alone knew Guerra's intensions. Even with all his ancient wisdom, however, in his frozen state he could warn no one.

Using a lift to help him with a small slab of travertine stone, Guerra was prepared in the event a guard asked what he was doing. He dropped a cement block near the fountain. Finally, the big man pulled the black bag from his truck and tossed the body over his shoulder. He then watched the black sack splash into the water near the base from where the wild horse eternally leaped. Done. His third and last disposal of a body in the night, and he was exhausted. Leaving his signs and tape around the fountain this time, he simply hopped in his truck and drove away. Rain and his preparations had dispersed the night's tourists and lovers normally drawn to this beloved Roman fountain.

There were still witnesses to the act but none understood what they had seen, the hour early in the morning. Unknowing witnesses buzzed from too much good, cheap wine. One tourist had taken a picture of a burly man at work, and she did not download her photographs until she returned to Germany. Even then, she never downloaded those particular images, unaware of the act she had marked.

~ * ~

By early afternoon, hours after officials had discovered both Miss Esposito's and Pavoni's bodies, the third black body bag containing the remains of an African immigrant, was found in the most illustrious of Roma's 2,000 fountains. Surrounded by plastic fencing, Trevi Fountain harbored an ugly leftover from construction and tourists were reluctant to investigate. No one called the *Polizia* initially. Then someone, an Italian passing by on his way to work, had already heard about the discovery of two bodies in the city. He walked closer to inspect the black bag. He noted uneasily, the bag was about the size of a small body. Putting his fingers to his lips, he texted a friend. "Something very strange in the water here. Could be a body." At last, a couple of students called Carabinieri, intending to call *Polizia*, but the numbers were too similar.

"I don't know, but it's weird to leave a black bag the size of a body in the fountain," a young Italian said to a Carabinieri answering his call. "I don't want to get a worker in trouble or anything but, still, this doesn't sit right. If nothing else, this mess will drive off tourists. Maybe someone should check it out." The Italian who made the call knew nothing about the other two murder sites already being processed. If he had known he would not have been so reluctant or nonchalant. By then, more visitors were drawn to the curiosity. The sun emerging and rains ceasing drew people to the attractions once again. The young Italian who had texted his friend finally waded into the fountain, deciding officials were taking too long. He was about to reach down for the body bag when *Polizia* arrived, ordering him out of the fountain.

Before the student called, casual observers supposed the dark material in the water was likely related to construction. Even though, in retrospect, visitors perceived something was very wrong even before Carabinieri and *Polizia* arrived. In fairness, security forces were already overwhelmed with the discovery of two murders, at major attractions, on the same morning even before someone alerted them to the black bag in the water. Panic had not yet risen its head across the city. Details of the murders were kept quiet for hours.

~ * ~

Both End in Speculation

After the discovery of the third body, the Mayor ordered restoration construction on the monuments shut down until further notice.

"No one touches our monuments, understand? If you see any construction around these sites, arrest the workers immediately. Get these corporate heads in here and find out who is responsible but, with some delicacy. We don't need to insult them."

Investigators brought in corporate executives who had given millions for the preservation of Roma's treasures, but they had much to explain. Interrogations, exceedingly polite, considering the wealth of the potential suspects, continued for several days until every last contractor and construction worker employed in monument restoration had been identified and their whereabouts on the fateful night accounted for. Bulgari had not sent out any employees on the particular evening in question. Location of trucks used in monument restoration were explained and resolved. Their workers had firm alibis. Not one of them was Martino Guerra or looked remotely like the image captured in cameras.

"What the hell is going on? We don't have murders in Roma!"

"Apparently we do, and three grisly ones in a single night," one of the *Polizia* officers said under his breath. The Mayor did not hear him but a few others did. There was uneasy laughter in the crowded room.

"What are you laughing about?" She had come to address the officers and make sure they understood the urgency of the situation.

"Nothing. We're saying we don't have any leads yet. It's not an easy case or cases."

"What do you mean we don't have any leads?" demanded the Mayor. "Find one. We have cameras; we have security. We have a city full of people. Someone saw something. Tourists from all over the world are ready to bolt. Do you know what these murders mean for Roma? For our economy? How do you think you get paid? And three murders? So gruesome. This must not happen here. Never again. This has to be solved now!" The Mayor was still struggling with acceptance of the reality.

"Ah, there was the suitcase murder."

"What?" the Mayor apprised the men around the room were mocking her in some way, but she could not find a way to prove it. "What did he say?" She pointed to a young officer with a narrow moustache and large, doe eyes.

The young man acted as if he did not know what she wanted.

"He was remembering the suitcase murder, the one where some Asian woman was found stuffed in a suitcase. He didn't mean anything by it, really." His commander rose to the officer's defense.

"Then there was an American student we found in the Tiber," another shouted this time. An uncomfortable ripple of stifled laughter was swallowed.

"Suitcase murder? Exchange student? Stop this listing. Do you understand how necessary it is we find the person or people who did this? Someone saw who committed this murder."

"We're doing everything we can," said the commander in defense of his men who apparently were expressing their discomfort with weird jokes.

"Like it or not, work with the Carabinieri. We are not looking for credit here but results. If we don't find this killer soon, we're all in trouble." She thought the mood and tone in the room were the result of sexism. They were all acting so insolent or lazy or exhibiting incompetence and disrespect. Would they come back with such lame excuses if she were a man? The room smelled of body odors, sweaty men who had no intention to bow before a woman.

The attractive Mayor breathed audibly to compose herself. The circumstances were not believable. Why did this have to happen on her watch? All the good she was doing for the city and now this? Turning a steely glare to them, she lowered her voice and tried to project menace, without adding threat. "Delve into this anti-migrant angle, even if no group claims responsibility. But keep this part of the investigation quiet. The last thing we need are riots and panic in the streets. Not a word of this detail escapes, but find who or what group did this and find them fast." She turned and left the room.

Other agencies were working in concert or, rather, overlapping and critical of the *Polizia*. *Polizia* were complaining about the military arm of policing, the Carabinieri. The new mayor had tried to remain professional, but she recognized herself to be a mess inside as she knew incidents like this would badly hurt Roma's economy and reflect on her leadership, unfair or not. Her margin of error was far less than the rope granted to men who held office. On the way back to City Hall, she found her hands shaking. No one would rest until the killer or killers were apprehended, and the tourists were assured all was, once again, safe for walking about.

Coordination of the many officers was expected to shorten the length of time needed to discover the killer, but the confusion of multiple agencies, security, and investigation personnel pushed evidence analysis into multiple directions at once. Voices overlapped and attempted to exert authority over authority.

~ * ~

Guerra counted on chaos. Operating within these dynamics his entire life he understood confusion offered him an advantage. Years earlier, the evening of his second killing, he set off a small, fairly unsophisticated car bomb in a town and everyone screamed terrorism. The authorities wound up arresting some poor black immigrant fool. If nothing else, thought Guerra, these Africans were good as scapegoats.

Developing his methodology, he came to perfect it: cause confusion, distract, divert attention, throw in a few red herrings, then disappear with the goods. No one had taught him these methods. His old man had barely spoken to him about his business in all those years before his father's sudden disappearance. A hit, Guerra theorized. His old man was not really likable, and he had never been around for long. Always off in the middle of the night on something shady.

Martino speculated at a young age his father beat people for someone higher up, roughing up slobs for lack of payments, debts owed. The boy had seen enough evidence over the years. Bruised knuckles, bloodied shoes, stains on clothing, a tire jack missing, a hammer with blood stains, locked trunks he was forbidden to go near. Most of all, his father never talked about his job nor permitted any discussion of what he did during his frequent absences. A question would lead to a cuff across the face or a kick in the rear.

As a boy, Martino was curious about whether his father had ever beaten a man to death and what the brutal act would feel like, but he did not dare ask. Somehow, he knew where the invisible lines were and which ones could never be crossed with his old man.

One morning when Martino awoke, sleep still in his eyes, his father stood at his bedside. "Take these and get rid of them," he said with urgency.

"I have to…"

"Now," the old man said with menace in his deep voice. "Make sure nothing remains." Then his father left, slamming the door. At the foot of his bed, Martino found a heap of bloody clothes. They smelled bad, he thought. Stretching his neck and flapping his arms in the cool air, he burned the clothes in a barrel several blocks away. Before taking the required action, he ignited another fire near a house to distract attention away from his disposal project.

Yeah, he knew his father was in the business; not too high up or important, but the old man understood enough about top lieutenants to give them cause for concern. Likely, his father's disappearance was collateral damage in a cleanup operation of some sort.

After the first time, there were lots of other errands to run for the old man: "Toss this knife in the Tiber. Bury this blade deep. Soak these clothes in gas and burn them." The first time Martino saw blood on clothing, he knew what the stains were even though the bright red had already turned brown. He also came to recognize the importance of eliminating trace evidence.

~ * ~

Lucky for Martino, his father had squirreled away a bundle from a lifetime of criminal dealings, payments for roughing up types who thought they could get away with not paying on time, and he left the money to his sole heir. No vast fortune, the inheritance was still surprising. They had lived as if impoverished. Martino found he had means, substantial enough to launch his seemingly respectable business and one in the sex trade, to boot. "Old man was good for something," he said to his store manager one day when talk turned to fathers.

"Not mine," said Tony. "Never gave me nothing but the back of his hand."

"Then he gave you something," said Martino in the most affectionate voice he had ever used.

~ * ~

Opening his gold broker shop on time, Guerra turned up the volume on a Puccini opera, put his feet on a cluttered counter, and hummed. He could have been an opera singer, he thought, if his life had begun differently. If his father had not been a low-level mobster and his mother some kind of whore who left her children in the care of an ignorant black laborer, never to return. Guerra could still smell his own sweat when he was locked in a closet for two days as a child. Black bitch told the boy she wouldn't put up with his foul mouth. He had cuts and bruises on his hands where he had pounded on the door and walls, silvers of wood embedded in his skin. He promised himself he would kill her, but when she finally let him out, his pants were soaked in pee, he was weak from hunger and fainted. He would never forget.

A month after the incident, Tiebe apparently tripped at the top of the stairs, hitting her head, suffering a severe concussion. She died a week later, never regaining consciousness. A blood clot, they said. His father did not question Martino. Local *Polizia* asked the boy a few routine questions, patted him on the head, and went on their way. Clumsy, stupid fool. Martino knew all it took was a diversion, then a hard shove when the heavy woman turned toward him, twisting her ankle, as he pushed his fist hard against her chest. He watched her open her mouth, in momentary surprise, before she went backwards down the steep wooden steps, tumbling over and over until she lay crumpled at the bottom. The tall boy stood at the top and looked on as blood flowed from her head, staining floors. Remaining still, he heard her moan once, then he went back to bed until his father woke him hours later, shaking him.

The African bitch who worked for his father, the one who had locked him into a narrow, hot closet where he cried, snot flowing over his mouth, because he was "unruly," paid the price. She was his first.

~ * ~

After returning from seeing Sabine's corpse, Vena could not get the horrifying image from her head. Had Sabine been holding Keats' last poem when someone killed her? If Keats really wrote a poem missing all these years, Vena considered, the poem was like William Faulkner's idea of the past, imploding the present, reemerging. If her student Sabine had actually found an original manuscript, then this *Poesia Mancante* would be a great discovery and have immeasurable worth.

Sabine did not meet her at the designated time and place, however. If Vena had been able to see her student before the fatal night, share the poem with authorities, take the pressure off Sabine, she imagined her student would not have been murdered.

Since talking with Sabine, a week earlier, Vena had been unable to stop thinking about either her bright student or the idea a previously unknown Keats' poem might actually exist. In her pause, the image of a jealous Professor Gould, her old nemesis, came to mind. He would have been apoplectic to find Vena might be the one to announce the discovery of a new Keats' poem. Difficult not to fantasize over the discovery, she was distracted.

"It's about the poem," said Vena. "The murders are connected through the missing Keats' poem."

"This makes no sense," Dante said.

"I thought you were interested in my theory."

"Yes, of course, I want to hear your theories but don't let speculation get in our way." Distressed, Dante corrected himself. "I didn't mean to sound the way those words just came out. I'm not trying to be condescending. I could use your help. I'm sorry, but this idea of a poem involved in the murders…"

Dante considered the victims' profiles they were compiling. Certainly, there could be a connection between the student and the professor, but the third victim? The African immigrant who was homeless? They had nothing on him. Perhaps he had recently arrived. Why was he in this mix of murders? Two people who might have helped migrants and the third victim a migrant? Perhaps a group opposed to the migration wave descending upon them was responsible, after all? But why had no group come forward to claim responsibility, as was their usual maneuver.

Dante and other Carabinieri hadn't ruled out organized crime, but neither could they find any real evidence of Mafia involvement. The Cosa Nostra had declared war on refugees in Sicily. Still, Roma tried to remove herself from the particular strife of the mob. Political statements about migrants in Roma? Drugs didn't seem likely. Bizarre and cruel placements of the victims set them apart from some tragic lovers' quarrel.

"Maybe the refugee saw something he shouldn't have seen," offered Vena. "He might not have been a target of the murderer, but incidental, even accidental fallout from a crime of which he knew nothing. If you separate him out..."

"Separate him? They had notes on their bodies about migrants. Fallout from what crime? How do we untangle this? There's nothing accidental in an arranged scene where the killer dropped the body. Why the Trevi Fountain for the negro? Has to be related to the other two. What is the killer telling us about these monuments? We're missing something in front of our eyes. I'm sorry, Vena, but we can't separate the third from the other two murders. They are all connected. This is feeling more and more politically motivated even if you don't want to see the politics of your former student."

"I'm telling you, she wasn't political. Nothing about Pavoni suggests he was helping refugees. You've interviewed his colleagues. I really think this is about Keats' poem."

"Your idea leads us nowhere. A poem? How does a poem connect this homeless man? Was he reading your poem at the time?" Dante had gone too far in his sarcasm.

"I'm asking you to use your imagination to speculate with me."

"The murderer or murderers knew them all. What we have to discover is an absolute connection between these three people. They knew each other, and the murderer or group killing them knew this."

Vena refused to give up so easily. "If he was homeless, as you suspect, this third victim might have been sleeping in the wrong location and woken up to see the murders or the killer dumping the bodies or even in the act of trying to cover up something. Maybe this African saw nothing, but the killer imagined he might have witnessed something. Don't you see, he doesn't have to be connected in the same way?"

"Security saw the bodies dumped," shouted Dante. "They didn't know what they were looking at. Construction truck, bags of cement, a large black bag of tools, construction fencing, they thought they saw, what? A hooded, dark figure. A homeless guy figures everything out and is killed?"

"Don't shout at Vena," Elio chimed in as his brother stood up and began pacing. He had been quiet long enough, he reasoned.

Dante turned toward Elio. "Really? We're worried about my tone and volume, right now?"

Vena brushed off Elio's defense of her. "I don't think the refugee figured out anything, but maybe he was in the wrong place with the wrong people or person. I don't believe this African homeless man knew Sabine or Pavoni, and he likely didn't know the murderer."

"I have to go. This is serious business." Dante left Elio and Vena standing on the street outside their little apartment in Monti. Unwilling to turn around, Dante immediately regretted the way he was acting. Why take it out on Elio and, particularly, Vena? He knew the tension of trying to solve the grotesque murders quickly but fumbled with entrance. He had trusted Vena could offer some insight. All she had for him was some crazy idea the murders were connected over a poem? How was a missing poem supposed to lead to horrific murder? The odd, political placement of the bodies?

*

Further down the street, his head cleared, and he thought about what Vena said, "the wrong place at the wrong time." Easier to think when he wasn't trying to defend his ideas. Suppose the migrant had stumbled onto something accidentally, as she suggested? The murderer might have killed the African and staged the body like the others to throw them off. The plan was working. Everyone was stumbling over everyone else in the case, talking about the migrant crises.

He'd covered enough cases to also know the weirdness didn't feel like Mafia even though there was one possible link he had considered. Canestrini knew the Mafia *Capitale* investigation had turned up Mafia involvement in siphoning off funds meant for migrant relocation and detention centers. Where a great deal of money was involved, you could never entirely rule out Mafia entanglement. As Gratteri had said, "Mobsters are where money and power are." When you have great money and power, the mob is likely behind it.

Yet, the African immigrant threw him off. If this could be connected to detention center monies, then maybe they had something, but Vena would not let go of this poem idea as motive. A poem? The belief of hers insinuated the absurd. Who would pay vast amounts of money for a poem whether by an English author or even an Italian one?

~ * ~

"I'm sorry for how my brother treated you," said Elio, turning to Vena after Dante left. "He asks for your help then yells at you."

"Don't be. It's all right. I'd be freaking out if I were him, too. He's not really yelling at me, anyway. He's frustrated and can't see the connections yet."

"Do you?"

"Nothing clearly, but I think Sabine and Pavoni were killed for the Keats' poem. I don't believe Sabine knew the third victim. It's also unlikely Pavoni would have had contact with the African refugee, particularly if he was homeless, as your brother says. Dante is right about one thing, though."

"What?"

"The murders are all connected, but perhaps their connection is to the murderer, not to each other."

"Stop worrying about all this crazy shit. My brother can take care of himself. This is what he does. It's his job, not yours."

"I know it's not my job, but three murders, horrifically public and gruesome in a city dependent upon tourism. There's a lot on his shoulders. Please don't forget, I knew Sabine and liked her very much. It's not as if I can forget what happened to her. I shut my eyes and see her battered face. I try to sleep and hear her voice."

"I know. I'm sorry. I hate to see you upset. Dante's not the Mayor. She's the one who better come up with this rogue. My brother doesn't face the same kind of political fallout, being in the military. He is perfectly capable of shouldering his responsibilities without your help or mine. You don't have to take this on, too." Elio stroked Vena's hair, running his fingers through curling ends.

"Ow." She pulled away from him, realizing how long her hair had grown since her graduate days in Rochester, when she kept her locks short and dyed purple.

"Sorry, sorry." He'd hit a snarl at the back of her hair and had inadvertently pulled. Elio was annoyed with himself. Even his attempts to comfort Vena were ending poorly lately

"It's nothing," she said, trying not to feel disgust with him. "The strangeness of it, Elio, is that I feel I have to figure this out. Maybe because I knew Sabine, and she was lovely and didn't deserve this. I cared about her. If she had given me the poem the night before she died, when she wanted to…I wish I had met her earlier."

"What then? You might be dead, too. I'm glad she didn't give the poem to you."

"I'm not."

"You don't have to make friends with all your students, you know. It's not really a good idea. Suppose you were there when this all went down? What then? You could be dead, like Sabine." Immediately, Elio wished he had not said out loud what he was thinking.

"If I had been there, I might have helped her take the poem to a Museum curator, removed her from danger."

"But you weren't. Let's go get something to eat."

Vena held his arm to slow him down. "I know you're being protective, but this happened, and I cared deeply for my student. I'm sorry you never met Sabine. You would have liked her, too." Vena recalled Sabine's reluctance to introduce her to Antonio. Was she, too, reluctant to introduce Elio to such a beautiful young woman? "Maybe it's because some switch flipped inside me when my friend was murdered back in the States, and his killer went free. After Michael's death, I couldn't let his murder rest. As you recall, my curiosity and persistence could have killed me then, too, but I did not die. I ran as fast as I could, flew all the way to Italy. He followed me, and I'm still alive."

"You don't have to run or fly anywhere." Elio could tell she was uncertain which bothered him. "So, you're telling me you're going to go about solving murders like the Carabinieri or *Polizia*? Do you want to be a tutor or an officer? Why won't you let this alone?" They began walking as rapidly as they talked.

"I don't really want to be the police. I know when I can't let something go. It's not everything. This case…I won't let go; I can't let this go."

"All right. I'll stop. Whatever you want. I'm not letting you go," he said, stopping and pulling her toward him, kissing her. Vena wiggled away, surprising both of them.

"I'm sorry, but I'm not in the mood right now."

Elio shrugged his shoulders. "I'm sorry, too." They continued walking, but his shoulders slouched slightly, and he lowered his head.

"Ah, where are we going, anyway?"

"I don't know. I'm following you. Don't get us lost."

"Lost is okay," she said.

"Don't get us killed."

Chapter Ten
Innumerable Shadows

Dressed in shapeless dirt covered clothing, worn for days unending, migrants moved in and out of cities looking for temporary employment, for shelter, slumping under an overhang, huddled in tents and make-shift constructs outside airports; these bottled up colonies of immigrants, strangers even to one another, even those who accepted them with suspicion…outside cities. Learning to move without being noticed, then suddenly calling out, they sold trinkets: an umbrella, a miniature Coliseum. Mastering the trick of shadows and light, they had learned to be both seen and unseen. Those were the lucky ones, the migrants who were not detained in sweltering, crowded camps or sent back to countries awaiting their arrival with a slavers' trade, robbers, forced conscription, death.

~ * ~

Across his face, there is anonymity. Beneath the façade, Fitsum wore mountains and deserts, never betraying leaving and loss. For a few moments of his solitary nights, the ageless Eritrean thought of the land he once called his home, but the memories faded further and further until he barely sensed place or saw a scene clearly in his imaginings. Hillsides terraced and dotted with cacti. Desert smells. He tried to recall the feel and vision of stark white against black: a boy sitting on a white rock outcropping. The child scanning shanties dotting the desert floor of the valley. There was a purity Fitsum never forgot.

~ * ~

Everything was brown and black, but the rock and the boy's white clothing stood out in contrast. Fitsum had startled him before the boy turned.

They became friends. Eferm was quick and clever, but when the time came, he, too, could not avoid conscription even though they were 15, not 18, like the soldiers said. Eferm was killed in a skirmish with some Ethiopian troops. He never saw the other man with the rifle, discharging the killing bullet. Sixteen-year-old Eferm never even had time to raise his weapon or consider the forces pitting him against another African in a quasi-war neither wanted nor understood. Fitsum ran and kept running. But he did not know when to stop. He was as likely to be murdered by another Eritrean as an Ethiopian, the military and the police, the Christians and the Muslims. Early on Fitsum learned, when everyone is your enemy, no one is your friend. The one friend he remembered was murdered. Fitsum saw flashes of ugly images: bullets ripping human flesh and bone broken, deprivation and starvation, the whites of his eyes red from the sun because he dared not close them.

~ * ~

If someone had asked him, Fitsum, could not accurately give an accounting of his birth or even his true age. His mother died when he was still a boy. His father disappeared several years later and never returned. The date of his birth had never been celebrated nor acknowledged.

"Watch out for your neighbors," his father told him the night before he left. "They will whisper about you, and suddenly soldiers are at your door arresting you. Go to your aunt's tonight." This was the last helpful advice his father ever gave him. He left his house and stayed with an aunt and ailing uncle. His uncle told him the next day his father was gone, likely dead.

What did his father's disappearance mean? This murder was before the migration, before he learned how to move quickly and quietly, undetected, with a few trinkets in his pocket, something slipped off a counter or, later, from the gaping hole of another's pocket. When he stopped moving temporarily, he sometimes smiled at the thought of tourists, their innocence and carelessness. How different their lives must be. They could stand staring up at a monument and never notice the hand slipping inside their clothing.

~ * ~

Smuggling people was much harder than picking a pocket, but the rewards were far greater. At first, he had taken the items and bartered them for migrants, helping them move through Italy. In the beginning, human smuggling had been about his own survival. Later, he found he was more than good at moving people undetected.

Since he loosely coordinated with individuals in NGO, things had gone easier for him, but the risk was still a constant. The non-governmental organizations set out in boats to rescue deflated rubber rafts, grab human beings spilled into the sea. NGO's plucked them from the water and brought them to shore where Fitsum and others waited. Even this operation was in constant jeopardy since prosecutors accused NGO's of coordinating with smugglers for profit.

Fitsum thought such accusations, however true in practice, were cruel and did not consider why men did what they did. He was a human smuggler, but he was also a man of honor, he thought. All men wanted a chance to live in the world. Whether or not the NGO's claimed a percentage was irrelevant to what they had committed of themselves in order to save lives.

"They're after us now," the European beside him said.

"Fuck Zuccaro," Fitsum spoke of the Italian prosecutor who had gone after NGO groups helping migrants cross the Mediterranean into Italy.

"You read about Zuccaro in Italian?" A worried humanitarian asked. "How many languages do you know?"

"Italian, English, Tigrinya, Arabic, a little French."

"Ah, good. We will continue in French. Italian is so clumsy for me. I'm more comfortable in my native language."

"Isn't everyone?"

The European smiled. "Doesn't matter if our motives are good and genuine, we can't afford to be caught. Amnesty International can't protect us all. Guillaume, by the way. Guillaume Desmarais," he said, extending his hand.

Fitsum answered, "Fitsum."

"No surname?" Guillaume asked.

"Fitsum is enough. You spoke of the dangers of being caught; don't get caught. Keep transponders off. Follow lamps. Avoid border patrol."

"You're Muslim, perhaps?"

"No religion. Once Christian. My name changed. I pretend to be Muslim when needed. The name will change again. Fitsum is not who I am."

Guillaume raised his eyebrows and said, "Good idea. Keep moving. You're from Somalia, Nigeria?"

"Eritrea."

"Ah, the Horn of Africa. I should have guessed since you already speak both Italian and English."

"The Hell," Fitsum responded drily. They both laughed uncomfortably.

"Life is difficult there. May I ask, how do you stay so calm?" They walked above the shoreline. Fitsum held his arms at his side but with his fingers extended as if prepared to grab hold of something, ready to fight or flee. Guillaume's hands were tucked in the pockets of his baggy pants, showing his trust or naiveté, thought Fitsum.

"Anything and everything has already happened." Fitsum shrugged. "I keep moving."

"I wish I could be so casual about it." Ironically, Guillaume stopped at the moment, stretched his long arms, folded them behind his head as in resting posture. Fitsum slowed and turned to his new acquaintance. He thought this Frenchman showed too much and exposed his belly.

"Not casual. What little I had is gone." Fitsum walked a few steps backward still facing Guillaume.

"I'm sorry for your many losses. We have time before the boat comes in if you want to tell me your story. It's a way to pass the time." He turned to the sea and held his right hand over his eyes to screen them from the glare of the sun on water. "Let's hope they make it."

"Too many lost."

"I heard about a boat…40-foot long, they said, with over 300 migrants crammed onto her. The Italian Navy saved them; otherwise, we would never know about them at all. How many attempt to cross and never make it?"

"The Italians can be generous or cruel, but the Navy can't be everywhere on those wide waters."

"Isn't the description fitting all of us? Generosity and cruelty. Tell me about you. How did you come to this place to help people navigate a new life?"

"You are a philosopher," Fitsum said as Guillaume smiled.

"No philosopher, not terribly pragmatic."

Fitsum stopped walking for a moment, then showed his suspicion. "Are you journalist?"

"Not at all. I thought about the occupation once. My parents told me I would be a good writer, but I'm here with Cimade, as a legal advisor. It's why I'm not on a boat but the shore. I expect the Italian border patrol will catch up to our boats—if the patrols are not already waiting when the boat comes. That's why I'm here."

"So, you tell them what exactly?"

"I will advise refugees as they are marched to relocation centers. I remind the border patrol of our rights as part of a NGO. Everyone deserves human rights. I want to make sure their rights are not violated."

"Too late for many of them. Much violation. Cimade?" The name meant nothing to Fitsum although he was by now familiar with NGO's.

"We're an NGO, not exactly welcome even in France right now and definitely not in Italy."

Fitsum laughed. "I'm not welcome either."

"Your story? How you came here? Why you are helping. You're alone?"

Fitsum did not really know this man, but perhaps anonymity made the telling possible. Where to start? Not at the beginning. Not when his Christian family had to flee from militants, not when he later deserted the military after the conscription and death of Eferm. Not when he ran from forced labor, not when he changed his name in captivity to a Muslim name to save his life, not when he buried the cross his mother had given him, not

Both End in Speculation

when some boys he knew were captured and ended up shooting men from their village, those foolish villagers unwilling to denounce their religion or throw away their crosses.

Muslim, Christian. Fitsum had seen both commit atrocities and torture. The political side of right no longer existed for him. The government of Ethiopia waging war, the government of Eritrea, all governments, were corrupted and the same to Fitsum. All he saw were images, not narratives flowing out behind him, his past a series of horrific pictures.

"Wool masks. They wore wool masks covering their heads and faces," he said after a moment, "showing the eyes. Militants. Other boys, really, some men, all hardened to kill." In the moment, Fitsum could taste wet wool. He had placed a mask over his head when instructed. He said nothing to the Frenchman about recognizing the eyes of one of the men from his village who had turned on his neighbors. He thought of his father's last warning again. Although his father had never been kind, his father was the one who told him to run to his aunt's house. The severity in his father's voice the last time and glare in his eyes were all the boy needed to obey. Fitsum thought again of the stars in the sky, the sand on his feet as he ran in the darkness.

"The men who came for you? The militants, were they Christian or Muslim?"

Fitsum did not answer the Frenchman's question but one unasked, addressing another raid many years later: "Their captives wore orange jumpsuits. They marched them to the shore then made them kneel, their heads bent."

"You witnessed this?"

Rubbing the top of his close-shaved head, Fitsum said, "I saw their bodies after the men left. Aaron, he was among the dead." He did not tell Guillaume. Aaron's head was all he saw, the body of a villager washed out to sea. Aaron's eyes stared up at him, told him to run and never stop. The smell of death brought him along the shore in search of someone from his past.

"I'm sorry. You were not captured then?"

"I was for a time. I escaped."

"Who captured you? Do you want to tell how you escaped?"

Fitsum considered the question. Frenchman likely thought his life was some kind of adventure rather than what darkness opened. There was statecraft of right and wrong, not one of a few corrupt men at the top of the world playing with their soldiers everywhere. Not a good story. An accident of distraction. Another man tortured, someone setting off an explosion, bullets flying, men running the other direction, and he was running again. He tripped on the outstretched leg of a dead man and fell into a partially dug drainage ditch. The wind knocked from his chest, he lay there and thought they would find him, shoot him where he lay, but they passed by him. Hours went by before he stood up slowly and saw they had moved on. There were still bodies burning, smoldering. Somehow, they had not noticed the skinny young man in a shallow incline in the chaos.

"Okay. Tell what you want."

Fitsum brought his fingers to his chin. He tried to imagine how he could tell such a story. A story he did not fully understand. He suspected even the leaders of the raids did not understand any longer what they hoped to accomplish.

~ * ~

As they walked again, the two men grew silent. Fitsum saw not the magnificent shores of Italy with the steep rock face hitting the sand at severe angles, nor the blue of the Mediterranean; but on the sunlit water, the wide, nearly endless creases of the Sahara rolled out in his mind, the unexpected face of a Sudanese man who picked him up in a rusting truck with bad springs, so long ago. The stranger had saved his life and Fitsum should have remembered his name. He did not. But the Sudanese, with deliberate scarring, those semi-circles framing his large forehead, and the whites of his eyes turned red, was a good man. Blues and greens in his colorful shirt were cooling. Colors and sensations are what Fitsum remembered of the time he hopped on the passenger seat of the rickety truck. The old vehicle carried him the rest of the way across the desert when he should have been left for dead. When he was riding in the truck, bumping along, after the Sudanese man shared his bottle of water, Fitsum

Both End in Speculation

thought he might see Europe, might escape running forever.

"Lucky for you I come by," the man said. "Too much death in the desert. Many think they cross on foot and end up a pile of bones." The words stayed with Fitsum. After all he had been through, luck again pulled him from imminent death. Not merely luck, however; his good fortune was more than coincidence: a man who had generosity and kindness in him. This was a moment to never forget.

This stranger, the Sudanese, would save his life and alter the course of it, turning Fitsum toward saving others. This is the story he wanted to tell Guillaume, the moment his life changed for the better, but the quiet between them had lasted too long to break silence again. Guillaume and Fitsum sat down until the sun set over the sea and the evening breeze blew in, chilling them.

~ * ~

The boat they awaited had capsized. Not even the captain, an expert swimmer, survived. All of those souls swallowed 40 miles from the Italian coast. One man, a Nigerian, had fallen overboard in his standing sleep state. Three other men tried to retrieve him, but they leaned too far and went over in the dark, as did their acquaintances, the men in the group they had traveled with, reaching out. Suddenly, the shift in weight, the surge of bodies desperate to save the drowning, unbalanced the boat. Many went into shock from the cold, lack of food, and dehydration before being spilled into the sea. Worried about miscalculating the distance, the captain yelled too late. The conscripted crew tried to pull some back, but by then, it was already determined: the boat capsized. Bodies flew against bodies. If the captain was not hit in the head and knocked unconscious, perhaps he might have been able to save himself. If the boat had not overturned so quickly, he might have been able to send an SOS.

Desperate migrants were entangled and trapped beneath drowning men, a sleeping baby flung from his mother and lost, the floundering woman screaming and swallowing sea water in darkness, still reaching for her son as she swallowed water. Men bobbed at the surface and tried to yell, but their mouths filled with the sea. A handful of strong young men survived for hours before succumbing, one by one, during the long night. Sharks finished a number who did not drown immediately.

~ * ~

Italian Navy vessels were miles away helping rescue migrants from another fishing boat overloaded with 180 men, boys, and a few women. All were exhausted and grateful as the Italians passed out water to the dehydrated migrants.

But those rescued were not the men, women, and children for whom Fitsum and Guillaume were waiting when they woke before dawn.

Chapter Eleven
Thief of Beauty

When Vena returned to Roma after a hiatus in the U.S. to visit her father and fiends, she made a list of the walking tours she wanted to take. Finding herself drawn to the Palazzos, she loved those open but people-hub spaces of the city. Vena felt almost at home in her chosen foreign land. If she looked up too long, a man would try to sell her a flower or some trinket, but she had developed a way of appearing intent on something in her hands while still taking in details from the surroundings.

Seated on one of the stone benches in the Piazza Farnese, Vena opened her journal, flipping to a blank page. Tucked between the open pages was a small copy of a painting showing Severn's work. Considering Severn and his art, Vena held out the print of Joseph's portrait of Shelley supposedly composing "Prometheus Unbound" on the ruins of the Baths of Caracalla. Shelley's drawing was influenced by Aeschylus's play, Vena remembered, and Shelley influenced Severn, both men drawn to Roma. All were inspired by the myth of an immortal chained to a rock and tortured by a scavenging eagle at the order of the gods. Prometheus meant "forethought" but symbolized man's hope for something better in the future, and his story was written: the perpetually tormented man forgave his immortal jailers. In Roma, mythology, legend, and history were so thoroughly intertwined, distinctions were often blurred to Vena.

She scrutinized Severn's portrait of Shelley for several minutes. In the print, the poet gazes out, his eyes connecting with the viewer, his quill resting in his right hand at his side while his left forefinger touches his face in contemplation. One foot balances on a crumbling brick wall, the baths surrounding the man are in ruins, while his other leg extends to the earth. This is another Roma in which hillsides and land around the city are still rural, grasses and wild flowers framing the English poet who appears completely within his element in this Italian capital. Such ease as a foreigner, Vena thought of Shelley, musing on her own adjustment, then thinking of the refugees who flowed into Italy. So much easier to be a foreigner when the color of your skin was similar, your nose easily mistaken for Roman, your lips and cheekbones obviously European in ancestry. Her manner gave her away as American.

~ * ~

Fitsum once told his tutor he would never fit in anywhere.
"Of course, you will," she promised. "Language mastery takes time, but you must not stop trying."
Fitsum wanted to be agreeable but said, "Easier once I stop wanting to be seen as human in the eyes of the other."

~ * ~

The day before Vena had seen Fitsum, she was worrying about the fears and hopes of the migrants moving through Italy. Were they afraid of being sent back? Nervous about finding work and food? They all longed for something better, but their "jailers" did not want them, wished for the tortured refugees to disappear without a trace. Such are the deeds and terrors of men and lesser gods, she wrote in her journal.

Ancient ruins of the Baths of Caracalla became her destination for the late afternoon, after classes and her sojourn to the Piazza Farnese. But first, she would get something to eat in the trattoria situated at a corner of the Piazza.

With her journal again opened, she ordered then dove into the rigatoni alla carbonara, not realizing how hungry she was until the plate was set before her. Back in New York she had loved Italian food without recognition of the fact she had never had Italian food. She had been fortunate to get an outdoor table against the wall, the place already crowded with patrons. "Alone at last," she said out loud, then laughed. One of the surprising delights she had found in Italy was dining alone almost anywhere. As long as the waiter saw you appreciated the fare and spoke

Italian, he was attentive. Sometimes it was wonderful to be in the city without Elio's presence, even though he was generally good company. She wanted to write and think freely before heading back to the apartment. Finishing her meal, she texted Elio and asked if he wanted to meet her at the Baths of Caracalla.

~ * ~

Even in fragments and ruins, the Baths were magnificent, grand in scope and design. After sitting down for a few minutes, she stood up again. Disturbed by unwanted and intrusive images of Sabine's death, Vena was aware she was no closer to solving the mystery of the murder of her student or the missing Keats' poem, if such a poem even existed. How did Dante do it? Return again and again to horrific crimes, many of which were never solved? This ability to immerse himself in a case, yet hold himself distant from the emotional impact, was a strength of Elio's brother.

~ * ~

The afternoon of the last time Vena met with Sabine, her student shared a secret. As soon as Sabine approached, late as usual, the young woman brought both hands to her mouth in a prayer like motion. Then she sat down out of breath. "I have something to tell you," she rushed the words.

"Let me guess," said Vena, "you're in love."

"Oh, yes, I told you, but my secret is not about love. I've already told you about my Antonio. No, this is something else, but we must be very quiet." She put one finger to her lips, scouting as she did so.

"All right. I already feel like we're in some spy movie, so what should we do? Would you prefer some place quieter with fewer people?"

"The opposite. More people, more noise."

"Lead the way." Both stood up from the café table in the street. Sabine grabbed Vena's hand and off they went.

"I feel like I'm your child here," Vena yelled to Sabine who finally slowed her pace.

"Oh, sorry. It's what I do when I get excited. Forgive me. Here we are."

They stood outside La Casa del Caffe Tazza d Oro where the line already extended into the street.

"You wanted noise. We have it," Vena yelled.

"Not so loud. We must talk softly."

"This really is a secret but apparently everyone in the city already knows about their coffee." She looked at the sign: Banco for service at the bar and Tavolo for prices when seated. Standing to eat and drink required getting used to when she first arrived in Roma, but leaning against the bar for espresso had become habit for her most mornings.

Sabine drank her espresso quickly and motioned for Vena to follow. They moved between patrons out into the street again. "Is this the best place for a conversation or the best place for espresso?"

"Yes, you caught me. I wanted to show you my favorite coffee bar, and the Pantheon and the Basilica of Santa Maria are nearby. We can walk slower now."

Vena was grateful for the change in pacing. "So, what is this mystery about? Are you getting an award for your scholarship at the university or something?"

"I wish. No, it's a discovery you will like."

"And another line, I see." Crowds of tourists had formed multiple lines at points of entrance.

"He is crying," said Sabine, pointing to the stone elephant at the entrance to the Piazza Della Minerva.

Vena turned and considered the huge sculpture with the weeping beast. "He is hardly little, is he?"

"Oh, yes, Bernini's 'little elephant' and the obelisk.'"

"He is weeping grime and a chemical reaction to the bronze."

"Chemicals? You know the story, don't you?"

"Ah, I don't think so, no."

"Why Bernini pointed the little elephant's ass toward the monastery?"

"All right. I'm guessing there were politics involved?"

"Father Paglia made Bernini change his lovely design, so Bernini complied but turned the elephant so he is disrespecting the monastery and their authority."

"So many good stories. You know, up close, the elephant's trunk is too long. See how the trunk twists around; there is an extra section of the trunk in this curve."

"Hah. So critical. Bernini would not have liked you any more than he liked Father Paglia."

"I don't suppose he would."

"And I have another for you."

"Prego, Prego," an Italian man dressed impeccably in Gianfranco Ferre all the way to his sunglasses, moved past them, brushing them slightly to the side, and they bumped into one another.

"He's in a hurry. We don't care, do we?" Vena followed the man with her eyes in amusement rather than annoyance. "It's such a good word, your 'Prego.'"

"What? Oh, yes, but my mystery."

"Do tell me, but he's dressed quite fashionably, even for a Roman."

"Ah, he's on his way to a photo shoot, I guarantee it. He's a model. I recognize him."

"Are we safe here?" Vena laughed but then saw Sabine lift her eyebrows and turn down the corners of her mouth.

"I don't know, so I will speak quietly, and you will have to lean toward me."

"Wow. This is some intrigue you've hit me with. What's going on?"

"You're a John Keats' scholar, right?"

"Not really. I mean I know his poetry but I am not..."

"Stop being humble. You know the poet. How expertly do you know his poetry?"

"I certainly don't have much of his poetry memorized. Why? Are you studying Keats at Sapienza?"

"Nothing like... I may have an original John Keats' poem."

"What?" Vena was struck by the fact she had yelled because everyone around them turned their heads to give her a reproachful look. They were now in the Pantheon, entering the rotunda, and already people displayed glares of disapproval.

"Sorry," Vena lowered her head in apology. Adjusting her volume, she asked Sabine, "What exactly do you mean?"

"I can't say it again if you're going to shout here."

"I won't. Let's try, please. I have remembered where I am."

"In my grandmother's house…my Nonna died last year, and my mother, Lia, was taking care of her. We all moved in with my grandmother many years back when my father hurt his back and couldn't work."

"Sabine, I'm not an impatient person but…"

"I know. It's…I have to explain first. My mother said we had to clean out her things, the upper floor where my Nonna lived was filled with all this stuff. I didn't really want to get into my Nonna's things. You know, taking everything out was weird, but then I found some wonderful objects, a little glass elephant, then this book of Shakespeare's plays. I could tell the book was very old, dust covering so thick, I couldn't even make out the name Shakespeare at first. I don't believe my Nonna ever opened the book, yet she kept the Shakespeare volume always."

"But Keats' poem?" She asked, stopping to stare up at the oculus.

"Inside. On a page in the midst of the play *Hamlet* was a piece of old paper with handwriting on it. At the bottom of the page was John Keats' name." Sabine stopped talking and bent her head back to stare through the hole in the concrete dome with her tutor. They lowered their heads together, and Vena released an audible breath.

"What?" Vena held her hand to her face in disbelief. "There could be a number of explanations, but I can't imagine at this moment how such a thing could have occurred. Keats died in Rome, but I would think someone would have known about this poem if such a work existed. Surely, Severn would have made mention of Keats' last writing even if he did not keep the poem."

"I don't think Keats intended to keep the poem private, but he must have died before saying anything. Maybe he was uncertain of the appraisal of the poem, at the time."

"No, humility is not like Keats. He believed in his poetic power. He would have wanted people to know, which is why…" Neither woman had moved in several moments, and tourists snaked their way around them with a growing level of irritation, a few mutterings in foreign languages

"But he believed his friend Severn would see it, read the poem as he always must have read him those words of Shakespeare. Severn might have given the book away after his friend John died."

"Possible, I suppose, but all this time…" Several people edged them from the center of the rotunda. "How exciting even if this paper turns out not to be Keats' poem. I get the feeling they'd like us to move along." Vena gently held Sabine's arm and proceeded across the expanse beneath the dome.

"I know. Exactly why I want to have the document authenticated. Would you like to see the poem first? Maybe you can tell."

"Yes, but no. I mean, I'd be honored to look at this poem, whether or not the work is Keats' original, but you should share the document with the University first, to make sure of what you have. I wouldn't have the means to know for certain whether or not you hold an original."

"I could show Professor Pavoni, my Classics instructor."

"Sounds like a good idea. After your professor has examined the document, I want to see it. Don't get too excited because the likelihood of this being authentic is probably very small, but then again, I would treat the paper very carefully."

"Trust me. I have the paper nestled in the pages of Shakespeare. I'm almost afraid to take it out."

"Are you sure you don't have a copy of a known poem?"

"I searched on the Internet and couldn't find anything similar."

"Possibly, it's a poem known with a different or original title. Of course, an earlier copy of a known poem would be worth a small fortune. But, it's entirely likely someone simply forged his name."

"If someone else wrote the poem a couple hundred years ago, why would they write Keats' name at the bottom?"

"A very good question. Do you remember any of the words?"

Sabine turned her head downwards. "You must think… I should have tried to memorize part of the text at least. I'm afraid…"

"Don't give it another thought. There are experts who will be able to determine what you have; certainly you appear to hold an old paper with a poem written if not by Keats, then by someone trying to imitate him. I can't imagine."

"Maybe this isn't any help, but I recall the names of gods and goddesses in the poem; Aphrodite and Nemesis, if I'm not mistaken, because we had discussed them in my mythology course."

"See, you remember more than you thought at first. Keats certainly wove mythology into his poetry. But, you could also have a good imitator, and many poets at the time used mythological allusions."

"Primordial," Sabine said.

"What?"

"Primordial was one of the words in the poem, I know, because I had to find an English dictionary. I wasn't familiar with this English word."

"Existing at the beginning of time."

"Yes, I found out, and's why I remembered the word."

"You have a real mystery here," said Vena smiling, excitement beginning to smolder. "Did the end of the lines rhyme?"

"Yes, let me think. Elemental, one of the words. Yes, the line after primordial."

"Keep going and we might have the whole poem."

"No, I'm afraid my mind is all jumbled right now."

"Is the poem an ode? Does the poem have the word 'Ode' in the title?"

Sabine said, "I don't think so. Tomorrow night, after I talk with my professor, I'll bring you the poem. You can see what you think. Does the arrangement work for you?"

"Of course."

"Where shall we meet?"

"Here. Let's meet right here, outside the Pantheon."

"The height to the oculus is 142 feet for you Americans," said an energetic tour guide as a tight group inched toward Vena and Sabine.

"I guess we are still in the way. Are we still meeting here tomorrow?"

"No, I've changed my mind. Let's go someplace where we can get a bite to eat. I'll be starving by then. I have classes all day at the University."

"Santa Maria of the Martyrs," Vena heard the tour guide state to gasps and the intake of expressed wonder. "The domed cella and temple portico are unique..." The tour group's guide continued as Vena and Sabine moved further out of earshot.

"Of course," Vena said. "What about Ciacco&Bacco? It's fairly close to Sapienza, I believe, and has good food. I'll call for a table for us."

"Oh, yes, I know the little place. They have arancini and a tiramisu I could dream about. But you are treating, of course?" Sabine teased to see how far her teacher would go.

"Listen, if you have an original Keats' poem, I'll treat you every day for a month. What time? They serve until 11:00 at night, so if you have a busy day and evening, we can meet later. What do you say about 9:00?"

"Ah, perfect. If I'm smiling, it means *Professore* Pavoni believes I have an original Keats' poem."

"And if you don't?"

"I will still be smiling because you've promised to treat me to strawberry tiramisu."

"You know I am a poor English tutor. Could we forget my earlier hyperbole and make my treat for a night?"

"Already hedging your bet? I see you now think I might actually have an original."

"I know nothing yet, but let's celebrate your find of a great mystery, perhaps of a great work of art. Let's celebrate you."

Chapter Twelve
Dust of Ages

The last time Vena saw Sabine they had been so joyful, and now Sabine was gone forever. Unable to believe what she knew to be true, Vena kept imagining Sabine waiting somewhere for her or, more importantly, for Antonio. Oh, Antonio. He would be suffering, too, Vena knew.

If she could go back and warn Sabine…Re-imagining the scene, Vena watched the approach of her student arrive at their assigned meeting place. But Vena was not there. How long would Sabine wait? Perhaps if she had called Sabine and they had met earlier. All of her speculation and imaginings led to nothing. Trying to alter the past was pointless. She had to convince Dante to let her examine Pavoni's office. Keep moving forward, she told herself, or somehow keep moving.

~ * ~

"There's nothing in there but a lot of dust. We went over everything with a fine-toothed comb. Nothing here offering clues or leading us anywhere. Whatever reason Pavoni was killed is not hiding in his office or his home."

"Please get me an entrance to his office. Let me at least try. What harm would it do?"

"I'm not trying to be dismissive, but our men are experts, Vena. They went over every paper, everything in his desk, on his shelves. You will not find what we are looking for. There is no poem in his office or any clue leading to motive. We might be wasting time on this theory of yours about a missing, valuable poem. The staging. The card referencing migrants…none of this information fits your theory."

"Maybe not, but will it hurt to let me try? Why not let me go into

Both End in Speculation

his office? Do you have a single lead yet?"

Dante shrugged, knowing he would allow her request, partially because he believed her digging around in the office could not hurt and partly because he ridiculously hoped she might actually find something. There was the enormous pressure of trying to bring the case to a close, and the investigation was going nowhere. Even his uniform seemed ill-fitting; nothing was quite right. He had not been home in too long, and this case would extend his stay in Roma without the possibility of leave. His irritation was evident in his face, his abrupt gestures and tone of voice.

"If I had a single lead, I would not be talking with you right now."

~ * ~

Professore Pavoni's office at the university was typical in its cluttered state of books and papers. *Polizia* confiscated everything in and around the man's desk. Vena suspected Pavoni would be more careful with a metaphorical map leading to his treasure or, perhaps, the poem itself. Dante had given her a small window to examine the room, and she had to move quickly. The task was not difficult. She knew what to look for, having practically lived at universities, both as a student and teacher. There wasn't so much a system in her approach as an urgency born of instinct. Where would I hide a clue if I wanted no one to find the clue but couldn't afford to lose it? she asked herself, feeling around under the desk drawers. Slowly, pulling out each drawer, she lifted them up and turned them all over to discover aged wood beginning to splinter.

Vena had been convincing in her arguments to Dante, selling him on the idea both Pavoni and Sabine knew about the poem which made their murders connected by more than shared location of the university. "Dante, suppose we leave the murder of the African refugee out of the equation for a moment. Do you see a possibility for a connection between Sabine and Pavoni? The fact she told me about this supposedly valuable poem makes it likely her Classics professor wanted to do something about it, too."

"Yes, I get it. She was his student, as you tell me, but we don't know if this is a coincidence, both their deaths on the same night? They could have been killed by different people, unknown to one another, however unlikely." Dante knew this was not true or helpful the moment the words came out.

"The difference between probability and coincidence is probability assumes an outcome with the right calculations."

"All right. Semantics. You teachers. We have the probability these two murders seem to be related, but I deal in evidence. Find me some evidence, and we'll talk about theories. I have to go, but if you come up with something, call me immediately. And, don't take anything out of this room, even if you think the material is inconsequential. Tell me what you've found. I don't need any screw-ups on top of all the pressure I'm dealing with right now."

"I'll be careful, promise. I'll let you know if I find something important."

"Let me know if you find anything. I'll decide whether or not it's important." Dante turned away from her then back again. "I will bring you some coffee if you'd like. I know you Americans prefer to drink coffee all day. But, when I get back, you're done here." The time he gave her might not be enough.

As soon as she entered, Vena searched for a volume of Keats' poetry or one with Shelley and Keats. The surface of Pavoni's desk was bare, and its drawers empty. Officers had done a thorough job. Perhaps there really was nothing to find? Then she looked again. In reading detective stories, she had come across methodology as to how a room is viewed in different ways. Something about using a flashlight at oblique angles to catch what might have been missed before, and three-dimensional aspects to taking in crime scenes. There had to be an angle the police had missed. Tilting her head, she scanned the room as if her mind was a computer.

On the fifth shelf, against the wall, was a volume of Keats poetry. No, the book was actually an anthology of both Keats and Shelley, but the discovery of the book emboldened her. Heart beating noticeably faster, she found herself slightly faint from excitement and exertion, moving things around to get a chair, pile a few books on the chair, climb on them, then stand on her tiptoes to reach for the volume.

In addition to excitement, she sensed her stomach churning in panic.

Both End in Speculation

If there was nothing in this book, Pavoni likely left no clue. Grabbing the anthology, she nearly unbalanced herself, almost falling out of indifference to her own safety. Investigators would have gone through these books, too, she knew, but perhaps they had not noticed something or dismissed possible evidence. Maybe something was written in code on a page. She wasn't even sure what she was searching for, although there was some part of her brain trained on a missing poem. Certainly Pavoni would not have left the original Keats' poem in his office. Yet, the missing poem was not in his home either, according to Dante. Maybe Pavoni never had the poem. If Sabine alone held the valuable paper, perhaps Pavoni had led the killer directly to her. All those thoughts raced through her mind in the instant before she determined to examine the volume.

Once the book was in her hands, she climbed down and sat at the desk, carefully turning the pages one at a time. Despite the illogic, she expected to find the poem harbored between pages, certain of discovery.

Disappointment was profound when she finished flipping over nearly all of the pages, finding no paper in Keats' handwriting. Pavoni had not even annotated poems in the margins of pages. At the end of the book, two pages from the back cover, however, there was a slight scrap of paper, a corner, on which was written a street address in Roma and the words *Compro Oro*. It might mean nothing, but Vena slipped the fragment into her jacket pocket. She knew she should tell Dante about the address, but then, what if he said the address was nothing and threw away the paper? She had to figure out if the location was of any importance to the case first.

Keeping *Compro Oro* from Dante was not deception but pragmatism. Vena continued to hold undisclosed information. Why put Dante in an embarrassing situation where he might have his officers surrounding the building of some poor bookseller or shop owner. *Compro Oro*...then she remembered the words meant, dealer in gold. Suppose this business owner knew nothing of the intrigue surrounding a missing poem? As much as she loved poetry, even Vena had to admit a poem was not gold. Assuming as much would be embarrassing to Vena, Dante, and the unwitting man or woman who owned the shop. Why did Pavoni have the name of a gold dealer in this volume of Keats' poetry? The address had to be significant, however.

"Find anything?" Dante stuck his head in the room. "Time's up. I brought you a coffee as consolation. We never drink coffee mid-day, but I remembered your American preference. I had to coax the shop clerk to make one for me."

"No, nothing, I'm afraid." Vena was sure Dante could see the red glow of her cheeks, but he pretended not to notice anything out of the ordinary as she grabbed the cup from his hands. "Thank you. Sorry to be of trouble."

"Told you. Let's go." Dante led the way out of the university building. "So maybe their murders had nothing to do with a poem. It's hard to let go of a theory, Vena, but you have to follow the evidence. Perhaps there is a jealous lover there somewhere in the mix, after all? What do you think? The professor threatens to kill the young woman's lover, but her other lover kills the professor?" Dante was heading straight back toward Antonio whether he knew it or not.

"Where does a homeless man fit in? I don't think he was the lover of either one. Maybe her lover…" Vena wrestled with her conscience about whether she should mention poor Antonio.

"Her lover? Do you know for certain if she had one? Are we referring to Sabine's lover? What about Pavoni's?"

"Suppose he had a male lover?" Vena asked.

"Are you speculating Pavoni went both ways? His lover tried to kill his other lover but killed Pavoni instead, or her lover killed his lover and her other lover in a jealous rage?" Dante tossed the absurdity out there, knowing how the words doubled back, but he hadn't slept in a while. Suddenly they both broke out laughing.

"I'm sorry. I shouldn't have," he said.

"No, I laughed, too. You're under tension. But let's assume for a moment, you're right about the first part. The case still makes no sense. Why would an angry lover seek such intricate and dangerous plans to carry out the staging? Why not shoot or stab them both and leave?"

"Could be like you said before, in the other case last year, turned out to be a red herring. This guy or these individuals do not want us too close to home, to the real perpetrator. So, let's say, he provides an elaborate distraction. What happens next in your detective stories?"

"They solve the crime."

"Too easy."

"Depends on what you're reading. Some are impossible."

"Give me the impossible."

"Does the crime have to be about a person?"

"Helps, but what are you construing?"

"Let me think."

"I'm afraid I need a quick something to eat. Let's stop somewhere." They walked into a trattoria and ordered. For a few minutes both were silent, listening to a crowd of voices around them. Thinking about the case appeared to provide no entrance. With a quick swallow, Dante turned from the bar and Vena followed.

"Calvino."

"Calvino? I've lost the…"

Bringing her hand to her chin, Vena said, "His story in which the pages are missing, and readers keep searching for missing pages to find other mysteries with missing pages, and the missing pages are not the mystery at all. Calvino's novel is about writing novels or a mystery about mysteries."

"We certainly appear to have missing pages. But I don't see how Calvino, whoever he is, helps. Hey, I'm still hungry. Do you want to get something substantial, too?"

"I ought to get back to see Elio and tell him how the case is coming or, rather, what I've been doing all afternoon. Do you want to come over? I can make a meal for us."

"I don't have long."

"I'll come up with something quick."

"All right. If you're nervous about being alone with a married man?"

"Not at all; besides, Elio will be there."

"No, I meant the two of us eating dinner together."

"No problem, but Elio has been waiting for me all day."

"Then you're worried Elio will be jealous. I knew it."

"Okay, you've found me out." They both laughed, but recognized Elio really might be jealous.

"At least you're honest. Let's go."

~ * ~

Sabine, her beautiful student, her friend, was dead. Her death still did not seem real. There was nothing she could do to bring Sabine back or find her justice. All Vena's instincts had failed her. As she teared up entering the apartment, Elio put his hands over her eyes.

"Surprise."

Vena did not tell him she felt blind.

"Why didn't you answer my calls or texts?"

"She was in the middle of helping with the investigation. Relax, little brother."

"I'm not your little brother." Everyone froze for a moment, then Elio twitched his lip before allowing his face to break into a smile. "I'm not little. So, what did you come up with…?"

"Nothing really. Vena was telling me about some mystery writer, ah, Calvino. She was no help at all." Vena shot Dante a glance to see if he was still joking.

"Italo Calvino. He's one of ours," said Elio, finally pleased to include himself in their discussion.

"Italian?"

"Latin Italian. He lived in South America," Vena was compelled to correct Elio slightly. She regretted the insertion immediately.

"Is he any good?"

"As a writer, yes." Vena answered but Elio was already nodding his head.

"At solving mysteries?" As much as Dante enjoyed their verbal interplay, he wanted to get back to the murders at hand. "But I'm afraid I need a real scenario here, not one imagined."

"Oh, he doesn't solve them at all," Vena said amused.

"Not helpful," Dante answered.

Elio opened his laptop and pulled up a quotation. "Listen to this: 'Reading,' Calvino wrote 'is always this: there is a thing that is there, a thing made of writing, a solid, material object, which cannot be changed

Both End in Speculation

and through this thing we measure ourselves against something else that is not present, something else that belongs to the immaterial, invisible world because it can only be thought, imagined.'"

"Now I know you like this Calvino, but what does he have to do with our murders?"

Squinting, Vena offered tentatively, "Elio is suggesting we are measuring ourselves, our ability to solve this mystery with something not seen. We have to use our imaginations in order to understand what is not tangible, what exists in the immaterial world, at least for the moment." With her left hand, Vena fingered the slip of paper in her jacket pocket. Preparing what she would say next, she wrapped her fingers around the address, in order to take out the paper and tell Dante about what she had found in the *professore's* office, when Dante's phone rang.

"I'll be right there." Turning to Vena, he said. "I have to leave."

"What? Another murder?"

"No, nothing so terrible. I'll catch you both later tonight, but no more quotations or famous authors, Italian or otherwise, please. I want to hear realistic theories around actual evidence we can follow. We need a motive where some homeless African migrant fits into the mix, and everyone ends up on top or at the bottom of one of our historical monuments."

"Easy," said Elio.

"I want to come with you." Vena had already grabbed her bag before Dante stopped her with a curt movement of one hand.

"Absolutely not. Stay here. I'll talk to you later, I promise." Dante said, not reading his brother's eyes but seeing Vena's determination and thinking about explaining what he had been doing to solve the case for the last two hours.

After the door closed, Vena looked to Elio. "What was the Calvino quotation about? I liked it, though."

"You two were talking about him; I thought I could help. I don't know. I guess I wanted to be part of this. You like Calvino, too. We've talked about his work, and I was feeling a little left out. I know Dante's married and all, but you're spending so much time with him, and I see the way he stares at you sometimes when he thinks my attention is diverted."

"Really? Come on. Of course, I love Calvino and you." She let go of the paper with the address in her pocket and put both arms around Elio's neck. In the moment of intimacy, she thought again of Sabine in the arms of Antonio, remembering they would never hold one another again. Then, she knew. She should have told Dante about Antonio even if the young man found himself in trouble as a result. She would tell Dante as soon as she saw him again.

~ * ~

Rubbing against the fabric in Vena's pocket, the address was kept hidden, even from Elio. I shouldn't feel guilt, she told herself. I am trying to keep this from becoming an embarrassing situation for anyone. If she had told Dante then, he would question why she didn't share the information earlier. Dante would, undoubtedly, be angry she had kept anything from him. She considered possible outcomes. The likelihood of the address leading to nothing of importance was great, and she didn't want to impede or slow the investigation. Her rationale played out slowly before her, unconvincingly.

Determining to check the location out first, she would find who or what resided at the address in her pocket. Perhaps the location held nothing more than an innocuous bookstore where Pavoni had purchased the Keats/Shelley anthology. But why the words *Compro Oro*? What was Pavoni's interest in a gold broker? Even if the address was connected in a significant way, what did gold have to do with his murder? A little exploring was in order. If the address led to something intriguing, she would call Dante.

Broker. The word rolled around her mouth, her lips forming an O when the impact of discovery made her pull her head back. She thought of it. Pavoni was attempting to deal. Did he already have the Keats' poem when he went to the broker? If so, then why was Sabine killed? *Compro Oro* suddenly assumed a sinister weight, and Vena could feel her heart beating, her pulse quickening. Still, she would not tell Dante yet.

Maybe she could offer something else, another bit of information. Yes, she determined to offer Antonio's name to Dante. The young man must have had an alibi. She would explain to Dante, she had forgotten about the conversation she had with Sabine. As to the address, she would alert both Dante and Elio as soon as she left for the location. A note on the table, not a text. It would take longer, but she would need the time. If she told them before venturing out on her own, Elio would insist on going with her, and he might interfere in some way or prevent her from going at all.

Step, walk back, step, turn again. She was moving along a fine line between caution and abandoning discretion altogether. Better to be cautious, but cautious detectives seldom get their man.

Chapter Thirteen
Melancholy Spirits

Crossing half-way across the majestic and perfectly symmetrical bridge over the Tiber River with Castel Sant' Angelo on the right bank, Vena stopped. Aware she was on the Ponte Sant' Angelo, or the Bridge of Angels, she pondered the mythical defense of the castle, the city. On the Bridge of Angels, Vena could almost see ancient invading forces confronted with an imposing castle wall. History was always rising up and riding into the contemporary scenes in this Eternal City. Even Dante Alighieri, the great poet, had written about this bridge, his pilgrims passing back and forth, some heading into the circles of Hell. They wished to pray in St. Peter's Basilica, but many were incapable of such prayer, according to the poet.

After the plague, legend told of angels appearing on the top of the castle, and the church renamed the span, the bridge of St. Peter. Legends, history, myth; all circled around one another in Roma, so much so, separating strands of fiction and fact became as complex and intricate as the men who wove them.

Vena did not feel either safe or particularly at risk. Rather, she was saddened, considering the beautiful bridge had once displayed the bodies of the executed. Their hanging bodies must have been a ghastly warning to all along the bridge over the river. Looking down through wrought iron grating, Vena watched the Tiber's muddy water swirl below her. She was not suicidal, but she could imagine jumping.

Ten angels graced the bridge, seeming to lift the arch with their wings; Vena could sense their frustration with man. Standing upon their marble parapets, inscribed with Biblical verses, the angels suggested movement, their marble clothing flowing like water below them. Yet, even the angels were supplanted years later, first commissioned by Pope

Clement VII. Vena knew enough history to be aware that more Clements were involved in funding Bernini's angels. Bernini himself was said to have directly sculpted two of the angels in marble, assigning the others to sculptors who shared his style and vision. The angel holding Christ's Crown of Thorns was the one Bernini brought to life, after the form and shape was carved by Cosimo Fancelli. Beneath the tenth angel Vena read the inscription, "You have ravished my heart," intended to remind human beings of the pain they caused Christ, and, Vena thought, continued to cause one another.

Bernini's statues were, however, too beautiful, and the next Pope Clement decided to keep those angels protected and inside, commanding copies be made. Those copies now stood sentry. Even ancient angels were vulnerable to the whims of capricious men.

Melancholy hung about Vena. Her shoulders were lowered, her hands questioning where they should rest, finally settling upon a railing. After a couple of years in Roma, she had made it a habit not to stand alone too long, but she had been walking all morning. Her adult business student had cancelled at the last minute, and another session with a small group of four students was cancelled by the school due to the students' failure to meet payments to the institute. But she was not really sad about losing her class.

Rather than worrying about her economic prospects, Vena stood on the bridge, hesitant. The Tiber snaked throughout the city in a way you could not avoid crossing the river if you spent any time in Roma. Vena was thinking about Sabine again, and how her student had been so bright and full of life. Where were the angels when Sabine was beaten to death? How could they have prevented what happened? How could she have stopped what happened to Sabine? No, she was giving herself too much credit and power. A whisper from one of the angels told her so, and she finally moved on and crossed over.

~ * ~

Lying in bed with Elio already asleep, she closed her eyes and could suddenly hear Dante breathing next to her. Arousal over imagining Dante was both desirous and terrible in stirring up guilt—not a place she wanted to go in the light of day. What made suppressing the fantasy more difficult was her suspicion Dante crossed into a similar dream. There was no reason for her to be attracted to Dante, she argued with herself, but the chemistry was there. The fact he was married was most likely part of the reason she let herself fantasize because, on some internal level, she knew she would never act on her inclination. Maybe the wild thoughts about Dante were nothing more than distraction from the horror of Sabine's murder. But Elio made everything too easy.

Every time a sexual fantasy distracted her or even lifted her spirits, an image of Sabine brought down from the Arch of Constantine flooded her with ill-ease and trepidation again. Sabine's terrible death brought back an old dread and the memory of the murder of her friend, Michael Lawler. The specter of Gould, the way she shuddered when she was in his presence, threatened to drown her if she did not shake off this engulfing shadow. Imagining what soldiers must feel after exposure to war, Vena sensed they would go right back to the event, replaying again and again with the sickness creeping up on them.

Why was it easier to imagine Sabine had been killed in a moment of jealousy and anger than for money? Could a poem really have caused her death? She understood why Dante didn't believe her theory. Her student did not deserve such a brutal and public spectacle in death, but Vena could no more stop thinking about the young woman's murder than her awful attraction to Dante. Yet she believed her mental affair with Dante would end once the case was solved. Elio had told her about the code of the Carabinieri in which affairs were not permitted. The Code seemed so silly in a country in which the men's eyes wandered so easily and freely.

In those early hours, Vena also imagined Dante's wife. What was Francesca like? Did she know her husband was spending much of his time with another woman? Would she be jealous or so confident in her love and the Carabinieri code, she would laugh at this American? What did Vena want? Agonizing over why she was always so restless, Vena was trapped by her own questioning, wanting something more without being able to articulate it. Murder, love, sex, history, death, jealousy, fantasy and unfaithfulness were congealed into surface tension she had trouble reading.

Both End in Speculation

If she had met both Canestrini brothers at the same time, Vena wondered if she would have immediately chosen Elio. He was closer to her age and beautiful. Clever and smart, Elio was naturally charismatic. Of course, he had a poet's soul, too. How could she not be attracted to him? Dante's military bearing even more than his uniform might have been off-putting, but she was also aware of Dante's subtle pull on her senses. Was it because he was out of reach, a married man, why she was so compelled by him?

~ * ~

Before she left for work, Elio had made breakfast while she readied for work. He had been reading her notes. Turning over a page in her notebook, he found a Tischbein print of Goethe at a window of his house in Via del Corso. "Why did you keep this print? These sickly Germans and Englishmen," said Elio. "First Keats, then Shelley, Goethe, and they all end up here in my city. Their intense fascination with Roma brings more tourists, more writers, more wanderers in the world."

"Why do you think I arrived here?" Vena asked.

"I'm not talking about you."

"I'm not in the mood for nationalist talk," said Vena sullenly, tossing her book bag in a chair already occupied by other books. She realized there was no place to sit except the bed, every chair occupied with books and clothing.

"I made breakfast for you."

"Thank you."

"What's wrong? You seem angry waking up." Elio regretted his tone and approach.

"Sabine's murder," said Vena.

Elio ducked back into the kitchen and boiled the water for her tea, a drink he did not like but knew Vena did occasionally drink when she didn't have an espresso.

"Here," he said, handing her the cup with the tea bag still in the water. "Tell me about what you're thinking. Sabine has been gone for a while, and you are solving the case."

"I've solved nothing," she said, drinking slowly.

~ * ~

"If you are so worried about losing her," Dante said to his brother while Vena was still pacing alone over the Bridge of Angels, "then why don't you make an honest woman of her and ask her to marry you? Two years is a long enough engagement."

"We're not engaged, and there are no time limits except those artificially imposed by others who feel discomfit. We are perfectly happy with our arrangement."

"Doesn't appear…never mind." Picking up a pile of books and putting them on the floor, Dante sat down.

"Who are you talking about…me or Vena?"

"Both of you. Stop pacing and sit down with me for a moment."

Resisting the urge to hurt his brother with a comment about Dante's long-distance marriage, Elio said, "Marriage doesn't prefigure adultery, but neither does marriage prevent it. I don't really think Vena wants or needs a proposal right now."

"She's your girlfriend. You ought to know her by now. What does she want then?" Dante honestly wanted to know but preferred to allow his younger brother to think he was simply guiding him to a life-altering decision. "Where is she anyway? Shouldn't she be home by now? I imagine you expected her earlier."

Elio winced slightly at the sting of, "You ought to know her by now," but simply shrugged again, feigning indifference. "Or, you expected her earlier. Say what you mean."

"I expected her? We're talking about a case together, but she's your girlfriend."

Blunt honesty slipped into the conversation. "I don't know for certain, but she might not want me any longer." Elio opened a bottle of wine and poured two glasses full. He held one in his hand and left the other on the table.

Suddenly empathizing with his brother, Dante stood up and clapped a hand on his shoulder. "Don't sell yourself short. Remember, you are the

Both End in Speculation

good-looking one every girl followed and adored, from our mother to the girls in school to every woman in the streets of our city." Interrupting himself, Dante said, "You know I don't drink, so you must be planning on drinking both glasses."

"Maybe I will...drink them both," Elio said, but knew the other glass had been poured for Vena. He still expected her back at any moment. "Why the comment about our mother? She loved us equally."

"No such thing, even when parents try."

"You love all your kids the same."

"Not really. Christine is my favorite, but don't tell the boys or their mother."

"Damn you, you're being snarky, I hope."

"I'm not. Vena is foolish to no longer be in love with you." Dante's comment was meant to console, but his words didn't come out the way he intended. Dante considered sitting back down, but tension prevented him.

Elio audibly inhaled. To hear his brother say such a thing out loud was so much worse than his mere speculative musings. "You believe Francesca still loves you, then?" He turned from compassion to cruelty, but his brother had gone there first.

"What bullshit game is this?" They were already positioned too near one another. Even his brother saying Francesca's name was annoying to Dante.

"No game. It's a simple enough question, like the one you asked me." Elio took a long draught of the wine, feeling the warmth all the way down. He seldom stood up to his older and bigger brother.

"Which I don't intend to dignify with a response. You know where my loyalties lie, and my wife is still in love with me, as if our love is any of your business, but since you so rudely asked."

"I didn't start this."

"If you allow Vena to come between us, you might want to rethink your loyalties." Dante stuck out his chest and pulled himself to full military bearing.

"The same could be said of you." The vein in Elio's temple was pulsing, and his hand involuntarily worked into a fist. Elio was still holding back, avoiding saying the worst things he could think of in the moment.

What had Dante said to anger him to this extent? He was already forgetting how the insults were crafted and what might have been intended.

Not wanting to fight his little brother, Dante would find himself willing, however, if the ass who had become his brother was going to come for him. Yes, a smack down could be arranged. Elio was not without physical gifts, but Dante knew he could still easily best him in a fight. Did he really want it to come to that? Without moving, they were beginning to square off in their heads as Vena entered the room.

"Oh, good, you're both here," she said sullenly with the faintest hint of sarcasm.

"You didn't answer my calls," Elio said, in relief rather than accusation. He gave her room and didn't approach or hug her as he typically did.

"Sorry, my phone was turned off at school, and I forgot to turn it back on when I left." She spotted a full glass of wine on the table. Elio lifted a glass to her. "You knew I was coming and poured wine for me? How come?"

"I didn't know. I guess I hoped you'd be back soon." They both suddenly smiled at each other, but Elio could not keep himself from grilling her. "Where were you, all this time? There was a call from the school: your class was cancelled."

"Yes. I might need to find another job."

"We'll be fine; we don't need your money," said Elio. But he could tell the way Vena turned her head sharply she did not want to hear his demeaning remark. "Where'd you go when you left school?"

"For a walk."

Dante snorted. "A lot of walking. Your boyfriend here has been worried about you."

Elio shot his brother a glance, telling him to shut up. "So, you wandered around alone?"

"I wasn't alone," she said, taking a slow sip of wine as anger in the room drifted out through a slightly open window, replaced by curiosity.

The brothers stared at her for several seconds before Elio couldn't resist. "Who were you with then?"

"Angels. I was on a bridge with the angels, talking to them for hours."

~ * ~

A plump waitress with a low-cut blouse, wearing thick black eyeliner, approached their table in Osteria Bonelli. She openly flirted with Elio. "And for you?" she asked, leaning into him and bending far enough so he could see the top of her breasts spilling from the shirt.

Elio was so used to this kind of attention, the flirting scarcely fazed him. "*Pasta alla gricia.*"

"I like a man who knows what he wants," she said, leaning against him.

"And apparently, he likes cured pork and cheese with his pasta, and me," Vena said in English, not rudely or angrily, simply factually.

Elio laughed as the waitress stepped away from him slightly. "And you? You want some spaghetti," she said in English, dragging out her syllables mockingly.

"*Riccota e spinaci ravioli.*" Vena's Italian surprised the waitress who was certain she had spotted *persona di inglese,* but now was not so sure. "By the way, your English is excellent, almost as good as my Italian."

Their waitress winked then vanished. She wrote Elio off to this nasty woman. "Spit in her dish," she said to the chef.

"Never," he replied haughtily. While he might have acquiesced to another waitress, this one was too bossy, and she had once spurned his earlier flirtations.

"They all love you," said Vena with a sigh.

"Not true. Some of them, yes, but why does their attention matter?"

"Because I don't want to go around being jealous all of the time."

"And you think I don't have to deal with this? Every man we pass, I have to decide, do I fight him if he makes a pass at you or grabs you? Do I try to laugh off their rude gestures?"

"We have a dilemma." They waited for their food in increasing anticipation of what the other would say.

"I know you like literature, and I'm a great beach read."

"That's ridiculous. I find you complicated and fascinating." She moved her hands from her chin and rested them on the paper topping the table.

"Now, you're flat out lying."

"Then why am I with you for two years of my life?"

"I don't know. I know I'm not as intriguing to you as Dante."

"What? What's this about? Jealousy over your brother? I chose you, don't forget."

"Did you? Have you chosen me?"

"Aren't we living together, or am I imagining something here? What's going on? Do you want to get into an argument with me or something?"

"I don't know. Maybe I do "

"Our waitress seems to think you know exactly what you want."

Elio frowned, but as Vena tried to suppress a smile, his lips curled upward. He broke out into a full grin.

Putting both hands to her chin and her elbows on the table, Vena said, "Tell me about your mother."

"What? I've already told you about her."

"You told me her name was Cecilia. She had cancer and died young; she cooked masterfully, and before she died she worked two jobs to keep you, and she sang around the house. She loved you, and your father left her. What you offered is an outline, not her story. I want to know her."

"Not so easy." They were both quiet for a few moments, then Elio said, "My mother, Cecilia, used to sing 'oh, oh, *Piccola* Katy,' a song by Pooh,'" Elio smiled, remembering the way she sometimes danced through a room when he was very young. "Oh, little Katy,'" he hummed. "I liked her singing. She wasn't a very good singer, but she loved to sing. Sometimes, she would be washing our clothes, then pick up one of my brother's shirts and dance around like the silly shirt was a man. My brothers and I would laugh, and we'd tease her, but nicely. My mother was a very good woman. She had a sense of humor even after my father left, but she had cancer. One afternoon, she poured wine for herself and my two brothers. 'A toast to me, your mother, the most amazing woman you will ever know,' she said laughing, then drank the wine down." Elio's gaze drifted away from Vena and the chalkboard menu, past the crowded wooden tables, out beyond onto *Viale Dell'Acquedotto Alssandrino*, further from the streets into the city, beyond Roma.

They were both silent for a time when the plates arrived.

"Thank you," said Vena to Elio, his eyes watery.

Chapter Fourteen
Endless Fountains and Drunken Nights

Guerra knew as soon as Pavoni told him about the supposed priceless poem whom he would contact. The American mobster Guerra had in mind had been to Roma multiple times and had frequented Guerra's gold broker business. Fostering their dealings was the fact the American was Italian, a criminal, and knew well the language of barter and Italian. Also, significant: his American client was a boss and wouldn't need to ask a higher up about anything. A price could be agreed upon without a third party. Guerra had always been an impatient man in all things, except his killings.

A quick call was all that was needed after cleaning up the mess from Pavoni. Guerra thought he really must be more careful. Pavoni's blood was spattered across the room. Bleach odors made him wince and stung his nostrils and eyes. He told Abramo he would be able to express mail the valuable paper in a few days. For this good service, Guerra wanted three quarters of his price up front. Abramo rejected the conditions immediately. He was unsure about the price and any definite worth.

"How do I know what this fucking poem will bring? It's a piece of paper. Because you tell me it's important? Send me some kind of verification, authentication or certification signed, then we'll talk numbers maybe."

"Already authenticated by a smart *professore* here. The *professore* and me finished our business," Guerra said, unable to keep his lip from curling slightly.

"You come into this paper, how? What professor?" Abramo suddenly changed his tone to accusatory. "Deal involve a burn? Is this what you're telling me? I want no part of anything sloppy or stupid."

"No concerns. Neat. Clean operation."

"I don't..."

"As far as price, this thing could go for an unbelievable amount. I have other buyers who might be interested, so you're either in or out." Guerra wasn't stressed about the gamble he was taking because he already had a couple of other potential buyers in mind. "I'm giving you first refusal. Think I've already proven my worth as a big earner." Guerra knew Abramo was pleased with the last two deals they had made, but Abramo continued his silence on the other end. "If you don't want it, forget it. But, you're maybe giving up a million American dollars." A poker hand, and Guerra had to be ready to play his cards.

"A million? That's nuts!"

"Give or take a couple hundred."

"No problems, right? This swag?"

"No trace. Like I said." Glancing around his shop, Guerra was glad Abramo couldn't see the mess.

"All right. Set it up. But 20%, not three-quarters." Abramo left off, "You dumb fuck," although the profanity was on the tip of his tongue, and he had to bite back those words.

"Twenty percent? I can't..."

"If it's worth what you say, then twenty's a good price for you."

"Up front," Guerra apprehended how much ground he had lost.

"Ten thousand. Nobody knows anything about this 'cept you and me? You don't have a partner, do you? I don't want complications." Abramo was suspicious again and ready to hang up.

Guerra knew Abramo didn't want others in the organization to know about this one, likely intending to keep the treasure himself. He could never figure out men who kept and held onto any kind of art, not as some collateral, but because they wanted to look at some painting or rare object. Their stupidity almost made him laugh when he thought of all the valuable objects in his shop. He gave little thought to their artistic merit, only considered how much each would bring in trade.

"Nobody else involved. This is a one-man operation. Thought you knew me by now."

"It's good to ask, never know when someone decides things are getting too much for the show."

"Ten thousand? Huh? How 'bout twenty thousand Euros up top?"

"Euros? I'm talking dollars here. Twenty? You go from ten to twenty? What kind of fool do you think I am? I should fuckin' hang up right now." Abramo was not a man even Guerra wanted to make angry. His connections in Italy were strong.

"Trying to get by. I've put some time and effort into this deal. Fifteen?"

"Eleven. As far as I go. The rest after I get the paper with some document of certification or whatever to show this poem is what you say, and I get it inspected. If the estimate pans out on my end, we'll finish *transazione*."

~ * ~

This hadn't gone quite the way Guerra wanted or planned, but Abramo offered quick cash and the promise of more to come. Even if Abramo stiffed him after he sent the paper, he was still up eleven grand. And he didn't yet have the paper in his hands. Sabine was next on his list, and he anticipated working with her would be an easy job, but he never knew until he was in the situation. Three murders for eleven grand and all the trouble he had gone through didn't seem enough, but he knew a contract murder might bring a couple thousand. "Eleven thousand for million-dollar art? I'm supposed to be happy here?"

"I don't give a fuck if you're goddamn happy. Take the offer or leave it. Find another buyer." Abramo was done negotiating. Guerra could hear shift in the way his voice rose to a pitch, making him sound like a woman.

"Wait. Let me think."

"You're done thinking or stalling. Now or never and don't call back."

"Deal."

"Send this fucking expensive paper to the address I'm going to give you in New Jersey. Insure the fucking thing, too. You don't get a dime until I have the paper."

Guerra slammed a gold-plated candlestick into a counter after he hung up, denting the candlestick and wooden counter. He had expected to do better, but the killings were not contracts. They were done to erase any trail of the theft. "Fuck, fucking Abramo," he said out loud, working himself up further. If anyone had been in his shop at that moment, he would have beaten the man or woman. Guerra thought it was fortunate for Abramo the American mobster was an ocean away. Even if he was connected Mafia, he would bleed as sure as the African and Pavoni.

Still, maybe the whole ordeal would earn him points in the future. If Abramo was pleased, a happy mob boss couldn't hurt Guerra who had so few connections to the power men in *Cosca*. He had the nerve and cleverness of the best of them, he reasoned, but no one to help bring him into the organization proper and move him up in stature. Maybe Abramo could help make those introductions at a later time. He slammed his fist down again, realizing he should have made such a demand as part of the package. Then he thought about the circumstances again. No one had ever taken him under his wing, allowing him to work his way up, first as a soldier. He realized he no longer wanted this entrance, even if he had hoped for it when younger.

~ * ~

Lying nearest John Keats in the ground was not Joseph Severn, as Vena anticipated, but Severn's infant son Arthur. The boy's marker is eternally positioned between his father and father's friend in the Protestant Cemetery. The English Ghetto, as Italians call it, in Testaccio. On a small gravestone between giants was an inscription to Severn's son, "Here also are interred the Remains of Arthur Severn." Found on the child's tomb are the words "Accidentally killed." Vena had to research to discover his manner of death. Little was written about young Arthur except the note, he had a "crib accident." Such a tragic fate must have weighed heavily on Severn and his wife. Joseph had lived a long and intriguing life. His self-sacrificing nursing of Keats in Rome was one of his many adventures in both metaphorical and literal poverty and wealth in the ancient city.

A gray cat curled at the base of Keats' marker, stretching with the sunlight tickling her nose which she scratched lazily before settling back in sleep. Smiling at the discovery of the feral cat, Vena noted the feline, too, had chosen to rest with Keats, as if siding with historical and literary preference. Unlikely Severn was jealous now or perhaps ever. Although Severn was a painter and had founded the British Academy of the Fine Arts in Rome among his many accomplishments, he was best known, rather unfairly, for being Keats' friend. Joseph returned to England after Keats' death, but Rome pulled him back again. He became British Consul in Rome in 1861, long after Keats' death, not the defining moment of Severn's life, after all, but a moment in which his name has most come to be regarded. Even on his gravestone, Severn forever holds the words, "Devoted friend and deathbed companion of John Keats."

Severn was evermore linked to Keats, Vena thought as she peered through the iron fencing in this place of solitude in the midst of a bustling city. She thought it curious and more than a little unreasonable, after all those years of Severn's own accomplishments and large family, the Englishman had such an inscription about Keats on his grave. Yet, his relationship with Keats assured Severn of immortality.

As she mused, the cat sat up, stared icily at Vena, licked her paw, then stalked out silently over the graves of all those non-Catholics buried in Roma.

If Keats did create a last poem in Roma, the event was remarkable because he was so weak with illness, and also because he was still seeing a foreign city with an Englishman's eyes. He was writing wholly inside himself while the Italian sun beat down outside his window. If Severn had found Keats' poem, as Sabine had asked her to believe, the paper tucked inside the volume of Shakespeare plays, Severn would certainly have hailed the poem as a great find. The discovered ode would have been published for posterity and likely a copy kept for Severn. Three months living in Roma, his last destination, allowed for the possibility Keats produced a few more lines. This disease of his lungs did not destroy his mind.

But the idea Joseph simply gave away the book of Shakespeare's plays gracing the bedside, in sadness or unbearable pain, returned to Vena. She could imagine Keats' poem squeezed between Shakespeare's voluminous and poetic words, starved of readers all those years on the top floor of an apartment building not so very different than the ancient *insulae*,

Both End in Speculation

What Vena was asking of Dante was to suspend his training as an investigator looking for concrete evidence and try to imagine this scene: Keats struggling to find lasting beauty in the act of creating as he coughed, spasmodically, a cupful of blood.

"My God, John," Severn wiped his friend's lips and drew the cup away.

"I don't have long, I'm afraid." Keats let his head fall back on the small pillow.

"Please don't say such things. You must believe you will recover."

"I'm the one allowed to be delusional here." Keats began coughing again, spurts of blood dotted his face and pillow.

After Keats' coughing calmed, he was deathly silent. Joseph leaned in to make sure the man was breathing.

"I'm here. Are you checking for my pulse or breath?" John asked with his eyes still closed.

"I was…let me get you something to drink." Joseph brought a cold cup of coffee to Keats' lips. "Here, drink a little if you can."

John swallowed a drop of the bitterness, then reached out for the cup and flung the contents at Severn. "It's cold. This is what you bring me? This is all you have for me?"

Joseph straightened himself and saw the coffee had stained his shirt and waistcoat. "Ah, I need to go for the doctor. John, you'll be all right until I return."

"I could be dead, and you'd return in the same amount of time. Leave the doctor. He's doing nothing for me."

Joseph left the room.

Keats sat up partially, picked up the quill pen on the little table and in his shaking but determined hand, he scratched out lines on a paper. "You will be surprised, my friend," he said out loud in the empty room. He was silent while he used his strength to concentrate, hurrying the words. He crossed out a few, chose others inked above them. He knew these words would be his last.

~ * ~

Dante turned away. "Simply not enough solid evidence," he would say. "This is conjecture about speculation or story-telling."

Not giving up, Vena weighed the idea this last poem by Keats would not have been his best work or even close to his great poems of genius. A poem, crafted in terrible circumstances, was certain to show weakness in many aspects as Keats finally gave in to the disease wracking his lungs. Also entirely possible, was the poem could have been incomplete, merely a fragment left by a dying man, one who was feverish and unable to distinguish art from artifice any longer. Yet, even a partial original poem, one not among his finest, would still be worth a fortune, she knew.

"I wish I could be of more help, but the idea of a missing poem makes the most sense for a motive."

"You never know what is helpful until an investigation is over."

"Antonio," she said.

"What?"

"Did you find out anything more about Sabine's lover?"

"No. The poor guy was stupid from crying like a girl." Dante checked Vena's expression, aware she would not have liked his sexist comment, but he continued. "He kept pleading with us to find her killer. Even if he wasn't convincing, he had a solid alibi. We were able to confirm it."

"I knew he couldn't have had anything to do with murdering her."

"So, what have we got? No love triangle with the boyfriend. A little checking on Pavoni, and appears he was still in the closet."

"Then, he was gay."

"No active partner, but several of his colleagues did more than hint. They didn't see him as violent. He was a loner, apparently. He could have deceived them."

"Are you always able to tell if someone is lying to cover up a crime?"

"Most of the time. Few people are as clever as they think." Dante nearly added, "except you," but he held back from the compliment which could be taken inappropriately.

"Do you think Pavoni could have been sleeping with one of his students?"

"Maybe, but his preferences don't appear to be relevant. The most his colleagues would admit was the *professore* was a deeply unhappy man. Deeply unhappy men are seldom sexually satisfied."

"Are you ever wrong?"

"We'll see. Not often." They both smiled.

"Maybe he was better at covering than you thought."

Elio re-entered the room. "At least you waited for me before theorizing."

"We're just getting started," Dante said.

Vena tossed her arm around Elio's neck, and he kissed her. She noticed a long hair protruding from his nose and stepped back slightly.

"I'll let you two alone for a while. Maybe some fresh air will give me an idea about the case."

Suddenly, Vena wanted to go out into the city, but she held back. "Please think about the poem angle again," she said as Dante pulled his coat over his shoulders.

"We'll discuss the case tomorrow."

"Let's do more than discuss it. How about we solve it?" Even as Vena tossed out the challenge, she had no idea of what lay ahead.

~ * ~

Returning home the next day to find Elio grading papers, Vena suggested they go out to a lively place for drinks.

"My kind of night and my kind of girl," Elio responded, quickly abandoning his class work.

Talking as they walked, Elio asked about her day, her visit to the Protestant Cemetery. "Was your walk to the cemetery everything you expected to find?"

"I don't know what I expected exactly, but I kept thinking about Severn rather than Keats, which is odd, I suppose."

"Severn? I don't know this man. Another Englishman?"

"Yes, but he lived most of his life here in Roma."

"A wise fellow."

"He was."

"So what troubles you about Severn?"

"Troubles?"

"I see them in your eyes, little wrinkle there." Elio touched her temple near her eye.

"I'm getting wrinkles now."

"Worry lines. How will this help your theory about Sabine's murder?"

Shaking her head, Vena wrapped her arm around Elio. "I am trying to imagine if such a thing as a last poem was possible from Keats, let alone a poem hidden for two-hundred years."

"And visiting his grave would relinquish this knowledge? Were you looking for a ghost?"

"I don't know. I guess I went there to think, to try to better imagine a last scene between those friends in a foreign country; one dying and the other feeling responsible for his care, yet unable to do anything really helpful. It's strange. There was a cat lying in front of Keats' grave as if even the cat knew the importance of the poet."

"Your ghosts and our ghosts. Those cats roam freely there." Elio said. "Ah, you are feeling helpless about your former student and this mystery which does not open, I see."

"Maybe you're right." Vena stopped walking and viewed the impressive fountain. "How many fountains do you have here in Roma again?"

"I don't know, a couple of thousand, I guess. This is a very beautiful one. Fontana dei Quattro Fiumi, but let's not stop here long—too many tourists, and already here comes a fellow selling roses."

"*Una rosa per la tua ragazza?*" the man moved into their space aggressively.

"*Non Rose,*" said Vena emphatically, almost cruelly, as she reached for Elio's hand and worked her way through Piazza Navona.

"*Cagna,*" shouted the man behind her. Elio turned, but Vena pulled him along.

"It's not worth it. He's trying to make a living."

"I don't care. He has no right to insult you. He insults you, then he insults me."

Quickening her pace, Vena tightened her grip of Elio's hand. "It's not really an insult. It's his defeat talking. We crushed his efforts, his hope. See?" she said, suddenly giggling, unsure of why she wanted to laugh.

Elio was confused about the change in her tone and spirits. "We'd better get you some food. You're sounding a little crazy."

"Yes, some good wine because I'm feeling a little crazy."

"No Dante, no murder case to try and solve tonight. You and me and plenty of Toscana Rosso."

"Agreed."

Elio and Vena drank plentifully, laughing and making love like the early days after they met.

~ * ~

Done. Bodies staged and discovered in confusion. Poem on its way to America. The money would soon be on its way to Guerra. Time to celebrate, but he was too bitter to go out and find a whore.

He opened a bottle of cheap red wine and drank long. "To Martino," he said mockingly, "To my many successes," he laughed, taking another swig, finally draining the last dregs of the bottle before opening another. *Polizia* had found broken bodies but not his expensive poem. Officials were running around in circles without a clue, he mused. Tourists were panicked, avoiding the most popular sites. Speculation about anti-migrant groups was not a focus, as he had hoped, however. Italian officials had kept information about his migrant signs on the bodies out of the media. One part of his plan had worked, but there was still time for the migrant distraction to leak out. Yet, Roma grappled with the chaos he created. He was pleased.

Neither *Polizia* nor the butt-of-jokes Carabinieri would tie the African to the girl or the professor, nor suspect what had led to their gruesome deaths, he thought. Sipping again, his lips nearly twisted into a smile as he recalled the painful labors of placing the bodies. This difficult action was most masterful and would continue to confound stupid authorities. He raised the bottle and slowly drank, savoring the taste at first until numbed. A long night of drunken celebration lay in front of him as he swallowed. Somewhere in the back of his roiling mind, he knew there would be a reckoning.

Chapter Fifteen
Secrets Further Down la Strada

Unopened on her computer, a message from Warren stared at Vena. Long-time friends and former lovers, they held their connections. She wore hers like a locket around her neck, unopened. Warren always got her notice, but this time she did not want to see his email. Why she suspected its contents, she didn't know. Elio was asleep, a soft purr coming from his lips, such a contented, beautiful cat. Then the email was open.

Vena, I know this sort of thing is better in person but, c'mon, when am I going to get to Italy? The band's doing great, but we're probably never going to be big time, touring internationally. And your once-a-year visit just doesn't work for me. Not that we thought our on again off again relationship ever did. I know you never considered me a boyfriend, except for about 15 minutes of our freshman year at U of R., but you also know I couldn't get you out of my head or heart. To be honest, you kind of messed me up. I'm not blaming you. It was my own damn fault, except for the times you came back around. Then, I'd have to blame you a little, too.

So, something surprising has happened. The girl you once told me about, the one who would be standing at the bar where my band was jamming, a pretty young woman was looking at me like you said she would be. She waited until the set was over and hung around while we were picking up. I finally found the nerve to go over and ask her name. "It's Bobbie, like a guy," she said, and she is really amazing. I won't go into details or go on and on about this, but I think I found her, the one I've been waiting for to take the place reserved for you all these years.

I'm not going to tell you anymore about Bobbie because it's not like you're going to become friends or anything. I wanted you to know. Mike told me to never say your name in Bobbie's presence because he said I get this stupid, glazed face when I do. He said I shouldn't mess up my relationship with Bobbie with shit from the past.

Damn, woman, you get under a guy's skin right down to his bones. Don't read anything raunchy into my statement because this is as close as I'll ever come to expressing my feelings for you honestly. I hope Elio understands how lucky he is. Anyway, I thought you might like to know your old friend Warren is finally happy. Really happy. This is the beginning of something very good.

Wishing you the best forever and always,
Warren

Starting to key in a response, Vena stopped and shut her computer. His timing wasn't right. The first thing she remembered about his message was he didn't sign "love" before his name. How did Warren know the best opportunity to tell her he had finally fallen head over heels for another woman was on a night she struggled with uncertainty over Elio, turmoil and uncertainty about everything in her life? Never mind the question she harbored was completely unfair. Warren was in love and no longer waiting for her. She could go home again, but knew her visits with Warren would never be the same. No, she wouldn't go to see him. She'd let Warren find his way into this new relationship without comparisons or distractions. Bobbie. Vena kind of liked his new woman's name, too.

Good for him, she whispered to herself, trying to mean it. "I hope she is right for him," she said out loud. She crawled back into bed, pushing Elio's leg over so she could stretch out. Not shutting her eyes, she listened to the city outside, sniffed in the dark and used the bed sheet to wipe her wet nose and eyes. Good for him. Be good to him, Bobbie.

~ * ~

In the morning, Vena moved to take actions. She wouldn't think about the murder case for a day. She wouldn't obsess over Sabine's murder or outline what Dante was doing. Go to work early, give her best skills to her students, return her damaged book, pick up fresh vegetables for dinner. She always made lists when things were bothering her. Listing held a kind of perfection, the ordering of the miniscule things in life she could control.

Both End in Speculation

~ * ~

"*Nessun ritorno*," the bookstore salesman said.

Vena tried again to explain in her best Italian why she was attempting to return the damaged book with the yellow highlighted pages. Useless. The neat, little gentleman with the red vest and thin wire glasses, curtly said, "No" in Italian. She flipped through, then pointed to the marked pages, setting the open book on his counter.

"We don't take books back," he finally said in English, as if he suspected her Italian was too weak to understand him. "How do I know it wasn't you who marked the page?"

Vena shifted to English since the man behind the counter had gone there first. "But it wasn't. Don't you want to keep a customer happy?" she asked. Trying an altered tactic didn't seem to be working either.

"There is simply no way for me to keep you or anyone else happy in this world. It is not within my power." He handed the book back to her.

"I'm dealing with a philosopher, I see."

"Hardly. I deal in practicalities, and as a practical matter, I can't take back used books, nor keep customers happy."

"You don't have to keep people happy in general. Merely keep them happy with their purchases of the books you sell. Is that too much to ask?"

"Yes. Suppose you don't like the book for another reason? Maybe the plot is too complicated, the dialogue peppered with annoying adverbs, the protagonist entirely smug and sexist? Should I take those books back?"

"There is no plot. It's not a novel but a book of poetry, and I'm not asking you to accept responsibility for content but for external damage to something you sold as new."

"Already covered. You might have scribbled on this page."

"Pages," Vena corrected him.

"How am I to know you didn't damage the pages?"

Vena studied him for a moment longer. There was nothing in his manner indicating he would bend or cave in defeat. "You're right. I might have been the one to create the mystery, demanding readers pass through doorways. I do wish I was the one to mark up the book because, at least, this would have been far more intriguing than simply returning a damaged book which was deceptively sold by you as new."

"I have other customers," the red-vested man said, his face growing redder as he turned away from her. She accepted defeat but continued to think about the book's previous reader, the person who had picked up the book, marked pages, damaged the chapbook, and proceeded to set it carefully back in place. Why hadn't she scrolled through the pages before buying? Why did it matter so much to her whether or not the book was read before, written in, streaked with yellow highlighter?

Admittedly, she had purchased the book for its intriguing cover, a child's scrawl. She didn't know the poet or his other work. When she first opened the slender book of poetry a week after buying it, Vena first found a page displayed with highlighter, the title drenched in yellow; the page number was also surrounded by bright yellow, and a line in the poem soaked in color. Curious, she flipped to the table of contents. So few poems in this thin volume, but there, the highlighted poem's title was again marked in yellow. Nothing else in the book was so designated. Why was the title marked, yet no other phrase in the book? "*Porte*" or "Doorways" appeared to be an innocuous opening to a poem. The markings could not have been an accident or stray colorings of a child because of the carefully repeated design: at every turn of the word, giving added significance. Wasn't that the way with communication all over? What was gibberish and meaningless fragments overheard by passersby could be of critical importance to the man and woman at the table. Likely, *Porte* had meaning, contained the entrance to something significant for the ghostwriter.

Although likely some kind of personal symbol to the first reader of the chapbook in her hands, *Porte* could also be an archetypal symbol, she reasoned. Was she intended to find the word and go through some opening, some passage, as the previous reader might have done? She read the poem again to be sure she had missed nothing, no element holding the peculiar meaning of symbols, personal or archetypal. Portals and doorways are, of course, archetypal in nature, yet she found none of this kind of meaning in the poem itself. Yet, the poem was not about entrances and exits at all. The 14-line verse, was not a Sonnet, but imitation offering a series of images of a willful child who was self-possessed in the face of unspecified trials. Had the unknown reader with the highlighter found herself or himself in the lines of willfulness, in the cluster of words and images trailing down the page? Now she owned another secret which could not be solved. Whatever the undefined reason, Vena knew her list of chores for the day was ruined. Order had disappeared, and chaos had taken its place.

~ * ~

At length, she gave the poetry book to an elderly woman reading another book in the delightful sandwich shop Baguetteria del Fico.

"*Perché?*" the well-dressed woman asked at the table next to hers, nearly touching her already, in the cramped and crowded space.

Vena shrugged. "You're reading poetry. I thought you might enjoy this, too. I've already read it."

The woman held the slender book in her hands and turned it over, tilting her head to the side in examination. Quizzically again, she narrowed her eyes ever so slightly, studying Vena.

"*Un regalo,*" Vena said, getting up to leave.

"*Grazie,*" the woman said, accepting the gift from a stranger.

As she walked along Via della Fossa, Vena considered the woman might be annoyed she had taken the book after she turned to the yellowed pages. Would she toss the chapbook out or relish the furtive?

Musing on this puzzle brought Vena to Sabine's story in which Severn had supposedly given the Shakespeare tome to a student descending the Spanish Steps. In both instances, the gifts had been castoffs, unwanted, but were willingly accepted. Did Sabine really hold a book in which a dying Keats had tucked away his last gift to literature? Conflating Sabine momentarily with the lovely woman in the shop, Vena nearly turned around to try to explain herself. She wanted to tell this stranger, "The yellowed lines and phrases may mean something significant after all. I couldn't figure out their importance but perhaps you can." What would the woman think about *Porte*?

All of these mysterious doorways, some were passages, but the murder of Sabine remained a closed door.

~ * ~

"You didn't buy anything for dinner?"

"No."

"We are out of fresh *pomodori*. I thought you were bringing something home?"

"I forgot."

"I don't feel like eating out tonight."

"We don't have to eat."

"You never forget."

"This time I did."

"What's the matter?" Elio dropped annoyance in his tone, hearing the catch in her voice, stopped writing in his notebook, and studied his girlfriend.

"Nothing. Everything. I couldn't return the book."

"What book?"

"The damaged poetry chapbook. The one with the yellow markings."

Elio laughed. "Really? Why do you care? An unreturned book can't be what's wrong."

"Maybe. I don't know the significance of *Porte* or why Sabine was killed or why I am still in Italy or why you love me or how I am going to make a living when they keep dropping my classes or why anyone thinks I can figure things out when I was lucky before, and I'm not lucky anymore." Suddenly Vena was crying, the kind of sobbing that shakes shoulders to stomach, an uncontrollable welling up of sadness springing from some inner volcano. She knew enough, even in her demoralized state, not to mention Warren moving on, not to say anything about her disquiet about loving Elio, the way back altered.

"Oh, my God, Vena. Okay, whatever it is, we'll figure this out." Elio pushed away from his desk and hugged Vena the way you would a child. She accepted his gift of compassion as intended.

After a few minutes, he said, "What you need is a good night's sleep." Elio moved her gently toward the bed, pulled off her boots, lifted her legs on the bed, and pulled the light cover over her.

"Yes," she said. "What I need," and she fell into disturbed sleep, knowing there was something important and dangerous she needed to do.

Chapter Sixteen
Murmuration of Starlings

At dusk, starlings flew over the city by the thousands, tightly flocked, painting the heavens. A black balloon shape swirled then flowed into oblong, turned back on itself, twisted inside out, as if the murmuration had become alien creatures capable of infinite transformations.

Transfixed, Vena let her eyes move, following patterns. The starlings' flight was designed for metaphors, for poetry, she thought. Having seen birds arrive en masse before, she knew the phenomena was quite natural over Roma in late fall, but the experience of witnessing their strange migration still unnerved her. Black birds invaded as if one gigantic lower form of life, becoming a smarm of insects flowing along rivers, amoebas in a sea, before they were ghosts whirling and swirling over the city's domes. Their undulating blocked out portions of the night sky. She thought about omens or what such wild black wings might portend.

In her pocket was a name and address she had worked hard to find. She knew she should have reported the little scrap to Dante or *Polizia*. After Dante's suggestion she forget about the poem angle of the murders, however, she remained silent on the information to everyone except Elio. Even with Elio, she did not immediately tell him she was going in search of a mystery address to see what she could find. He would have stopped her, called his brother, followed her. In a moment of clarity, however, she jotted down the street name and number on a note to Elio and left the address on the kitchen table. She wasn't sure what time he would get home, but there was no reason to call and bother him on his afternoon out with friends.

~ * ~

Nearing the location of the address, she suddenly changed her mind and wished Elio had come after her. She wished she had told him directly. When she was rounding the corner to approach the shop, she finally placed a call to Elio and a text to Dante, giving them the address again with greater urgency. Finding her would not take them long, she calculated incorrectly. Then, she hit the button on her silly recording pen, the one Bill had given her. Perhaps Bill's atonement for not giving her gifts as a child would be of some use now.

Before she knocked on the door, Guerra had already swung the massive door open with such force Vena was nearly pulled in by displaced air. Guerra shut the door after her and positioned himself between Vena and escape with a motion so quick and skillful, he conveyed dancing.

"Oh, hello, I've come to..." she said mistakenly in English, her agitation and nervousness causing her to revert to her native language.

The big man grimaced, then smiled in one nearly simultaneous twitch of his full lips. "You have come a long way to bargain," he said in Italian. "From America? You're the tutor."

"No, I mean, yes. I have an item to barter, but I live in Italy now." What was she thinking? How could she have been so careless? "How did you know?"

"I know more than you will find in all your books."

Surveying the room without appearing to do so, Vena could see a window with bars across it, not allowing escape except through the door she had entered. Boxes were everywhere along the walls on shelves. All appeared disorganized except the beauty of antiques in full view. She knew so little about gold trading in Italy: the government had liberalized retail gold trading in 2000, and the market plunged downward in 2013. Gold brokers still operating in the city typically had some other enterprise going to stay afloat.

"You said I was a tutor? Why would you say...?"

"A little bird told me." Instantly, Vena knew this little bird.

"I'm afraid I've..." The back of Vena's neck prickled with sensation.

"It's late in the day. I don't play games," Guerra said, moving closer as she tried to back up. "What do you have?" Still, he would not allow her access to the doorway. With one seamless movement, he pulled the window shade and flipped the door sign to "Closed."

Vena knew her moment of escape, of changing her mind about the whole adventure, had already passed. Yet, one detail did not escape her notice: although the shade was pulled and the Closed sign faced out, Guerra had neglected to lock the door in his haste. Information she stored. Trying to distract him, she lifted a necklace from her jeans' pocket, then dangled it in front of him. Even if Elio and Dante burst into the room, what would they find? She was trying to make a legal deal with a gold broker? She had to get Guerra to say something which would incriminate him then get out again. There wasn't enough time, but the interval was either too long or not long enough.

~ * ~

Bill had given her the little necklace, telling her, "It's not much, I know, but it's real gold, plated I mean, over sterling." His daughter puzzled over why her father always confessed such things when there was no urgency. It wasn't as if she believed he went out and spent an extravagant amount of money, money he did not have, on his daughter. "They said it's 12k gold finish," Bill added. "I thought you would like it. It's nothing but a trinket, something to remember I love..."

"Of course, I love it." She laughed when he stumbled with the gift in his hand as she was leaving him again, heading back to Rome. His gift reminded her of the necklaces and bracelets given in Catholic sacraments, but they weren't Catholic.

~ * ~

Guerra snorted at the locket as he yanked the chain from her. "This? It's not even real gold. Plated."

"What?" she feigned disbelief. "I was told the necklace was gold."

"I'll show you." He turned the locket over and pointed to the letters HGE. "See this? These letters mean gold plating…electroplate." He closed his fist around the locket as if to crush it. "Why did you really come here?"

"I was hoping, I didn't realize, I'm afraid I've made a mistake," Vena stepped back instinctively as Guerra lunged toward her. In disappearing space, he wrapped his big arms around her and pushed her down onto a chair. Pulling the necklace around her neck, he choked her until she stopped struggling. "I'll take this," he said, grabbing her cell phone from her pocket and tossing her lifeline across the floor.

Within a few seconds, he had already wound a rope around her hands and the chair. Strangely, even greater than her fear was her mortification at her inability to see how quickly everything moved from mystery and intrigue into life-threatening danger. She had been completely inept.

"Better. Relax," he said, lessening the tension on the necklace. He finished tying her hands and arms. "Now, let's talk about why you are really here. I don't like liars, and I don't like wasting my time. What do you know about this poem? It's why you came, isn't it?" He brought the necklace back to her neck and pulled, cutting into her flesh, then releasing slightly, choking her slowly.

How had Guerra known this? She fought her panic more than the metal against her neck. Struggling to speak, Vena turned her head slightly to meet his eyes. She tried not to show fear but curiosity. "Ah"

"You want to talk. Go ahead." He released the necklace again. "Better make it quick. But, to be sure you aren't heard screaming…" Guerra touched a button and music filled the room, an opera.

Vena knew little about opera in the moment except the volume, and she should have yelled a few seconds earlier.

"I…opera?"

"Wrong question."

"I won't scream. I want to know why."

"Oh, you'll scream; you'll beg and cry, but your tears won't matter."

Vena struggled to speak, "Why?"

"Why, what?"

Stall, stall. Vena stared at the floor…vinyl tile, not Carrera marble, and she thought of all the fakes, dirty gouges here and there, where some object had struck the floor with great force. This little shop was a place of violence. She focused on the fact the longer he let her live, the possibility of Elio or Dante arriving increased.

Her eyes widened again, realizing she was putting Elio in danger if he arrived without Dante and the Carabinieri. So many mistakes. Such amateurish sleuthing, she thought, still analyzing her errors rather than thinking ahead to avenues of possible escape. "The composer? This style? You surprise me. I didn't expect Sabine's killer to like opera."

Guerra showed no emotion at the mention of Sabine. "You know Puccini. It's Tosca, and why should my love of opera surprise you?" Guerra blew air between his lips in a great release of disgust. "You know nothing about me. You think you know me because I killed a girl, but I know everything about you, all you little, arrogant fools. You, American girl. You're weak and stupid. This, this is my music." He struck her face hard with his open hand rather than his fist.

Shocked but regaining her voice, Vena feigned calm. "The style…verismo?" Searching for something to keep him talking and not hitting her again.

"Verismo. What does an American know of opera?" Vena's turn to surprise him. He had hit her hard. Usually a woman cried and screamed at his violence, but this helpless woman acted as if she was not helpless, not about to be killed, asking questions about opera.

"Verismo is akin to Naturalism, an American literary genre, and the subject matter…the lives of the disadvantaged become the center," she said coolly, with blood from her nose flowing over her lips.

"Hah. So, you think you know, but you are too pretty to understand, teacher. You walk right into my trap without any honey."

He knew. How? Vena couldn't believe Sabine had given her killer the name of her tutor, but Sabine must have done so. Aware of her peril, Vena determined to at least trap him into giving up more information, remembering the silently recording pen in her pocket. "You killed Sabine. For the poem? Did you know her at all?"

"Your pretty student told me she had an English teacher friend who was helping 'verify the poem,' she said. She told me all about you. Your name, where you taught. She betrayed you. What do you think now? I beat her while she begged."

"She did not betray me. She was fighting for her life. Sabine offered what little she had as exchange. You take pleasure in hurting women, don't you?"

Guerra struck her again, this time with his fist.

Stunned, Vena struggled to hold her head up in defiance. "Did you even hold Keats' poem before selling it? Do you know what it is you have or had?"

Guerra almost laughed. "You don't know me or what I do. All this before—what did you call her—Sabine? tragically died. So young, pretty, until…" He wrapped his hands around Vena's neck, gently at first then with increasing strength and intensity.

Loud, strident chords filled the small room causing the blood vessels at her temples to throb in revolt. An image of an Ambrose Bierce story, she had read years ago, came to her in the moment. She was Peyton Farquhar in northern Alabama on the Owl Creek bridge, attempting to escape with her mind even as the life was choked from her. If she could reach the door... "Wait," she gasped.

Strictly out of morbid curiosity, he released her and let her speak. "What am I waiting for?"

"Perhaps I am aware of more than you give me credit," she said softly, forcing the big man to lean over her in order to hear. Alcohol and onions mixed in his foul mouth as his breath dripped down.

His weight pressed against her, his forearms a thick thud against her head. Again, he hit her with his arms rather than his fists, but the force produced the same effect. Dizziness and nausea pushed up inside as he twisted her tied arms before laughing.

"You have made my rotten day so much better," he grinned, his lips now nearly touching her own. His brows were wild, tickling her forehead as his yellow teeth grazed her lips. "First, we will have some fun," he snarled, pushing his hand between her legs. He was panting now in anticipation. "You will beg for your life, but I will fuck you—"

The unlocked door opened, and Fitsum motioned to Vena with his finger brought to his lips to silence her. Opera blared from the speakers as if a tragedy was being played out in front of them all.

While her eyes widened, Vena willed herself to train on Guerra who loomed over her, his wicked smile turning to an oval before blood suddenly drooled over his chin, his mouth twisted in shock, his brows raised, his fat lids opening and closing, then opening too wide. Fitsum had sunk his knife deep into Guerra's back, hitting the liver, before twisting the blade and thrusting upward. In less than a few seconds, Guerra turned, still on his feet, and faced his assassin.

"You, Negro."

"Yes. All of us at once…every black man you ever insulted and beat or murdered." Fitsum finished the job with another stabbing motion near Guerra's heart before shoving the dying man to the floor. Unable even to catch himself, Guerra was felled like a tree and his surprise was total. *Such a small man, a little Negro killed me,* was his thought as he hit hard surface, knocked out.

During the next few moments, Fitsum opened the boxes in which Guerra kept forged passports. Moving quickly, he unlocked the safe. Every awful conversation with Guerra had been spent memorizing the big man's motions at the safe.

Vena turned her head, amazed to find he somehow knew the combination. The Eritrean stuffed the pockets of his jacket and backpack with money and gold trinkets from drawers. In all of his encounters with Guerra, he had carefully surveyed the room, knew exactly where Guerra placed his valuables away from the register. How carefully he had paid attention in Guerra's shop. Working quickly, Fitsum said nothing as Guerra twitched below him.

He glanced over at Vena who looked as if she wanted to tell him something but could not, blood pouring from her mouth and nose.

Vena watched her student's methodical thievery then glanced down at Guerra groaning, reaching for her foot. The felled man was regaining consciousness. As she tried to pull back, Fitsum kicked Guerra and pulled Vena in her chair further from the dying lump of a man.

"Please, untie me," she said, shaking her head again.

"No. If they find you standing over a dead man, this will not be good for you. When they come to this sewer and see you are tied, they will know you could not have killed this pig."

Vena couldn't argue with his logic and knew leaving her tied was

Both End in Speculation

the right move. Still, her panic rose with her incapacity. "Wait." She realized she must not identify Fitsum. Hoping her voice pen was still recording, she closed her lips tightly and turned her head to him, looking down toward her pocket.

"I'm sorry. I have nothing for you." Fitsum misunderstood and finished tucking the money and gold possessions away.

Except my life, she almost said, but instead mouthed the words, "They will find you."

Fitsum expressed bitter amusement. "They never see me even when I am right in front of them. I disappear." Vena noticed he was wearing gloves.

She motioned to her pocket. Fitsum seemed to understand and said nothing more. As quietly as he entered, he slipped back out through a back door, leaving the door partially opened. The incomplete movement did not trigger an alarm which had already been shut off by Guerra when he entered. The death rattle from Guerra's throat filled the room.

For a moment, Vena could not believe how impersonal Fitsum had been, but then she was grateful he had not given himself away.

Reviving slightly, Guerra stirred. "Fucking Negro." Guerra said, spitting blood. He made no attempt to regain his feet.

"You killed her for a poem? You killed Sabine for a piece of paper? Say it."

"Skinny bitch was easy. For your Englishman's stupid poem."

"Yes, the poem. You killed them both, you murdered Sabine for nothing. She could have given you the poem. You killed her professor, too."

"I killed them, yes. Hah. I kill Pavoni..." Guerra stopped, out of breath then breathing shallowly, "for many reasons, but the poem...worth more than you and her together." Guerra halted again, and Vena thought he had died, but suddenly, he spurted out, drooling blood: "Girl told me about poem. Thought she could save herself like her faggot professor. I bashed her. Stupid girl grabbed the paper after it was in my hands, tore a piece. Angered me. I mutilated her. I would have killed Pavoni for nothing."

"How could you? She never hurt anyone."

Guerra winced in pain, summoning what strength he had left,

faltering now. "Easy," he sputtered. "Too easy."

"The other man? You killed a black man, too? Why? What did he have to do with anything?"

"Negro in my doorway. Oh," he said in pain. "I kicked him. He was in my way. Accident, but how did you like?" Guerra was hesitant in letting go of each word as if it was his last.

"Like? Staging? On the Arch, in the fountain? Why so elaborate? What was your meaning? To confound?"

Guerra attempted to laugh but choked. After a moment, he tried again. "Threw off everyone except—except you. They never told about my signs: 'fucking migrants' on the faggot."

Good for the police and other officials, thought Vena. They were trying to keep tensions from rising to hysteria over the flood of migration into Italy. And Sabine's body on the Arch of Constantine, a red herring, Vena thought, suddenly remembering her conversation with Dante and his dismissal of her theory. "Keats' poem? What happened to it?"

"I had the paper in my hands."

"Had? What did you do with the paper? With his poem? Was the poem really written by Keats?"

"Hah. Cast…cast out my spirit with words fundamental." He stopped, and Vena was confused about his language. Guerra began again, "A covenant distilled with myrtle, primordial."

Then Vena knew. He was trying to recite a few lines from the poem he had seen. She attempted to analyze the lines he spoke, even in her panicked state. "At my window, a sparrow's…a sparrow's sweet song elemental." Guerra struggled to speak, a gurgling sound released as blood choked him.

"You know the poem? You memorized it?"

"No Aphrodite," he choked, spurted blood. "I find Nemesis/ Goddess divine to punish presumption…" Guerra attempted to smile once more at his trick, then coughed in a much more violent spasm, his heaving machine shutting down. His eyes further widened in recognition of the end.

Vena could almost hear the next line with "consumption" in her head. How could this man Guerra have made up such words? He would not have known English in a manner allowing him to create poetry. Even if they were not Keats' lines, the words and phrases had come from a poet.

Silence filled the room. Odors of death already invading. Vena wanted to shake him awake again...if her arms were free, her own fears dissipating, giving way to intense anger and curiosity mixed with revulsion. Did he still have the poem? "The rest? Where is it? Keats' poem? Is it here in your shop?"

"I sold," Guerra spurted again, out of breath, wincing in great pain. "But you get—nothing."

"Who? Who did you sell the poem to?"

"To fat American. Not like you. Rich. Maf..." Between his words, a few seconds of shallow breathing halted the flow. "Very rich. Brid..., Conn..." With those words, Guerra shuddered, his body in involuntary spasms, and died.

"Bridge, Con? Bridgeport, Connecticut?" Vena asked stupidly, knowing Guerra was already gone. "Ahhh," she yelled, as much from frustration as horror. "Wake up and tell me," she shouted at the dead man, then let loose with a proper, raging scream of frustration as much as from fear, release of tension, and exhaustion. The opera playing in the background had come to an end, and the only sound from the room was Vena's full-throated scream.

Chapter Seventeen
Waking Dreams

In the seconds during which Vena thought she might be killed, her mind seemed to flee, digging into her past. Guerra was dead, and she was still a captive, tied and helpless. What had led her to this point? She searched for something tangible.

~ * ~

A year earlier, Vena had been walking in the hallways of the Vatican Museum with Elio when Dante caught up to them. Her neck ached from staring up at elaborately painted, curved ceilings and taking in the Galleries of Tapestries and Maps. Along one wall were giant frescoed maps in brilliant blues suggesting the *Ligure* and Tyrrhenian seas surrounding land. At the top of one golden framed map was the label Sicilia. Another was labeled Calabria in elegant red and gold. In these antique maps, commissioned by Pope Gregory XIII, man's artistry, his prejudices, his glories, and his foolish superstitions were expressed on a grand scale in which monsters loomed as large as sailing ships. Mountains on land mirrored waves of the sea.

Christopher Columbus rode in an emperor's gold chariot driven by Neptune who was holding his trident, the god once worshiped as a creator of horses. Vena was drawn to the powerful horses in the painting, those beasts appearing to struggle to keep from drowning as they charged ahead through water, an impossibility no more absurd than the gods themselves. One horse had turned back toward the chariot in rebellion or panic, and Columbus' oval mouth acknowledged fear. Here, again, history, myth, and pagan beliefs converged in *Galleria delle carte geografiche*, this Christian passageway to St. Peter's. The whole of lands surrounding and later comprising Italy had been painted in relief by the Roman friar, mathematician, and cartographer Ignazio Danti in the late 1500s. History rising up again, over and over in Roma.

After coming to the end of the long hallway of deep blues and greens, Vena felt she had been swimming under surfaces of seas, yet could still sense the golden domed sun above her.

"I could stay here all day," she whispered, but they were propelled by masses of visitors, a group of Chinese pushing hard against them. She was yet new to Roma in those early days and excited by every discovery. Elio caught her arm when he spotted Dante.

"I thought you were going to meet us in the Piazza San Pietro? We waited 20 minutes for you before coming inside. I had these tickets, so we wouldn't have to wait." Elio's gesture to his brother could be read rather than heard in the bustling of bodies and muffled myriad voices.

"I know. But I have my own means of cutting lines. Sorry. Couldn't be helped. Glad I found you. Fewer people today with miserable weather, thank goodness."

"I assume you mean the crowd control and not the weather?" Vena smiled, rubbing her sore neck. Elio and Dante stepped to the side, pulling Vena with them, to allow the crush to move past.

Turning to Vena alone, Dante asked, "What did you think of our magnificent square?"

"Couldn't take my eyes off the statues looming over us at the top of St. Peter's."

"Yes, thirteen statues of Jesus, the Apostles, and St. John the Baptist. They are indeed watching over us, where the Pope confers his blessing to the masses."

"Watching, looming?" Vena said out loud, musing on the differences in connotations both brothers ignored. "Perhaps you must be Catholic to feel the difference between looming and watching?"

"We are all Catholic. You cannot know Italy until you have been to St. Peter's Basilica," said Dante, pleased to find them and offer his counsel. He was not about to quibble over semantics. "St. Peter's is the largest Catholic Church in the world and the most glorious. No one else has Michelangelo's painted ceiling in the Sistine Chapel. We are almost there.

Don't forget, we can't speak once inside, and no pictures." He was leading now to the obvious annoyance of his younger brother.

"Vena's not Catholic," said Elio, either in her defense or condemnation. Vena was not entirely sure, although she suspected he was defending her since he assumed the mantle of disgust with his brother.

"Oh, Americans are never Catholic in the way Italians are, but I mean Catholic in the larger sense."

"As in all-embracing, universal, not institutionally religious?" Vena asked out of curiosity not sarcasm.

Dante smiled. "In the larger sense of Catholicism within the Roman Catholic Church."

"Does it ever strike you as odd or even a bit heretical, the Catholic Church acquired, to put this kindly, acquired and displays all of this beautiful pagan art?" Vena was genuinely curious. "We saw a statue of Artemis, the Egyptian fertility goddess. Are those her breasts or hanging fruits?"

"It's a little strange," admitted Elio.

"Yes, I've seen the statue. Those are representations of severed testicles of bulls," Dante said without embarrassment.

"Sacrificial bulls," added Elio, not to be outdone.

"Makes sense to have this glorious pagan art housed in the Vatican, how exactly?" Vena suspected the brothers' defense but wanted to tease them.

"Perfectly reasonable testament to the powerful consolidation of the richness and earthly, and heavenly, reign of the Pope of the Church." Dante settled for the official line in defending the Church, and Elio shot his brother a look suggesting Dante was going too far.

"Since when did you become a tour guide?" Elio stuck his chin out, realizing the gesture would have earned him a beating by his brother when they were younger.

"We'll have to save this argument for another time," said Dante. "We're entering the Basilica shortly, and we're not supposed to speak."

"You already told us," Elio said.

"So many rules here," said Vena, still happy Dante had found them in the crowds as Elio reached over and squeezed her hand. "Before we're not allowed to speak, what is the metallic, iridescent sphere in the courtyard? What's the name?"

"Sphere within a sphere," said Elio, moving slightly to complete the forged link with their hands.

"*Sfera con Sfera,*" Dante corrected Elio with the Italian name and positioning, partially blocking Elio from Vena again.

"A bronze sculpture," Elio jumped in, "part of a series of spheres by Italian sculptor Arnaldo Pomodoro."

"Who's the tour guide, now?" Dante smirked with his back to his brother.

"Appears broken and breaking down inside," Vena said, pleased to be in their company on such a grand stage. "A symbol of our fractured world?"

A group of tourists turned around and frowned at her, apparently understanding her Italian and English mix of words or annoyed with her tone and volume.

"Perhaps I should save my irreverence for another time and place," she said.

"Good of you," replied Dante.

"I guess I was a little loud," Vena said, pulling her head and neck in slightly like a turtle.

"Our complexity, the bronze globe's symbolism," offered Elio.

"*Fragilità.*"

"Maybe both," Vena delighted in the brothers who were obviously competing for her attention.

Elio wanted to ask his brother, "Don't you have a wife and child to go home to this weekend?" But he kept the last indictment to himself as they moved into the hushed crowd flowing into St. Peter's.

~ * ~

Vena recalled the seemingly faraway day in which the brothers vied for her attention a year earlier, in the Vatican Museums. Dante was a married man, but he clearly was attracted to his brother's girlfriend. By now, she knew much more about the code of conduct for the Carabinieri. Instinctively, Vena knew she should not encourage Dante in any way, but she could not help smiling at the thought of the two handsome brothers trying to squeeze next to her in a cathedral a year earlier. Since Dante had been assigned to Roma, he was spending more time with his brother and Vena and less with his family. The arrangement could not be a particularly good thing for any of them, Vena considered, even as she recognized her growing attraction to the older brother.

~ * ~

In the hours before seeking out the dangerous Guerra, Vena was almost enjoying the challenge and balancing the affections of two brothers. If Sabine had not been her friend, then the case could have been as pleasing as an academic puzzle.

~ * ~

"What do we have so far? Nothing," said Dante. "This case is making fools of all of us. Three murders, one seemingly unrelated. No real leads. Blurred images on a camera giving us nothing but a hulking figure."

"But we have some information. There was a stolen poem. A young woman who told her professor about this supposedly valuable poem, and his murder."

"Not again. Vena, this idea about a valuable poem is taking us nowhere. What poem? One from a dead girl's imagination, perhaps?"

"Whatever Sabine held in her hands was stolen. You saw the tiny scrap of old paper in her fingers. She talked to me about finding a Keats' poem. Not imagined but something she touched, even if incorrectly ascribing the poem to Keats. Someone else, likely the killer, seems to have believed her. Even if the poem was suspected to not have been written by Keats, it would have potential worth. Sometimes even the belief of a great price is enough to get a person killed."

"Sounds like a lot of speculation to me, Vena. Sometimes, potential, belief…these are not terms inspectors use to solve crimes. I trust your instincts, but where are we? We're circling around abstractions."

"I use what I have."

"Speculation is helpful up to a point. We've reached a dead end." Dante turned from her. "I have to go in another direction. This is where we part ways for today." He left Vena at the espresso bar.

~ * ~

Walking alone, trying to sort out what she might have missed, Vena decided she must visit Sabine's family home in Trastevere where her student's mother still lived. The neighborhood had become trendy. Difficult to envision one family remaining on the upper floors of a building all of those years. How was it possible? Wouldn't landlords have forced them out? Families staying in one spot, in one building, generation after generation?

~ * ~

By the time Vena arrived, Sabine's mother Lia had barely a few minutes to talk with her. Vena apologized for her delay due to heavy traffic.

"I'm afraid I have to leave for work in a few minutes. I don't know what you want from me, *Signorina* Goodwin. I really have nothing to give you. Can you bring back my daughter? No. What is left?" Lia opened the door without moving and spoke abruptly.

"I'm so terribly sorry for your loss. Your daughter was my friend," said Vena in front of the arched doorway.

"Ah, *avanti, avanti*. Yes, she told me, or I would never have permitted this visit. I'm done talking to officers and prying neighbors who are morbidly curious about my murdered child."

"I understand how difficult this must be for you. How unfair and unkind my questions might seem, but I want to help find her killer. If I may, could I see the Shakespeare text Sabine believed held the poem?"

"A horrible book. If Mamma had rid herself of that thing years ago, my baby would still be alive. I plan to throw the book in the trash."

"Oh, please don't. I will take the Shakespeare book if you really want to be rid...do you know why your mother kept the Shakespeare volume all this time?"

"For her own mother. Some stupid story about my Nonna given the book by her *fratello*. If he hadn't died, Nonna likely wouldn't have kept it. She could no more read English than me. Come with me." They ascended narrow, winding stairs surrounded by stucco walls until they reached the room where Sabine's grandmother had lived.

"I've barely had time to clean her room out. First my husband Gianluca, then my mother, now my daughter Sabine. It's as if God is punishing me for something I've done." Reaching to steady herself, Lia lowered her head and sobbed. Vena wrapped her arms around Lia and held the shaking woman. They remained in an embrace until Lia breathed more regularly and pulled herself straight again. She patted Vena's arm. "I'm sorry, so sorry. I'm not myself. Sabine would be angry with me for treating you so poorly. She was very proud of learning English well, and she spoke highly of you."

"Don't be. You have nothing to apologize for. Is there anything I can do for you? Can I get you something? Some water, perhaps?"

"No water. There is something. Find her killer. Bring the man, or men, to justice."

"I..."

"I'm sorry again. It's not for you to do. See, I'm out of my head. You'll have to forgive me. I say things I shouldn't say lately. There," she said, changing her tone. "The book you want, right on the end table. Take. Don't ever let me see..."

Vena turned from Lia and picked up the beautiful, mottled calf leather-bound volume of Shakespeare plays. The book was no longer dusty, and Vena was aware of a shameful excitement at holding the text with Lia still in the room. "I will do whatever I can to help with the investigation into Sabine's murder."

Lia lowered her head in defeat. "I must go. Take the old book with you. Please."

~ * ~

Vena had turned the pages of the beautiful Shakespeare volume slowly and carefully as if expecting to discover another treasure hidden somewhere in the rich, dense Elizabethan English. When she found the page with the play *Hamlet*, she stared long at the opening. The faintest shadow from another paper was barely visible as foxing, a faded outline inside the book.

~ * ~

Nearly a lifetime recounted in seconds as she waited tied and bleeding with a bloated Guerra at her feet.

Chapter Eighteen
The Bargain

A block down the street, Ignacio Mariani was working up the courage to pawn his mother's earrings. She'd been dead for a few days, but he desperately needed the cash. Ignacio's sister Lauretta had wanted those earrings, but he told her their mother must have lost them.

"She kept hiding things. Too bad she hid the earrings, and no one will find them," Ignacio lied to his little sister.

"Someone will find them, and they will be richer for it. You know, she promised them to me." Lauretta turned from her brother, still suspicious, and picked up a lace doily. "This is what she left us," she said bitterly. "This old doily and unpaid bills."

~ * ~

Turning around twice on the street with the gold broker, Ignacio tried to stop himself from making a decision he would regret. Would his mother see him in this betrayal, even beyond the grave? His sister suspected he had the earrings, but he managed to confuse her. Then, hearing the sharp cry of a woman, Ignacio lost all momentum in his internal debate, running the rest of the way down the street, and burst in. A woman was tied up, struggling at ropes binding her hands, and yelling. A bloated man lay dead at her feet. Blood covered the floor and was spattered about in the horrifying scene.

"*Mio Dio*. What happened here? Are you okay?" he asked stupidly. Moving a step closer, he tried stepping around Guerra but couldn't help noticing how dark the blood was. Then, his feet wouldn't move, and he thought perhaps he had entered some movie scene. This could not be real. In all his short, uneventful life, Ignacio had never been a hero or villain.

"No," she yelled. "I'm not okay. Untie me!" But the stranger couldn't take his eyes from the dead man. Knowing he was rude, even wrong, Ignacio swallowed hard then forced himself to speak.

"How did? Who killed him? Is this...was this the gold broker?" Maybe there was a reason he should not untie her. If he hadn't felt partially paralyzed, he would have turned and run out the door again.

"What difference does this make? He's dead. Yes, it's Martino Guerra. Untie me."

Hesitating, Ignacio questioned what role this woman played in the man's death. This was exactly the kind of thing he had feared as he wrestled with his conscience in the street moments earlier. He thought of his mother. Was this a message she was sending? Run, my son, run. Don't look back.

"Please," the young woman finally said more gently, recognizing her anger was getting in the way of the actions she wanted. Her altered tone woke him from his stupor, and he moved toward her then behind her, touching the rope at last, fumbling and not knowing where to begin with multiple knots.

"Get away from her before I kill you," Elio yelled, rushing toward Ignacio and knocking him to the ground.

Dante and Elio had burst in on the scene. The trailing brothers had also heard Vena's screams.

Unintentionally, Elio tracked through Guerra's blood, staining the souls of his shoes.

"Hands up," Dante ordered. The young man complied, trembling, as he attempted to get back up with both quivering hands in the air.

"No, he did nothing." Vena yelled. "He was trying to help untie me. He came in."

"Stop moving about," Dante told Elio, realizing his brother had already smeared blood across the floor.

"Jesus, Vena," was all Elio could manage. "Jesus, Mother Mary."

"Stop," Vena cried. "He arrived. Please listen."

Stuttering momentarily, Ignacio finally found his voice. "I...I found her like this," the baffled man said. "I heard a scream and was trying to see if someone needed help," he frantically offered as Dante made a move to handcuff him.

"No, listen," cried Vena. "He is innocent. He heard me yelling and came in to help." Suddenly everyone looked at the hulking dead man at their feet.

Dante put both hands on his head, realizing how terrified he'd been Vena was in danger or already dead. He then reached out for his brother's shoulder, whether to calm him, too, or steady himself, he was not certain. "Untie her, Elio, but watch where you're stepping." Dante commanded. Turning his attention to the stranger in the room. "Your story first. What happened? Why are you here?"

"I don't know anything," Ignacio was incredulous he had somehow been drawn into something so nefarious as a murder and more. "I heard a scream. This woman here...I don't know her...was yelling, and I ran in. There was a dead man." Bloated Guerra, his face smeared from blood, had spouted like a fountain as he had spoken his last words.

"All right. All right," Dante said to Ignacio. "Your full name? Why were you passing this shop?" Fortunately for this young Roman, Dante had seen him enter the shop ahead of them as they were sprinting up the street, or he would have been more suspicious of poor Ignacio.

"Ignacio. Ignacio Mariani," he said hesitating at first, then firmly. "I am fully cooperating. I was walking by when I heard screams."

"Walking by?" Dante had to cover every scenario. "I don't think..."

"Wait. I'm not...I am an honest man. I came to pawn something, I admit it, but the broach was my grandmother's, and she left the jewel to me." Ignacio was puzzled. Why had he lied about pawning his grandmother's broach when the earrings belonged to his mother? What kind of stupid lie did he tell? If they searched him, they would find earrings rather than a broach. Did he think one more generation removed and a change of jewels made his act less awful? "I required a little extra for an emergency...a health problem, you see. My sister has been very sick." Now the lies were again flowing. Ignacio's face reddened with his tale. "I hadn't even reached the door when I heard this woman scream." Ignacio pointed to Vena as if they would demand clarification or there were multiple women tied up in the room. He hung his head, let his shoulders fall, and his mouth moved downward. Guiliana would be so ashamed, and Lauretta would never speak to him again.

"Yes, yes. Better. A little honesty." Dante jotted down his information, asking the nervous Ignacio to wait outside.

"Okay. I will wait. I'm not in trouble?"

"If you've done nothing wrong, you have nothing to worry about. Step outside the entrance for a few minutes. But don't move beyond the front of this shop or we will find you and arrest you. We will have more questions. I'm afraid you'll still have to come to Questura Centrale." Ignacio accepted the command with such gusto, he expressed joy at the invitation. As he stepped beyond the immediate reach of the Carabinieri, Ignacio fingered the gold earrings in his pocket. They were still there. His life was not yet ruined. He knew then he could turn things around.

On the other side of the closed door, Ignacio leaned against the building, his heart still beating rapidly although he realized how events had changed once again. He suddenly understood he would give the earrings to his sister. The story of how he found the missing gems was still forming.

Inside the shop, another story was creating itself. "Who the hell is he?" asked Elio, motioning to the dead man.

"Apparently, the man is Ignacio Mariani," said Dante, not looking at Elio, believing his brother was referring to the man who had left their presence moments ago.

"No. I mean the dead guy. But, while we're talking about the other one, what was he doing here? Why are you here? What were you thinking coming here alone?" Elio demanded, suddenly turning to Vena.

Dante considered whether or not Vena had done something illegal and should be extricated before his officers arrived. Better for the stranger outside the door not to overhear what Vena had to say about their encounter.

"What went down here?" Dante asked cryptically as soon as he checked to make sure the door was shut. He glanced out to be sure Ignacio was still standing against the shop front. Elio had finally managed to untie Vena and was attempting to hug her, kissing her face and hair.

Pushing aside Elio's loving arms, Vena pulled out her voice recording pen and shut it off with some urgency. Elio's obvious confusion and pained expression caused her to wrap her arms around his neck and kiss him.

"Time for your affection later," Dante barked.

"I came to ask him…", as they all looked down at the dead man once again, "about Sabine's murder, about the Keats' poem, or, at least I thought I might find someone who knew about John Keats' missing poem, and about what happened to Sabine."

"Do you have any idea what you did? How dangerous? Why? How did you know about?" Again, he indicated Guerra with a motion of his head. "Right now, Vena, straight answers. All of it. Everything you know."

Vena did not hold back any longer. "Guerra's address was on a slip of paper in Pavoni's office."

"Let's be clear. Are we talking about the deceased? This corpse is…was named Guerra?" Dante asked.

"Can't you see she is hurt and tired. Let her answer these questions later."

"I'm afraid not. Shut up, Elio. Vena…"

"Yes, Guerra. His name was Martino Guerra, and he killed Professor Pavoni and Sabine. And the African refugee. The refugee first, by accident. Then Pavoni, and Pavoni led him directly to Sabine who held the Keats' poem."

"By accident?"

"Yes, killed the migrant, kicking him from his doorway. Guerra would have killed me, too, because Sabine apparently gave him my name and description under torture, most likely, but Guerra already had taken the poem from her. It wasn't essential he kill me or at least try to find me, but I came to him." She gulped, taking a quick breath. After the rush of adrenaline left her body, she began shaking uncontrollably. Elio put a protective arm around her.

"Back up," Dante commanded.

"What?" Elio asked.

"Not you. Vena. Go back over everything quickly. Guerra's address was in Pavoni's office? You knew all this time? Why didn't you tell me? We could both be in trouble for this." All three of them looked down at the dead man as if he, too, was listening, and they were awaiting his response.

"I know. Stupid. I'm sorry, but I tried to tell you…twice. The day in Pavoni's office, then in our apartment. Guerra's address was in a book on Keats and Shelley. An anthology on Pavoni's shelf, the top shelf in his office at Sapienza. And to be fair, I didn't know what the address meant or if this location would lead to anything at all. I'd never heard of Guerra or didn't know what he did. Then I checked the address and found a gold broker."

"My men went through everything in Pavoni's office. *Polizia* turned over everything, too. How did you?"

"Almost nothing, really, a scrap, a corner torn from a page, with nothing but an address with a single name. I had a hunch the paper might be important but…"

"Important? Because?"

"Because the address was tucked or hidden in an anthology on the page with 'Endymion,' 'A Thing of Beauty.' It's a Keats' poem," she answered, finally composing herself to think more clearly. "I had a feeling the placement was a clue left by Pavoni."

"If you knew this was a clue, why didn't you…"

"I told you I tried, but you didn't listen," Vena protested.

"You could have been a bit more persistent." Dante was more annoyed with himself than Vena, but he couldn't tell her this yet.

"I had no proof of anything or assurance of evidence, a gut feeling the missing Keats' poem was related to this scrap of paper. But the idea a simple torn paper would lead to the killer also resembled the ridiculous. A ripped, little piece leading to a rare treasure and a murderer who had thrown the city into turmoil? I thought you wouldn't believe the address meant anything, believed you'd take the paper from me, crumple it up, and find nothing. Then we could go no further in the investigation. The address was all I had. If I had told you, then I would not have even a scrap to go on nor have been able to find Sabine's killer. We'd know no more about Keats' missing poem or the murders than we knew before."

"Not your job. You could have been killed," Elio was suddenly angry.

"When have I not listened to you?" Dante was trying to figure out how he was going to present this in way which did not implicate Vena or reflect poorly on him. Why had he given her permission to search Pavoni's office in the first place?

Standing up to the two brothers, Vena said resolutely, "When I told you a poem was at the heart of this whole thing, these terrible crimes, you listened at first then decided the concept at the heart of such heinous murders was ridiculous. You thought an anti-immigration group or far-right follower was somehow behind everything."

"I thought, I had to have time to think the evidence through. Your idea sounded dumb or maybe unbelievable. Not you, just the idea." Dante knew he should have conceded to Vena, giving her more freedom to explore her theory under his protection.

"Do you or the other investigators still have the slip of paper you found in Sabine's hand?"

"I believe so, although I don't know what good a blank paper would do."

"Would help determine the date of the paper, lend some credence to the idea it was a Keats' poem they were after."

"I don't see how a small corner of paper could determine anything," said Elio.

"They were still making rag paper in the early 1800s. Wasn't until after Keats died that wood pulp papers began to be mass produced. If the little corner is rag paper...," Vena said wiping the blood from her face with her sleeve. Elio studied her with dismay. He should have been helping her more, he thought.

"I get it, but this place is going to be swarming with Carabinieri and *Polizia* in a few minutes. How did this bastard die? Who killed him if you were tied up and Ignacio outside is really some innocent?" Dante glanced outside again to be sure Ignacio was still standing there.

"I honestly don't know," Vena said with conviction. She knew her acting talents were called upon again. This was her toughest choice because it meant lying to the brothers who trusted her, one of them her lover. "Guerra grabbed me, threw me on the chair, and tied me up almost as soon as I came in the door. He recognized me before I knew what happened. Then he intimated he would torture me for fun because he already had the poem."

"The poem really exists?" Elio jumped in since she had rebuffed him.

"I believe so, yes, and so did Guerra and so did the person to whom he sold the Keats' poem."

"He sold the Keats' poem? Who has it?" Elio couldn't stop himself.

"Let me ask the questions," Dante commanded his younger brother, shooting him a scolding glance before turning to Vena again.

"First, Guerra. How did he end up like this?" Dante poked his foot at the corpse. "Let's start with when you were tied up and..."

"I was so frightened. Thought I was going to die..."

"Why didn't you call me before?" Elio demanded, angry since Vena was now out of danger. "A text a little earlier, really, Vena? All you had to do... I would have been with you."

Dante raised his hand to still his brother. "Leaving a note, we don't find right away. You could have been dead by the time we saw it. You're lucky."

Vena acknowledged her foolishness. "I know."

"How did this—this Guerra die? What did you witness? And I have to ask, were you involved?"

"No. I was not involved with his death," she considered what to add. "Except to the extend I was an unknowing distraction when his killer entered."

"Did you know or recognize whoever came through the door?"

"When I was crying and begging Guerra not to kill me, he choked me. Someone came through the door at that moment. Guerra was a big man, and I couldn't really see what was happening behind him. I honestly thought I was going to die. I was close to blacking out. When suddenly he turned, Guerra's face was contorted. Then he turned around again—full circle, and I could see blood everywhere, all over his back, soaking through his shirt. There was a black man, partially obscured from my view, who was holding a knife."

"A black man?" Elio had a momentary panic at the thought of her Eritrean student.

"He didn't say anything. He came in and stabbed Guerra again before he raided those boxes." Everyone looked toward the emptied and upturned containers along the shelves against the wall. "He opened a safe, too."

"Could you describe him?"

"Thin, very dark, wearing black clothes, I think, or dark loose clothing."

"How tall? Any distinctions? Tattoos? Piercings?"

"I didn't notice any tattoos or piercings, but everything happened very quickly, and I can't be sure of what I saw. Not tall or short. Average height, I guess. I don't know. I was scared, and he was dark. Short, close cropped hair. Then he was gone." Vena understood the description she gave was a fair one of Fitsum, but one that could also be a description of countless migrants and would appear accurate to the Italians investigating.

"Did he say anything to you? This black guy?"

"Let me think. I asked him to untie me, and he shook his head, then left. I never heard his voice." Vena never hesitated in her lie. She knew her vague description of Fitsum could belong to any African immigrant to these two Italian men, and the description would be believed. To them, the African immigrants were all alike. They might have all been twins.

"You said nothing more to him?" Dante was still incredulous, fighting disbelief, wanting to trust his brother's girlfriend.

She knew her lie was not good enough, and remembered there was the recording on the pen. "Wait. Yes, I remember. I did ask him to untie me again, and he said something like, 'no.' Of course, I tried to get him to release me. He might have said something else, maybe. I don't know. I asked him, but he mostly ignored me. Then I asked what he wanted, but he moved to the boxes as if he knew what was in them, grabbed some things, then left. I told him you—the police—would find him, and he said something about no one ever noticing him." Vena knew Fitsum had taken files, gems, and other papers. A haul of passports, Euros, gold, and a laptop. There would likely be little or no trace of the Eritrean man's interactions with the gold broker because Fitsum made certain. Then she remembered as if a movie was playing back in slow motion. Fitsum had been wearing gloves, and he knew the safe combination.

"It's good he didn't untie you," said Dante at last. "He opened the safe. He must have known the combination, been here before, maybe in with Guerra on all of it. He could have been one of his partners. Maybe this is a double-cross."

"He didn't touch you, did he?" Elio jumped in again, turning Vena's face to his own. "Your face is bruised, your nose, your eye…" Elio was more carefully inspecting her face.

"Guerra hit me, hard, but I'll be okay."

"You're okay?"

"Yes."

"Why did Guerra tie you up? I know what you said, but his actions toward you make no sense."

"He was a monster."

"What did you expect to find here?" Dante's tone was far less gentle than his brother's.

"I told you already. I found this address in Pavoni's office. At first, I didn't think the paper with the address meant anything. At least, I had no reason to believe a location was evidence or would lead me anywhere. I wanted to follow the trail first and find out if the address was important, then let you know. I wasn't trying to keep you out of it. In fact, I left you the address and note for both of you. I was trying to keep you from being embarrassed if this had led nowhere."

"Stupid and dangerous," Dante said, spitting as he spoke. Elio looked at his brother with annoyance.

"I know. I'm sorry." But Vena also knew her actions had led to Guerra's discovery and confession of the murders.

"Still doesn't explain why Guerra would tie you up."

"Hasn't she answered enough questions for now?" Elio was exasperated with his brother but knew he held no weight here.

"Not nearly enough. Don't you understand, *Polizia* and Carabinieri investigators will ask many more later. You must be consistent and unwavering in your answers. If you change your story, it suggests you have something to hide." Vena understood then Dante was questioning her to protect her, to prepare her for what she would face upon formal examination.

"I'm afraid I was right about my suspicions. Like I said, Sabine must have told Guerra about me before he killed her, likely tortured her to get the poem. He created the impression he recognized me when I came in." She turned her head up to stare at Dante who was now towering over her. "Remember the tiny slip of old paper in her hand when they lowered her from the Arch? She had been clinging onto something for dear life."

Nodding, Dante frowned, realizing he should have believed Vena's theories. "Maybe I should have paid more heed."

"He would have come after me, likely found me from what Sabine told him, except he already had the original Keats' poem. See, he didn't need anything else. He had the poem and sold it. I don't know, but the second he opened the door, he had this facial expression which told me I should have turned and run like hell."

"God, Vena." Elio was breathing hard. At the point he had finally calmed down he understood how close Vena had come to being another of Guerra's murder victims. "What kind of bargain did you think he would make?"

"He must have decided since I had found him, he couldn't let me leave. He would have killed me, too. I'm grateful to the man, the black man, who saved my life."

"The thief?" Elio jumped in.

"I don't even know if he was a thief. Maybe what he lifted from Guerra belonged to him. He seemed to know where to go."

"They very likely knew each other, did business together," said Dante, making a note. "We'll have to find Guerra's files, his computer. He will have records which may lead back."

"A thief maybe, but he's a hero to me."

"Perhaps, but definitely a murderer and a thief. A robbery of opportunity, escalated by circumstance. *Omicidio*. Yes." Dante called in the murder, kidnapping, and theft, turning away from the two momentarily. "We will have to arrest your hero when we find him. Perhaps the judge will consider the fact he saved your life and what Guerra had done, but we will find him, Vena." Dante was already searching around the desk area for a computer nowhere to be found.

Vena was not at all sure they would find Fitsum. "There's something else you should know," she said, turning on her voice recording pen again.

The brothers looked at her intently.

"Listen. I taped Guerra's entire confession." She hit the button.

Dante smiled widely for the first time in days.

"Smart girl," Dante said. Elio heaved a sigh of relief, then put his head down because he was feeling nauseous.

"You're a spy," said Elio. "When did you get a spy pen?"

"They're all over now." She thought about telling them about Bill's silly gift which turned out to be invaluable.

They heard Guerra confess to all of it. Dante clutched her pen. "I'm going to need this, I'm afraid. Let's hope you don't have to use another one for a while."

"Can't you listen to his confession and give my pen back?"

"Not how this works. Evidence."

By the time they heard Guerra again confess, betraying himself in his dying words, Carabinieri and *Polizia* officers rushed in, holding Ignacio by the arm but not handcuffing him.

"What have we here?"

"We have the hero who solved the murders," Dante said drily but with a tinge of pride in his deep voice. "Listen to this." Then Dante played the recorded voice of Martino Guerra in his death throes, confessing to the murders of three Romans, a student, her professor, and a homeless black refugee who happened to have fallen asleep on the wrong doorstep.

Vena could have sworn she saw Guerra move.

Chapter Nineteen
Leaving the World Unseen

With outstretched hands and an unclouded conscience, Fitsum firmly placed papers and Euros into the waiting arms of fellow travelers. No one needed to say, "These documents offer you a new life," but it was understood with simple gestures: a nod, a longer stare, grateful eyes, a hand on the shoulder in gratitude. Once out of Italy, they would part. There were a few names and addresses of houses, names of friends, if they were able to go far enough to reach them. Who would be waiting was as mysterious as the day they had left their homes in another time.

Night had been long with fleas and ticks or bed bugs biting all of them. Old mattresses on an earthen floor offered minimal comfort, but there was no way to keep used, discarded mattresses clean or free of vermin. They smelled from sweat and blood and feces of humans and animals. One woman briefly considered the mattress, then decided to sleep on the ground, her arm her pillow. Her teenage son put his jacket over his mother and crawled next to a stranger for warmth.

The day before, they had slipped out of a tenement house where they slept on mattresses arranged in rows on the floor. Italian protesters had broken into the government housing for the migrants and set fire to some of the mattresses. While in the street, protesters shouted at them, then screamed, "*Questo è stato,*" this is war. A Syrian woman starred dully out an upper floor opening, looking at the angry faces of men, anticipating which one she would have to fight in her last battle against death.

Firemen and police arrived to ward off what could have ended in a massacre, as agitated protesters armed with clubs waited outside for migrants to try to flee the fire and smoke. Police, however, prevented the ugly scenario, using their own smoke in the form of tear gas. Rocks were thrown at police for protecting the migrants, and arrests were made after the scuffle. Someone threw a firecracker, and several protesters were tackled to the ground by riot police wearing gas masks.

"*Questo è il nostro paese.*" "This is our country," protestors chanted even as police threw tear gas at their countrymen.

"*Uscire, stronzi africani.*" "Get out, you African fuckers."

Two policemen and twelve protesters were injured. A handful of migrants looked out window openings on the slow, violent quelling of the riot. The rest of the migrants huddled in a corner of tenement apartments furthest from the fires, covering their faces from the smoke. Another long day and night in an endless journey.

After the majority of the protesters were temporarily moved, buses arrived, and migrants were marched to the buses under police protection where they rode to an abandoned school to begin the long wait again. Walking into the large open space, migrants saw mattresses covered the dirty floors, but the eyes of the women and children and some of the younger men were still wide with fear. In the eyes of mature men, there was hate. How long before the protesters found them again?

When a small group of migrants decided to make a run for the north and cross the border, they met Fitsum who was already waiting with papers.

"Too many at once," said Fitsum, siding with the huddled émigrés and shaking his head. They had to travel fast and light.

After much discussion between members of the group, a few broke away and motioned farewell to the others. They went on alone and were soon picked up and returned to the abandoned apartment building where the fires had been quenched. Smoke hung in the air, and they hung their heads, not defeated, still desperate.

The people who went with Fitsum found themselves in an alleyway with a few mattresses lined up on the ground. Sometime in the night, after arriving, they collapsed, and a couple of the adults slept fitfully. Children, however, slept as they were carried, a mother or father pacing the night.

Fitsum woke after closing his eyes briefly, surprised to find he had been bitten. A small bite, so unlikely a rat. He was so used to infestations, the wound scarcely registered. But a lone child was crying and scratching incessantly, digging into his skin until he bled. His mother was too exhausted to comfort him. Finally, a man, not a relative, picked up the child and rocked him until the child fell asleep again.

Rats always ran through the alleys the migrants slept in, but rats seldom bothered Fitsum. One particularly large creature, nearly the size of a cat, ran so smoothly along the base of the wall upon which Fitsum leaned, its shadow could have been mistaken for running water. Fitsum moved out of the way as the rat challenged him with its eyes, then scurried on its way. There were children with them, one child in the arms of a grown man, or the rats would have been more of a menace. Still, someone yelped at the size of a rat, and another tried to chase the animal down before the monster vermin disappeared into a grating behind another building.

Looking at a woman's reflection in a pool of stagnant water, Fitsum noticed she adjusted her head scarf self-consciously. He thought this might have been the first time she had seen an image of herself in many days, perhaps weeks. She was crying silently.

"Don't stare too long," he chided her, really teasing, trying to get her to forget all the pain.

Although she said nothing, she backed up from the water and turned away, embarrassed.

"And you? Where will you go?" asked a fellow Eritrean, coming up and offering him a cigarette. Fitsum nodded, thinking part of the money he had given the man was now being returned to him in a dirty cigarette which had been passed from the bony hand. Before daylight, they would be on the move again.

"As far as I am able."

"So, there is no promised land? There is the road; streets are what you promise us?"

"I make no promises. I move you from here to there. What you make of our journey is up to you. There are lands and opportunities where we take them. Be ready for yours. You never know." Listening to and speaking in his native language again was surprisingly comfortable and soothing. The other man lit his cigarette which glowed like a firefly in the dark.

"If they arrest you, or pick you up and send you back?"

"I will be in motion until I die. Sending me back would be futile, but then again, I am an invisible man, so they do not see me."

"We wish to be invisible, too." A few young men had gathered around him, somewhat menacing in their slow forward movements, but Fitsum knew the desperation in their eyes would never disappear. Although not directly asked, he thought to remind them: "I have given all away. I'd give you more if I could, but you know how to find what is essential now. Invisibility is a skill you will learn by habit, not by what you do but how you are 'seen' by others." There was no quiver in his voice, no fear, and the tone altered the steps of the men who stopped moving toward him.

Not wanting to dispense advice which could fail them, Fitsum preferred to deal in material things. "You will be too many; confuse them, overwhelm them. Ask for nothing but work. Take what is unattended from those who have abundance. There will be plenty in some places, and you'll be tempted to stay long but keep moving until offered work. They will offer because we work for less than their countrymen." The Eritrean who had given him a cigarette moved his head slightly in response, perhaps indicating he would fight with him, if necessary. The young men changed their aspect again and moved off, satisfied Fitsum had nothing more to give. Even his fellow Eritrean had left as Fitsum decided to catch a little sleep before the sun rose.

Fitsum fed their resolve to take what they could along the broken path. Watching them until they were past a grove of trees, Fitsum motioned for a teen, a tall boy, to come to him. The boy had been studying interactions of others at a distance, ready to turn and flee. He had no fight left in him to defend the weak or helpless with the exception of his mother.

Drawing out a few more Euros from a pocket sewn on the underside of his shirt, Fitsum slipped them into the palm of the boy. "Don't waste them on cigarettes or alcohol," he said, sounding like his father when he was a child. Fitsum knew there would be stops in Germany, questions and surges of panic. Even overturned, Fitsum had become a vessel which could not be sunk. "The train stations have tourists," he told the boy. "Be quick and be silent. If you are caught, say nothing, admit nothing. Fight if you have a chance to get away."

"Thank you," the boy whispered and moved off to join a woman and small child. Although still very dark, Fitsum could detect movements of the boy's hand giving his mother something. This boy, somehow, had not been hardened by his perilous journey. He still believed in family and obeying his mother. Good, Fitsum thought, as he closed his eyes momentarily.

The night was long, and Fitsum slept like a cat with one eye open. He heard another approach of footsteps, and said, "You will be tired by morning if you don't rest."

"Where are you from? You Muslim?"

"I answer to no one, not you or any man." Fitsum lit another cigarette, taking a few draws before offering the smoke to the other man who held the cigarette for a moment before putting it between his lips.

"Fair enough," the man said. "Sizing you up. Can we trust you?"

"I have given you papers and wages you have not earned. Asked you for nothing in return but barter items. What do you think?"

"We gave you our possessions. We accepted what you paid."

"More than fair," said Fitsum.

"We must take your word. Semhar. Eritrea. One of the men said you were from Eritrea, too."

"A thousand years ago," Fitsum said smiling, but the man could not detect his smile in the dim light.

"Never forget where we have come from," said the weary Eritrean. "I overheard you giving advice to the boy."

"Better not to remember and better still not to overhear." But Fitsum put out his hand and rested on the other man's shoulder. "Brother." The other man laid his hand on top of Fitsum's as in a pact.

Short exchanges punctuated their leaving. It would not be practical to adopt these refugee children and grown men. The few women hid their beauty until beauty could be of use again. On the road, such extravagances were an invitation to attack or worse.

Giving the kind of advice he always gave, Fitsum reminded them to be like shadows, visible to Europeans, they would require work, but unidentifiable. "We all look alike to them, remember. Read faces of these European strangers before striding out into light. You will know if a man is waiting to hire you or beat you before you ask."

~ * ~

Both End in Speculation

If he had a genius, Fitsum thought, his genius was for disappearing again and again, leaving one world after another largely unseen. Vena had seen him, he remembered. Yet he did not think she would identify him to the authorities. He had left her tied and helpless, but Guerra was dead and would not hurt her any longer. Perhaps if he had not decided to kill Guerra, he might have remained in Italy longer, moving without detection. Italy had been warmer than these northern countries. Perhaps if he had not been following Vena, she would be dead.

The decision to take Guerra's life led to this path and leaving Italy for good. Even if Vena did not turn him in, and he believed she wouldn't, his actions made a continued stay in Italy nearly impossible. Yet Fitsum understood without analysis, his decision to move was not because he would be recognized for a crime but because something in him had once again changed.

Like a mole, he would go underground, raising the earth ever so slightly, making his way in darkness with an expertise honed in perpetual danger. He was neither immoral nor amoral but a moral man bound to do harm by circumstances and terrible choices.

"You have saved my family," a Syrian man said roughly, with his chin pressed nearly to his chest in embarrassment as they rose with the pale pink sky. This Syrian wanted no part of thanking an Eritrean, but here he was expressing gratitude.

"No. I have done little. You have saved your own family, but you must keep this information and walk every step with no one but your wits and your family. Good luck to you. The Europeans," he said hesitantly, as the Syrian turned back around to him, "their women are better than their men. If you must trust anyone, trust a woman first. Better yet, let your wife come out of the shadows to speak to a woman first."

Flashing either anger or confusion, the Syrian lowered his eyes before he walked away, pushing his wife and child along.

Odds for all of them were long. The Syrian family would likely be detained in Germany. Simply harder to move around undetected with a child. Fitsum was not a fortune teller or prophet, but he knew their fates were based on the odds. Others would be caught up and languish for an interminable time in unsanitary, crowded camps. Some would fight each other or hostile Europeans and die. Fitsum had read about the siege at Bicske station in Hungary in which 500 migrants had rioted and broken out. Nearly all of them were captured and returned to the camps, waiting to be extradited back to their home countries once identities were roughly or approximately sorted out. A few would make the passage to Belgium where they would sleep in a room with other men and listen to anger build and fall like their chests. Two Syrians were charged with murder they had not committed. A Nigerian would push a tourist into a canal after taking his money at knifepoint. Some of the women would be raped by men outside their group. The children bore the scars and buried them in their minds. All this and more awaited them. Yet, there was the hope.

Fitsum was never caught or exposed as a smuggler in Italy. He never questioned his actions the night of the assassination. Of all the men he had seen, those who had robbed and killed, those who had raped others, Guerra showed himself to be the most deserving of an ugly death. Fitsum was merely the messenger. The message was not from God or the gods, but from other men: these things you will no longer do to men or women. Although he was unafraid when he fatally stabbed Guerra, Fitsum knew the act made him no more powerful. The execution was necessary and completed. His quickness and the element of surprise permitted him to best the stronger, bigger man. Little boxes in Guerra's shop yielded far more than he hoped or expected. Such bounty consented to his generosity this last time as the migrants made their way.

~ * ~

Outside another train station, Fitsum passed out forged passports and papers to the Africans and Arabs who were without identities and wished them good fortune. One dirty and ragged boy with eyes too large for his head, stood up and smiled. Fitsum motioned to the boy and slipped an extra coin in his hand. What good would one more coin do? Yet, the child ran to his father or older brother with his good fortune, seeming as resilient as the land itself. With his beautiful face, Fitsum thought, the boy could make a living for his family by begging. He hoped the boy would not be used in the sex trade, but knew the possibility.

Their journeys had been long and so familiar to one another, even when arriving from different countries. Taken again, Fitsum thought one journey blended into all—without distinction—until this last one because he had no intention of returning. Shortly after leaving Rome, Fitsum arrived with a group of migrants in France, stuffing shirt pockets with Euros. His backpack was growing empty, and the money he wore around his chest, under his clothing, was rapidly disappearing.

Some moved on to Germany. Belgium was preferred by young men from Yemen. In their home countries, none of this band of travelers would have interacted. They might have killed one another as enemies, but on the road, the migrants became like brothers, perhaps distrusting ones, but nevertheless still a weirdly tolerant family.

~ * ~

Finally, they waited where they could until discovery or disappearing into low paying jobs and crowded little flats dispersed. Fitsum continued on. He had not come all this way to live in another camp or with ten foreigners on a hard floor, dirty sheets over the windows, water boiling to cook some undesirable, unidentifiable vegetable.

Unlike his mentor teacher Vena, Fitsum had never read Henry James, but the Eritrean carried a quotation written by James with him on a slip of paper in the pocket of his Italian jacket: "One's destination is never a place, but rather a new way of looking at things." At first, Fitsum had held onto Vena's little gift of words to practice his English, but now, he carried the quotation for its meaning. Every once in a while, when he could tilt his head back and breathe in the middle of the night, he recalled Vena with a smile. She had taught him well, but mostly, she had not belittled him or given him away. He saw her face, her head shaking in warning. This look kept his voice silent in the place of Guerra's trade. Looking back on the scene, he pondered why she warned him to be silent. He wanted to tell her he would have been silent anyway. Passing through a town in France, he dropped a note card in a post box. The card held an image of a woman reading on the front. The postcard illustration was from some famous

French painting. Inside, he scratched out a short note. He left no signature. Few things ate away at him, but it continued to bother Fitsum he left his tutor tied in a chair with a dying or dead man at her feet. He hoped she had already forgiven her student. Vena did not know he had followed her to Guerra's. He had previously identified the address led to a monster, the one which had fallen out when she gave him the quotation. Although he said nothing to her at the time, Fitsum understood she was in danger if she planned to visit Guerra. He had watched her movements for days before she walked down the street with such trepidation. Guerra was dead, Fitsum was certain. He had learned to use a knife when still a boy.

~ * ~

The Euros he reserved for himself made his passage easier, eventually enabling him to cross into England and finally to land in London. His clear command of English eased his passage, fooling many about his identity and place of origin along the way.

When he arrived in London, Fitsum had become Sammy of his forged passport, "God heard," he would tell people when asked how he came by his name. With his papers, passport, and a small stash, Sammy determined to rent an apartment. But first, he stood on the brick pavement outside the Royal Academy of Arts, a place he had seen in a book Vena shared with him. He laughed. No one looked long at him, but his gesture had drawn a few stares. He did not believe England was any kind of holy ground, but worn pavement marked the end of a long passage.

His smile eased suspicions of him, the Caucasian men who moved quickly along. Fitsum's first move was to buy a meal, then he proceeded to purchase better English clothing. When he looked less threatening, he thought, he completed the steps necessary to living as a Londoner. From employment as a delivery man to a rented space. A beginning.

~ * ~

Walking a city was something he was used to, but he saw men had bikes, and decided he wanted to try this method. But he needed a bank card to ride one of those bikes, and he didn't have a bank card. Sammy watched a video of a man named Adam who gave step by step procedures as to how to open a bank account in London. Sammy was a careful note taker. Here, he was building a very different life from the one he was used to in Italy, and the many lives he had known since he was a boy.

Before long, he walked up to a docking station terminal, and Sammy used his new bank card to rent a Santander Cycle.

Looking around and finding no one there to arrest him, he hopped on his rented, public bike to make his way in the crowded city, a quickly moving man on a swarming island in the wide world.

Chapter Twenty
The Eternal City

Escape brought Vena to Roma. Escapism was also why so many writers and artists fled to the Italian capital over the centuries, but Vena had to decide if she was still running and from what or from whom. No, she was not fleeing any more. If she decided to stay in Roma, the act of faith would be because she loved the city more than any other place. The pull was strong. There was Keats at the end of his life, Shelley, Goethe, Virginia Woolf, Byron, Nietzsche. Even Shakespeare, who never left England's shores, imagined his characters in this Eternal City. In a metropolis with more tourists than residents, Roma was overwhelmed, but the ancient city had lived her long life under such circumstances and benign, as well as violent, invasions. For Vena, however, as for all of those ex-pats before her, Roma was also myth and legend, history walking out of texts, all made tangible by exposed remains of the past.

Would she stay in Roma? Would she go back to America? Of course, but perhaps not to live. She would travel to visit Bill in the spring but not see Warren. Her former lover had finally moved on with his life, and her entrance into his new relationship would cause him sadness and problems. Letting Warren go in her mind was far more difficult than it had been to let him go in body as she stood on the Via dei Condotti across from the Spanish Steps.

She ventured out again, walking at a brisk pace before halting and looking back at a group of students, visiting from Germany. Laughing, posing, posturing on the Spanish Steps, the Germans all wore the same white cap on their heads, easy to pick out amongst a crowd. There were a couple of adults with them, likely their teachers, who looked spent, their heads down, their forearms resting on bent legs as they leaned forward. The students behind them looked ready to conquer the world, Vena thought before proceeding. Although in physical years, she was not far removed from those teenagers, she saw herself as worlds and time apart. In the moment, she imagined herself as old, not yet ancient like the city but weighed down by time and experience.

Deciding not to return to the Keats Shelley House again, she was keenly aware of Keats and his stolen poem. The thought occurred to her: she could write about the poem and its disappearance after the murders. If she could get such an article published, then attention would be drawn to the search. Perhaps such notice would cause the buyer to be uneasy, even give up the poem to a museum, but more than likely, he would hide the stolen words in some temperature controlled safe in Bridgeport Connecticut or some other port in the world. The clues Guerra left were so fragmented, and any truth they might carry was suspect. Yet, something told her she was not done searching for this missing Keats' poem, and looking for it would take her from Italy.

Hoping Sabine was now at peace, Vena recognized her own restlessness. Occasionally thinking about what might have been, she mused on an alternate ending. One in which Sabine shared the Keats' poem with her. They brought the document to an appraiser, and the reward Sabine received for finding the poem paid for the entirety of her education. Sabine remained her lifelong friend, and Vena stood beside her, jittery with excitement, as Antonio kissed his bride. A once possible future was now foolishly imagined. Yet, Vena sometimes smiled thinking of Sabine and an altered ending.

~ * ~

A bright green, white, and red flag waved in the slight breeze. Italy's colors were always on display, offset against the rich, layered ochre of buildings. The blue of the Mediterranean caught and put out on display in hand-blown, colored glass orbs hanging in decorative fishing nets near restaurant doors, reminding inhabitants the sea was never too far away from their minds, their hearts, and their *Italiano* heritage. Although Vena had become very comfortable in Italy, she was aware Roma was not her heritage.

On cooler days, when she ventured out to the ancient Capitoline Hill, Vena loved to wander to *Palazzo dei Conservatori* where the Capitoline Wolf forever suckled the twin boys Romulus and Remus, those mythical founders of Roma cast into the Tiber and rescued by the She Wolf. This was a legend more than half believed by the population. The symbolism appealed to her poetic sensibilities, and Roma held within her enigmatic heart the wildness of the wolf and the naked ambition of the foundling boys, one of whom murdered the other out of that ambition. What once recalled Roma's empire was now in ruins, glorious and glorified.

Even with its myriad problems, Roma offered so many reasons for her to stay. A young woman had been elected Mayor, the first woman and first from the Five Star Movement, and Vena told Elio she would have voted for Raggi if she could have voted. Elio was not sure about this woman, he said, even though he complained about the city's outgoing Mayor who had been removed due to criminal investigation into corruption. Although she knew little about Virginia Raggi, other than the fact she was a lawyer, Vena already liked her, liked the fact Raggi was a decisive leader in what was still such a machismo context swirling around her. Italy itself a male construct built from the love of women.

~ * ~

Dante was on leave and had returned to his family. Francesca would be waiting with open arms at the door. His daughter and sons would wrap themselves around the long legs of their tall father and ask for a ride as he pulled them along laughing. Nearly a perfect scene of domestic bliss. Something in Dante's smile was unfamiliar, however, and the awkwardness of his initial movements toward her troubled Francesca, but she said nothing at the time.

In bed, when the children were asleep, and after they had made love, Francesca asked him. "You were gone a long time. Did you sometimes see yourself never coming home to us?"

"Never," he said with conviction. "You and our children are my life."

She wanted to believe him, and so she did.

~ * ~

Before he left, Dante told Vena she should consider marrying his brother.

"He is crazy about you, you know. Time to make this legal."

"I know he is," was all she said.

"Then try not to hurt him too badly," Dante said, kissing her cheek, his hand around her waist as if to pull her to him. She leaned back ever so subtlety, but her movement away from him was detected.

"I guess I should not be giving you advice."

"You love your brother, and he loves you."

"There's more to the equation." They were both silent.

~ * ~

The next morning, Dante called and offered to take them to lunch before heading back to his home for the first time in months. "It's a celebration luncheon," he said cheerfully. "For solving the case."

Elio did not really want to go. "I don't feel like celebrating," he said glumly.

"It's the last time you will see Dante for a while; you should go."

"Do you want to see him?"

"To say, 'good-bye?' Yes." They met Dante in the Monti area at one of their favorite restaurants, *LaTaverna dei Fori Imperiale*.

"Order the white-truffle ragu," Dante said in what was taken as command to Vena.

"It's homemade pasta," Elio offered, rather reluctantly. "She knows, though. We come here often."

She heeded their advice, but the thick, too rich, truffle oil aftertaste unpleasantly stayed with her.

Holding up a glass of seltzer water, Dante offered the toast: "To Vena, her uncanny instincts, and solving murders."

"How about, to all of us, then?" she added.

"No, you figured this out, and you almost were killed for your efforts. To Vena," said Elio.

"I'm not going to toast to myself," she laughed.

"All right, to solving the case; to justice served," said Dante, and they drank.

"I still don't understand why Guerra killed the African. Part of the mystery was never solved. I mean we have him on tape confessing to kicking the man in the head, but he never stated a reason. Really made no sense and never will." Elio said, looking toward Vena for an answer.

"Oh, yes, I didn't tell you a couple of things we learned after autopsy," said Dante.

"Tell us what?" asked Elio and Vena simultaneously.

"Turned out Pavoni had given money to some organization helping migrants come into Italy, but he was not any sponsor of note, and unlikely Guerra knew of Pavoni's migrant involvement. There was the paper. A little scrap of paper in the murder victim's hand," Dante said.

"Sabine. In Sabine's fingers?"

"Yes, they had the paper tested…rag paper or paper made from rag pulp which they stopped making in the early 1800s. I don't know if this proves the paper had a Keats' poem on it, but at least, part of your theory was right, Vena."

"Oh," said Vena.

"And?" said Elio. "You said there were a couple of things you found out."

"Guerra did not kill the Negro but possibly thought he did."

"What?" Vena leaned toward Dante.

"Autopsy showed the homeless man died of cirrhosis of the liver and subsequent heart failure. The blunt force trauma to his head was inflicted very near but after the man's death."

"Then why did Guerra stage the body? To throw off the investigation?"

"Makes sense. Either Guerra thought he killed the man, who might have looked as if he was sleeping, or he knew the man was dead and used the body as a red herring, as you would say," Dante said.

"He didn't know the man in his doorway was dead," Vena said. "Guerra thought he killed him and didn't care." She remembered Guerra's dying words better than she wished.

"To use an already dead body to confuse a murder investigation—it's either brilliant or lucky," Elio mused.

"Or perverse," said Vena.

"Definitely perverse," Dante added.

So, you have your answers," Elio said.

"Not quite all of them. We never did find the African who killed Guerra, the one who likely saved your life. I'm not sure if we would have arrived in time."

"He did save my life," said Vena.

"We weren't far behind, but we have to thank him for those actions. I'm afraid this information won't alter the fact he is a murderer."

"He did the State's work. He executed a vicious killer," said Elio.

"He should get a medal if you ever find him," Vena said, trying not to betray her feelings.

"I'm afraid we won't be giving him any medals. We'll get him at some point. They always slip up." Vena never even blushed as Dante said those words about Fitsum. She did blush, however, when Dante leaned over and kissed her good-bye on the mouth. "*Fino alla prossima volta.* Until the next time."

~ * ~

The day after Dante left Roma, Vena picked up her mail from where she had worked, her box still receiving notes from former students. She found a curious envelope from France without a return address. Reading the brief, almost coded message inside the card, she immediately understood. "Known address. Monster waiting. Followed you. Looking for Keats." The card was from Fitsum. He had seen Guerra's address when the slip of paper fell from her pocket. Somehow Fitsum knew the address led to Martino Guerra. Fitsum had followed her to Guerra's. Saving her life wasn't a coincidence or good fortune. He had been protecting her. Last three words on the card, "Looking for Keats," could mean several things, but Vena thought Fitsum was telling her he was heading to England. She didn't think he was searching for the missing poem, but the idea was intriguing, particularly if one of the papers he had taken from the gold broker contained some clue as to whom Guerra sold the Keats' poem. Guerra had said something like Brig, Conn for the location.

She wanted to keep the card but was nervous Elio would see the note and question her, so she set the card on the stone lip of a window as she walked home from work. Even though she knew she should have tossed the card away, Vena couldn't bear the act of destroying it. She anticipated the person who found the enigmatic note would consider the mystery as she once had the yellowed lines in the book of poetry.

~ * ~

In the evening, Elio told Vena they were going out.

"I thought we'd make dinner at home tonight. Buy some veal and fresh cheese," she said.

"I want to take you out. The two of us. It's been awhile." Vena understood Elio meant they were eating without his brother along. She realized how much Elio had put up with. He was a man naturally given to jealousies.

"We'll have time for lots of dinners at home," Elio said, less certain than his statement implied. "Come, we should celebrate your new employment, this rich corporation can afford to pay you a regular salary."

They laughed. "Ah, yes. It's good to be gainfully employed," she said.

"Do you miss him?" Elio asked.

"Who?"

"Stop it. My brother, of course. You know you miss Dante."

"We worked together for a while, and I like him. He's your brother, but I will not miss him," Vena said, lying calmly. She hoped to be convincing.

Elio disagreed. "You'll miss him and solving cases. You want mystery in your life. He's the Dostoyevsky novel or the Faulkner, for you Americans," Elio said more quietly. "I'm the feel-good beach read. Could be a problem for us."

"What are you talking about?" Vena tried to laugh. "Ridiculous.

Besides, do you have any idea how many people prefer the beach read every time?"

"Maybe, but you don't. I couldn't be my brother if I tried."

"Don't ever try. If Dante was willing to be honest, I'm sure he wishes he was you, sometimes, too."

"Because I'm with you."

"No. I don't want to hear about you wishing to be Dante again." Vena used her sternest voice, holding off Elio's further protests.

"Maybe you're right. Dante is so self-possessed, and I know women find self-assurance attractive. But he'll never leave Francesca, even if he stops loving her. Not simply the code of the Carabinieri prohibiting affairs. My brother has a severity about him. He was born with it. As he said before, he's not Vincenzo."

"And neither are you." Vena wrapped her arms around Elio's neck.

The exchange settled nothing but left them happy for a time again.

~ * ~

Standing near the center and looking up at the domed ceiling designed by none other than Michelangelo, Vena let amplitude enter. Twenty-eight meters above the floor, the unadorned, curving ceiling was breath-taking. Pink, Egyptian granite columns surrounded the walls. Bianchi, she was told, had a great circular hole carved out of the roof through which the sun cast its light on a sundial across the marble floor.

She was not formally religious, but this space precipitated tingling up her spine and the sensation of being blessed in the moment. The Basilica of Santa Maria *degli Angeli e dei Martiri* had seen all: tribute to the Christian martyrs, then Christian judges martyring those who did not believe, but Santa Maria had come to be a place of forgiveness for all who entered into such grace.

"You feel it, don't you?" Elio whispered, inching closer to her. "They built the basilica inside the emperor's great construct, the church named for the Christians who supposedly died in the making of the Baths of Diocletian."

Vena already knew this, but let Elio be her guide again. Located on the smallest of the Seven Hills of Roma, the original baths had been built and rebuilt hundreds of years after their first construction, and still, ancient history. Even the building of the basilica, commissioned by Pope Pius IV, was a fragment of what once was. Vena knew the original Baths of Diocletian were also said to have contained libraries, and she could picture Romans bathing and reading, then walking out with their books beneath the beautiful semi-circular doorways into sunlight. She looked at Elio and wanted to step away with a book into light.

~ * ~

"You're going to leave me, aren't you?" Elio's expression was both accusing and plaintive. They had gone to San Lorenzo for *pizzeria*. Formula Uno on *Via degli Equi* was known to the locals and considered inexpensive, as Elio said. Even without Elio's help, Vena could have easily afforded the six Euro pizza *capriciossa*. Biting into the thin, crispy crust, Vena watched Elio's eyes widen. Aware her indecision made her more desirable to him, she suspected he both hated his lover and never loved her as deeply. Elio admired her American independence and feminist rebellion, but not in relationship to him.

Elio summed up an inner strength in order not to say, "I want you to be someone other than who you are." He looked at her impatiently.

She swallowed preparing to say something but nothing came. She conjectured why he had to force the answer. If he had given her time?

Her prolonged hesitation in answering confirmed his suspicions. She held the crust between her teeth, her mouth partially open. Without debasing himself further, Elio thought of causing a scene then talked himself out of it, in silence. He stood up, turned once…not so much to look back at her as to check himself in the impulse, before walking out the door. Vena's eyes followed his exit, but her mind was already somewhere beyond the door, her heart racing. She wouldn't cry, but the moment was horribly sad. Running after him would be a lie and perhaps a worse cruelty. Dropping the pizza slice and lifting her hand to her lips, as if to work on the shape of the words later following, she squared her shoulders. Then she tossed her hair back and looked out at the streets. Her eyes welled with tears, but she did not cry.

Already Elio was lost in the crowd. She did not choose to find him in the mix. He was there somewhere, however, walking wounded but resolute, striding long steps, steps not taking him back. Reasoning the break had been coming for some time, he knew he had no choice but to let her go. Why had he been so stubborn to force the issue. If he hadn't demanded an answer? If he had left things as they were?

"Don't be so very hurt," she heard herself say aloud after he had left. Elio, she whispered, but there were too many uncertainties. She deliberated as to whether, like Michel Butor's character Léon Delmont in *A Change of Heart*, she, "did not love him without Rome or away from Rome." Elio had been her entrance to this city, and her associations of Elio and Roma would continue to be conflated. She would always love this city and always love Elio. By allowing him to walk away, however, she had indirectly chosen a new course.

Even if she went back to him, and she would later, their relationship would not be the same. Her failure to respond to his plea had been a kind of answer, a resolution for both of them hung in the air until she packed her bags and moved. But the dramatic action of final farewells was a few weeks away yet. Elio would blame both Vena and his brother Dante. He would not trust a woman for months before he would fall in love again.

Vena blamed no one.

~ * ~

In the weeks leading up to her final break, their conversations became more stilted. Yet, they slept in the same bed, sometimes still made love in the early morning. Neither one of them thought the act of making love would change anything in the long term, but lovemaking was comforting if no longer fun. Everything had changed.

Roma's sunlight cast long shadows through their bedroom, touching gold like spider silk on a desk lamp, a pen, a necklace Elio had given her. Vena rolled over and looked out before getting up. Sunlight fell on cars and motorbikes in the streets, fountains in the Piazzas, mixing with ancient dust rose and fell every morning and evening, and always on the

River Tiber. Thousands of years of untouchable gold on the Tiber.

What am I thinking? Vena's change in jobs enabled her to have regular hours in one location and better pay. She finally had enough money. She could clearly afford her own small studio if she decided to leave Elio and continue to live in the city. The independence would be welcomed but unsettling.

~ * ~

Yet, somewhere out in the world, there was a stolen poem, likely written by a dying John Keats. For now, for a little while longer, she would stay, but qualification hung in the air. This was a city she loved, but she had known and seen Sabine brutally murdered here. Images of Sabine's damaged face, her broken body stayed with Vena and resurfaced at unexpected times. She was curious as to whether or not re-experiencing the murder scene was similar for Dante, too, or was he simply used to the act of identifying victims, grown indifferent to their individuality and horrific exits from the world? Yet, this was no reason to leave a city. There was no escape from ugliness and brutality. Every city, small town, and rural landscape revealed such atrocities committed by men. Roma also held a multitude of fantastic secrets embedded in her long and deep history.

~ * ~

After waking, she slipped out, leaving a note for Elio, and walked without pre-determined destination. On cobbled alleys wet and shiny from a recent night-time rain, Vena watched a crumpled piece of paper tumble past. But there was no mystery to this scrap of paper, merely a tourist's discarded receipt. A plastic bottle stirred and swirled in the early morning breeze, and some piece of food turned sour and rancid in the sun. A paper cup, a remnant from someone's drink the night before, rolled past. A broken bicycle was abandoned and leaning against a structure in which stones ached with the weight, crumbling at the edges, a little more dust falling.

You have to get used to a bit of decay, she thought, before grabbing an espresso from a coffee bar and easily making her way through a business-bound crowd. All of the faces looked determined, ready to climb the ladder, while she merely pretended to be on her way to a destination.

Roma was forever steeped in the fluidity of time. Fragments calling up conquering and conquered soldiers, the victorious and defeated in an endless cycle, Roman citizens walking through the baths, in and out of Diocletian's abandoned libraries, achievements and death. Olive oils and basil in a bowl, emperors and popes vying for power, ash and dust in the air. Vena could suddenly see an eighty-six-year old Michelangelo hunched over a table outlining his last project, the great cross-vaulted ceiling of the Santa Maria Basilica, mysteriously held all those meters above her. Would Elio see Vena sometimes as he walked through a crowd? Nothing and no one ever completely left Roma.

From one end of the street to the other, an invisible pull caused her to turn her head. She could hear again Guerra's last words, his intended cruelty, his indifference to the murder of a beautiful young woman. She could also hear his rasping clue to a possible, original Keats' poem, a few lines Guerra could not have created floated over her, past the Piazza and Palazzos with their fountains, over Roma's white domes, the mountains, and into France or England where they disappeared, perhaps boarding a plane for America. Every suspicion of those words' origins made her move a little faster, knowing she would pursue the enigma.

Vena Goodwin walked the long distance from an apartment she had shared with Elio Canestrini directly to Sapienza University where she gifted the old volume of Shakespeare's plays. Turned out, the single book of a rare, two-volume set, published in 1806 by William Miller and printed by Savage and Easingwood, was worth upwards of 9,000 Euros, due to its rarity, age, and pristine condition. Vena was offered a finder's fee which she gave to Sabine's mother.

~ * ~

"So, our Nonna knew something about English book's worth," said Lia.

"Perhaps she did."

"Thank you for the money." She stared at the Euros in her hand before finally looking up. "Much more, thank you for caring about my daughter."

~ * ~

After leaving Trastevere, Vena headed back to the center of the city where she walked to Roma Termini, boarded a train, checking her seat number. Twenty-one. Ah, she thought, the number of perfection and the next chapter of my life. Then she set out, moving past fears and caution, into uncertainty.

About the Author

Author, poet, and educator Nancy Avery Dafoe lives in Homer, NY. She writes across genres, including fiction and has published seven books. Her books, essays, and other writings have earned local, state, and national awards. In addition to her Vena Goodwin murder mystery series, including You Enter a Room and Both End in Speculation, Dafoe has written nationally recognized short stories. Her poetry has earned first place in the William Faulkner/Wisdom creative writing competition. Other published books include a cross-genre memoir and poetry book An Iceberg in Paradise: A Passage through Alzheimer's and texts on education and writing: The Misdirection of Education Policy; Breaking Open the Box; and Writing Creatively. Her chapbook of poetry Poets Diving in the Night was a Central New York Book Award finalist.

Also by the Author
at
Rogue Phoenix Press

You Enter a Room

Heroine Advena (Vena) Goodwin does not set out to become a detective. She is more interested in untangling a literary mystery, writing her dissertation, and falling in love, but the young man who fascinates her has killed himself or, as she suspects, been murdered.

A smart, resilient young woman, Vena attempts to trap the clever murderer Professor Gould by using his over-sized ego against him. With no one believing her suspicions at first, she is on her own in dangerous territory masked by a scholarly campus setting.

This upmarket murder mystery takes place in the settings of Rochester in upstate New York and Rome, Italy. The crimes, murder and theft, are interwoven with a literary puzzle the protagonist solves even as her life is imperiled.

Chapter One
You Enter a Room

"Poems are what? Dirt, death, fondue? Answer the question." Professor Roald Gould demanded with intensity that pinned us down from the opening of class. Silence followed. No one even took off coats or backpacks, no one adjusted seats or papers. We froze in nervous anticipation because the class could not possibly begin and end with such dramatic confusion. Our professor kept us waiting until we started to look around at each other in confusion. Were we in the right room? Roald Gould had a reputation that preceded him, but we were momentarily startled even after all of those years of schooling and every manner of introduction. Disorientation, apparently, was our lesson for the day.

"Poems are?" Gould repeated after several minutes of absolute stillness that held reticence rather than peace. In the aftermath of that interminable absence of voice, Gould spoke again; "poems are death unless they are a moving shadow, a woman making love, a boy fishing." We waited again before our instructor finally asked, "What did Leroi Jones suggest in his poem "Black Art?" What is his first line?"

I was again orienting myself to the Africanist presence in English Literature, but I knew Jones' work was not in the curriculum.

"I don't think he was suggesting at all," said the typically silent Michael Lawler. "Jones' lines are urgent and brutal and direct. Jones is really demanding and stating that poetry must be, must feel as critical as breath, as violent as a punch to your gut." Michael, who usually sat hunched over and pensive in class, was bolt upright for an instant. His face and confident voice were so altered that I almost didn't recognize the handsome but shy guy from my graduate level English classes.

Gould met his eyes, and the exchange happened as if no one else was in the room except the two of them. You could discern competing forces that were drawn together as the rest of us were involuntarily pulled into this tension. At the time, it was likely that none of us could define those dynamics of repulsion and attraction. Only later, would I realize that I had witnessed a struggle between independence and submission, between bravery and cowardice, between dominance and questioning, between sexual attraction and repulsion, and between good and evil. The interaction was not about knowledge or lack of knowledge as Gould framed their meeting.

"As a figure of speech, the simile by its nature is suggestive, guiding us to make the connections laid out in the construction." Gould was talking only to Michael, and the rest of us waited to see how Michael would respond. "And I note you used the word 'as' a total of four times in one sentence, apparently unaware of the signifier as simile and suggestion. Jones used the simile to suggest the relationship between violence of the physical world and signifiers. Read Doty's essay on metaphors." A number of students started looking through the syllabus, fearing they had missed the first day's assignment. "Don't check. It's not in the syllabus. Read Doty for your own edification; read Jones' poetry, and get a better grasp of signifiers and metaphors. Such a lack of delineation at this point in your academic careers is startling," Gould said with evident disdain.

Just as I wanted to cheer Michael for his precision about wording and poetic interpretation, as well as facing our esteemed professor on seemingly equal footing, the young man slumped in his chair and lowered his head slightly. Body language was everything. Those of us still standing, finally sat down. Michael had not simply given up the argument, but the room. No one was looking at him any longer except for me. Here there would be no wild spinning out of a disturbed magnetic order, at least not on that day.

Gould scarcely emoted in triumph but betrayed the slightest curve invading the lower corner of his lip. "Thank you for at least being aware of his poetry," he said as the rest of us wondered if we would be able to catch up. Many students fidgeted in relief that someone had dared to face the formidable instructor head on, even if the dialogue had ended poorly for him. I thought I knew Michael would regret his challenge. No one had assigned Leroi Jones, and his poetry wasn't part of the course, although I was suddenly wishing that the poem was. I wrote down the poem title as soon as I took out my pen.

Even though Michael had been humbled, as was typical in a Gould class, I was still impressed he had read "Black Art" somewhere along the way and could quote lines from memory as well as Gould always seemed to do.

Looking back on that time, I am reminded of Professor Gould's many lessons that were not only occasionally cruel but full of surprise and insight, even spontaneous discovery. All of the poet/educator's talent, ability, knowledge roared into rooms with him as the force of his personality was greater than a single attribute. "There are students and there are scholars," said Professor Gould, turning toward the class again. "The key difference lies in the word 'aptitude.'" He looked at all of us as if appraising which of us were merely the lesser. "What have you read lately? Do you know Charles Simic and Seamus Heaney as well as you know Robert Lowell and Berryman? Are you as familiar with Rainer Maria Rilke as Tony Hoagland?"

If having read works you were not required to know was about scholarship, then I had much work ahead of me. I recognized all of these poets' names but knew only Lowell's work well. No, wait, I had read some Heaney poems too, and I'd come across a few poems by Simic that I suddenly recalled. I started to calm down, but then I thought about the fact that our instructor only mentioned male poets. This pattern was part of a larger picture that Gould, knowingly or unknowingly betrayed, one I was slow to recognize. What did I know by Heaney? Recalling a poem entitled "Gifts of Rain" that I remembered liking, I thought better of mentioning it. Gould offered his own pick: "Has anyone of you read "Strange " by Heaney?" Most of us looked around at each other at a loss. Then Gould added, "Perhaps you should examine your heads to make sure they are still attached." He turned his own head slightly as if he was amused only with himself. I looked up the poem in the interim and discovered the related phrases in Heaney's poem. The image was macabre enough, but, at the time, I didn't connect the loss of ahead to our professor directly, only wondered at his choice of lines to memorize.

    I shot Michael another glance and gave him an encouraging smile. There was an attraction I had sensed on other occasions, but that morning, I grappled with his retreat before Gould. I wanted to sit down next to Michael, but he had placed his book sack on the chair beside him, and the wall was on his other side. I finally sat down two rows in front of him, turning only once to see him glaring at Gould.

    Our professor had already moved on and was lecturing, speaking rapidly, as he wrote notes in shorthand on the white board, his back turned toward us. In that instant, I understood I had already fallen behind. I needed to forget about Michel and focus on Gould. Then I realized that I was in deep water and would have to start swimming faster. There were some in the class who already knew they were drowning.

***FOR THE FULL INVENTORY
OF QUALITY BOOKS***:
http://www.roguephoenixpress.com

*Rogue Phoenix Press
Representing Excellence in Publishing*

*Quality trade paperbacks and downloads
in multiple formats,
in genres ranging from historical to contemporary romance, mystery
and science fiction.
Visit the website then bookmark it.
We add new titles each month!*